SPINSTER
OF THIS
PARISH

Also by Ann Purser

Pastures New

SPINSTER
OF THIS
PARISH

ANN PURSER

KNIGHT

The right of Ann Purser to be
identified as the author of this work has
been asserted by her in accordance with the
Copyright, Designs and Patents Act 1988

First published in Great Britain in 1995 by
Orion
An imprint of Orion Books Ltd
Orion House, 5 Upper St Martin's Lane, London WC2H 9EA

A CIP catalogue record for this book is
available from the British Library

ISBN 1 84429 069 7

Typeset by Deltatype Ltd.
Ellesmere Port, Cheshire
Printed in Great Britain

This edition published 2004 by
Knight, an imprint of
The Caxton Publishing Group

For Philip

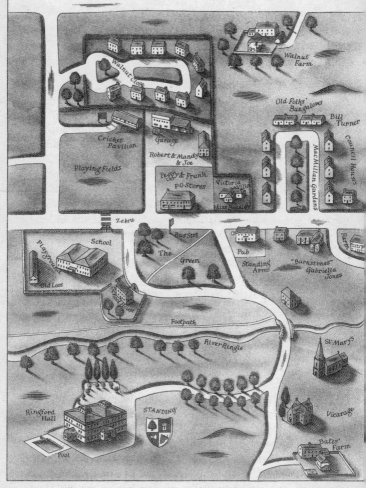

ROUND RINGFORD

CHAPTER ONE

Ivy Dorothy Beasley marched smartly up the sandy path to the vicarage, pushing her way through overgrown, budding roses which sweetened her way in vain.

It was late spring, a warm, gentle morning, and a song-thrush serenaded her from the great mulberry tree in the vicarage garden. But Miss Beasley did not hear it, having a number of important matters to discuss with the elderly Reverend Cyril Collins, and being determined to get some definite answers from him.

Ivy Beasley had lived all her life in Round Ringford, an unexpected gift from God to her parents when both were in their forties. Her father had been a railway inspector until he retired at sixty-five, and her mother continued to keep house to a strict regime until arthritis had forced her to hand over duties, but not control, to her only daughter Ivy.

Ivy had been much loved, but her mother and father were of the generation which believed that sparing the rod spoilt the child. They niggled and criticised and cut her down to size, all for her own good, and blighted her childish optimism. Worse, she was never sure of their approval, since shows of affection were rationed with care.

'You're no better'n anybody else, Ivy Beasley.' It was her mother's favourite phrase and Ivy had grown up without self-confidence, resentful and rebellious. She never defied her formidable mother, eventually nursing her to the end, and

I

then, without any change of direction, continued her inhibited, spinster life in the village where she was born. Her sharp tongue and fondness for malicious gossip had put her in a position of power in the village, and she was treated with cautious respect.

She reached the vicarage porch and stopped, fanning herself with the notebook in which she had made a list of subjects for discussion.

Well, at least he's at home this time, she thought, finding the heavy front door ajar. She pulled the bell lever and heard it ring deep in the heart of the vicarage. Nobody came, so she lifted a stiff black iron knocker and banged twice. Still no answer, and, determined not to be put off again, she pushed open the door and walked into a large, black and white tiled hall.

In the heavy silence, Ivy stood still and listened. No sound, except for the distant barking of a dog at Bates's Farm, and cawing rooks high above the churchyard.

'Yoo hoo!' shouted Ivy. 'Are you there, Reverend Collins?'

Ivy began to feel her senses prickle. It was a special kind of silence, and she had experienced it before.

'Oh dear me,' she said quietly, and began to climb the stairs. She went straight to the main bedroom door and knocked softly. She expected no reply and got none. Pushing open the door, she walked slowly into the dimly lit room and over to the big bed.

The Reverend Cyril Collins, MA BD, was lying on his back, his eyes open and, as if in prayer, his hands folded across his chest. As Ivy Beasley had anticipated, he was not breathing.

'Dear me,' Ivy repeated gently, and expertly closed his eyes with one respectful sweep of her hand. She then drew up a chair to the side of the bed, and sat down. With her eyes on the mortal remains of the village parson she had known so long and so well, she composed herself to keep him company on his last journey.

One hour later, Ivy Beasley got to her feet, brushed down her skirt and replaced the chair. She walked to the foot of the bed and looked down at the pale face. 'He's gone peacefully,' she said, 'gone to meet his Maker.'

A couple of sniffs and a quick shake of her head, and she walked firmly out of the room and down into the hall, where she picked up the telephone and began to dial, first Dr Russell in Bagley, and then churchwarden and local squire, Richard Standing. The old doctor was sympathetic and reassuring, saying he would be over as soon as possible, and Ivy, confident that in these hands of authority everything would be taken care of in a proper and official manner, spent a few minutes tidying and straightening the bachelor vicar's kitchen and study, then crossed the hall, and locked the big door carefully behind her. She put the key in her handbag, ready for Dr Russell to collect, and set off for home, down Bates's End, past the ancient, squat church where Cyril Collins had ministered to the parish for so many years, and on towards the stone bridge over the river.

Round Ringford was a small village in the middle of England, and, considering its proximity to motorways and main railways, its rhythms and routines had remained remarkably undisturbed by modern incursions. A strong sense of rural isolation felt by visitors from town was heightened by the green hollow in which the village had settled, and by the wooded hills surrounding it. Only the narrow roads leading from it and the bright length of water in the River Ringle flowing across the far end of the Green were reminders that Ringford was, in fact, as much in touch with the outside world as it wished to be.

Halfway down Bates's End, Ivy Beasley saw a figure on a bicycle approaching her, and she frowned in disapproval as she recognised Gabriella Jones, slim and blonde, wearing a short skirt and showing long, smooth legs.

Gabriella had been tempted out by the sunshine, savouring the warmth on her bare skin, and she pedalled slowly, touching the lacy heads of cow parsley in the grass verge, and shaking her long, pale hair like a switch to disperse the cloud of gnats that hovered round her head as she wobbed over the river bridge. She was on her way to discuss the hymns for Sunday with the vicar, a meeting she looked forward to, finding the old man gentle and charming, and always grateful for her enthusiasm.

Gabriella was Ringford's church organist. She had taken on the job when the ancient old widow who had done it for years finally died and no one else had come forward. Gabriella played with more energy than accuracy, but her optimism and beauty had brought sunshine into the twilight of Cyril Collins's life, and he had adored her.

Ivy Beasley knew exactly where Gabriella Jones was going, and stepped out into the road in front of the bicycle, holding up her hand like a comic-opera policeman.

'Excuse me, Mrs Jones,' she said firmly, 'but if you are going to see Reverend Collins, I must just have a word.'

Gabriella put on her brakes hard, and the bicycle skidded on the gravelly lane. 'Gracious, Miss Beasley,' she said, 'you nearly caused a crash there!' She was nervous, alarmed by Ivy Beasley's stern face, and her voice sounded falsely jocular.

'It is a serious matter, Mrs Jones,' said Ivy reprovingly, and told Gabriella in blunt sentences of the death of her friend Cyril.

'But he wasn't ill . . .' said Gabriella, looking dazed. She straightened her short skirt in an unthinking gesture of respect.

'The authorities have been informed,' said Ivy Beasley primly, 'so no doubt we shall hear the cause in due course. If you ask me, it was his heart, but as he was up there on his own, there may be further investigations required.'

'Poor old Cyril . . .' said Gabriella to herself, and Ivy Beasley looked at her sharply.

'Reverend Collins,' she said with emphasis, 'was a good age, and had lived a good life. You can be sure his Father in Heaven gathered him in when the time had come, and his reward will be awaiting him. We need not sorrow for Reverend Collins, Mrs Jones, only for ourselves.'

Gabriella began to feel tearful, and, not wanting any more wise words from Ivy Beasley, got on her bicycle and rode off the way she had come, back home to get her tumbling thoughts in order.

CHAPTER TWO

Her business with Cyril Collins now indefinitely postponed, Ivy Beasley returned home to Victoria Villa, and, quite composed, prepared to bake a sponge cake. From her cool, stone-floored larder she took out flour, sugar, margarine, and milk. She looked in the old yellow mixing bowl where she kept her eggs, and found only one left.

I knew I'd forget something, Mother, she said to her empty kitchen. And them two coming for tea. I shall have to nip next door.

Forget your head one of these days, you will, Ivy, said the voice of her ever-present, long-dead mother. Feeling chastened, Ivy pulled on her old grey cardigan to fetch eggs from the shop.

Ivy's plain red-brick house was next to Round Ringford Post Office and General Stores, and both looked over the wide village green, an expanse of springy turf bordered by a narrow road, with tall chestnut trees giving shade in the hot summer.

'Looks like a queue,' said Ivy, climbing the stone steps to the shop door, 'just when I'm in a hurry.'

The Stores had been kept for the last year or so by Peggy Palmer, who, with her husband Frank, had moved from Coventry, using Frank's redundancy money to start a new life. Tragedy had struck when Frank was killed in a road accident, and Peggy had taken the difficult decision to carry on alone.

There were four people in the shop, a crowd for Ringford Stores, and Ivy Beasley stood tapping her foot impatiently, waiting for her turn to be served.

' 'Aven't you 'eard, Peggy?' The speaker was a bent old woman, wearing a loud orange and green jacket, her head cocked on one side like a colourful old parrot. She looked enquiringly at the small, plump figure of Peggy Palmer, friendly and attractive in her pink-checked overall.

Peggy Palmer, Ringford's postmistress and shopkeeper, confounded the old image of a grim, impatient face at the Post Office window. Everything about Peggy Palmer was feminine and pleasant. Her greying fair hair curled around her face, and her clear blue eyes looked out steadily from soft, creamy skin where colour came and went in the uncontrolled way of a sensitive schoolgirl. There was something perennially young about Peggy.

She smiled, said, 'You tell me, Ellen,' and tipped three red apples into a brown paper bag, pushing them over the counter to the old woman. Ellen took coins out of her peeling leather purse and repeated her question to the shop in general.

'It's all over the village,' she said. ' 'e's definitely goin', soon as possible, I 'eard.'

'Who's going?' said Ivy Beasley, 'and how come you know and I don't, Ellen Biggs?'

Fred Mills, an elder of the village, in the shop to collect his pension, took his evil-smelling pipe out of his mouth and said, 'Known for weeks, I 'ave. Vicar told the churchwardens and I 'eard soon arter.'

'Reverend Collins retiring?' said Peggy. 'Well, that's not exactly news, Ellen, we've all know he meant to go this year. He's well past the age, poor old Cyril.'

'Past more than age,' said Ivy, with perfect timing. 'He died this morning.'

There was a gratifyingly shocked silence, and Ivy said nothing more, letting her news sink in.

'You tellin' the truth, Ivy?' said old Ellen suspiciously.

Ivy bridled. 'Since when have I told lies?' she said, and there

7

was no challenge to this. It was well known that Ivy Beasley did not invent things, but had a gift for editing the facts.

Peggy Palmer took a deep breath. The suddenness of this had knocked her off balance for a few moments, reminding her of that other time, that dark winter's evening when her husband Frank had crashed into a tree.

She frowned, shrinking away from the inevitable talk of death, and said, 'No doubt we shall hear more details later, but I'm sure we are all extremely sorry. He was a very good man. Now, who's next with their shopping?'

The shop emptied slowly, speculation mounting on the cause and circumstances of Cyril Collins's death, until only Ivy Beasley was left, carefully picking out the biggest brown eggs. She took them to the counter and paid for them, saying, 'The trouble is, Mrs Palmer, there's nobody to mourn for him. He had no close relatives, and he is entitled to the respect of a decent mourning.'

Peggy looked her straight in the eye. 'I am sure we all mourn for him, Miss Beasley, and not from a sense of duty. He was much loved.'

Before Ivy could reply, the door opened and a big, burly man with a shock of greyish hair and deep-set eyes came in with a rush of fresh air.

'Morning, Ivy,' he said, but his smile was for Peggy, warm and welcoming behind the counter.

'Good morning, Bill,' said Ivy, noticing everything. 'How's your Joyce this morning?'

Bill only nodded in reply. He was used to Ivy's loaded questions and knew that whatever he said would be mis-interpreted. Born and raised in Round Ringford, he worked at the Hall and was always about the village. His marriage was an unhappy one, but he tried to keep his private life to himself.

It's not right, Mother, Ivy said, back in her kitchen and weighing out flour in the old kitchen scales. There's Bill Turner with eyes for nobody but Peggy Palmer, whilst his poor wife is shut up night and day in that poky, dark little house on her own. Something should be done . . .

8

The voice in her head agreed with her. You might have been the one to do it, Ivy, it said. Ivy, hearing a knock on her front door, did not answer, but went to give the vicarage key to Dr Russell. At his suggestion, she postponed her baking, changed her cardigan for a grey flannel jacket, and went with him to meet Richard Standing at the vicarage, a last call on their old friend Cyril Collins.

'Fancy, Greg,' Gabriella said, sitting down heavily on the sofa next to her husband, 'it could have been me that found poor old Cyril.'

Greg Jones was relaxing in the morning sunlight streaming through their big windows, drinking coffee and leafing through a pile of accumulated newspapers. The Joneses had lived in Ringford for several years, the first owners of Barnstones, a sympathetically converted granary on the main street.

'My dear Gabbie,' said Greg, putting his arm round Gabriella's shoulders, 'don't upset yourself, old Cyril must have been on the way to eighty if he was a day.'

Greg was a geography teacher at the comprehensive school in Tresham, and, like many in his profession, talked to everyone as if they were eleven years old. His voice was loud and odd in tone, a result of losing his hearing at the miserably early age of eight. But the handicap had spurred him on to tackle a constantly challenging job, and his results were good. All his friends had marvelled at his apparent ease with girls, and could scarcely believe it when he led the prize peach, Gabriella Rogers, to the altar. Greg, however, had not been in the least surprised. He had grown a dark, piratical beard, kept his slight frame in good shape, and soon discovered that a handicap could be attractive to some girls. He made the most of it.

'Gabbie, dear, if you had discovered a lifeless body in the vicarage,' he said, smiling tolerantly at his lovely wife, 'it would not have harmed you. This is Round Ringford, not down-town Chicago.'

Octavia Jones wandered aimlessly into the room, a sixteen-year-old replica of her mother, but with a disagreeable expression that her parents hoped would vanish with the end of her teens.

'Shame about poor old Cyril,' she said.

'Reverend Collins to you, Octavia,' said her father, 'and I wish you wouldn't eavesdrop. Your mother is very upset. She was very fond of the old boy. Think what a shock it would have been if she had got there before Miss Beasley.'

'Oh, I don't know,' said Octavia, 'she might have been in at the kill.'

While her parents were reeling under this remark, Octavia continued, 'I'm hungry, Mum, can I have a piece of that cake in the kitchen?'

'There are times, Octavia,' said her mother, sighing and getting to her feet, 'when I wonder whether you are really our daughter, or were switched at birth in the hospital.'

Gabriella loved her daughter, of course, but even in her most maternal moments she could not deny that Octavia was a difficult child.

CHAPTER THREE

'Looks like rain,' said Doris Ashbourne, stepping into Ivy's narrow hallway, and taking off her grey mac. 'No good thinking we've seen the last of bad weather yet.'

The day had begun too well. The morning's clear skies had given way to slowly advancing clouds, thickening over Bagley woods, and casting threatening shadows over the fields with the freshening wind. By the early afternoon the sun had gone, and Bates's cows were lying down in the lush spring grass of the glebe close, expecting rain.

Doris Ashbourne had owned Ringford Stores before selling to the Palmers, and she now lived in an old person's bungalow in Macmillan Gardens. She and Ivy, and Ellen Biggs from the Lodge, met for tea each week, taking turns to play host. None of them would admit how much they looked forward to these teas, especially Ivy Beasley, but it was rare for a week to be missed.

'Come in, Doris,' said Ivy, 'you're the first.' She looked out of her open doorway across the Green. 'There she is, Ellen Biggs, late as usual, hobbling over the Green.' Ellen had been cook at the Hall for many years, and now lived in retirement in the damp and draughty Lodge.

Ivy's front room was spotless, no speck of dust and every surface polished until it seemed an affront to put even a handbag down on the table. A photograph of Mr and Mrs Beasley, unsmiling, stood on a bureau by the fireplace, watching Ivy's every move.

Each piece of furniture was solid and well-made, the pictures on the walls were respectable prints of Scottish glens and lochs, and the curtains heavy maroon damask. There was nothing frivolous, no rash purchases made on seaside holidays, no cushions with embroidered kittens, no laughing snaps of the Beasley family caught enjoying a joke.

'There's Ellen,' said Doris Ashbourne. 'Shall I let her in, Ivy?'

Ellen Biggs, breathing fast from her walk and the ascent of Ivy's front steps, took off a light purple garment, which in its day had been called a duster coat. She pulled her beige lacy cardigan well down over a sugar-pink cotton skirt and looked at herself in the hall-stand mirror. Her thick brown stockings had wrinkled a little over comfortable canvas shoes, but on the whole Ellen was pleased with the general effect.

'You bin cooking, Ivy?' she said, her eyes taking in the small table set with a fresh white cloth, and a perfect Victoria jam sponge in pride of place.

'Just had time to bake a quick cake,' said Ivy casually.

Doris raised her eyesbrows and smiled at Ellen. Ivy was an excellent cook, judged the produce classes at local shows, and singlehandedly kept alive the spirit of jam and Jerusalem in Ringford WI.

'That were quite a bombshell this mornin', Ivy,' said Ellen, when tea had been handed round and the light sponge cake broached and served on Ivy's mother's best china plates.

'Poor Cyril,' said Doris, 'I remember when he first come to the village, a young man all alone in that great vicarage. Many's the time he sat having a cup of tea and a warm in my kitchen.'

'Pity 'e never married,' said Ellen, 'though some say 'e 'ad plenty of chances.'

'It isn't given to all of us,' said Ivy grimly. 'Some people get on quite well without being wed.'

'Quite right, Ivy,' said Doris, 'and come to that, Ellen, none of us can remember the late Mr Biggs . . .'

'God rest 'is soul,' said Ellen devoutly. The truth was that

12

Ellen had long ago been very nearly married, and had felt no guilt in subsequently taking on the honorary title given to all cooks in the kitchens of great houses.

'Well, it's one more gone from the village,' said Ivy. 'Makes you wonder who'll be next for the grim reaper.'

Doris Ashbourne delicately wiped crumbs from the corners of her mouth with a paper tea napkin.

'That's quite enough of that, Ivy,' she said. She had noticed a shadow cross old Ellen's face, and judged it time for a change of subject. 'There's still a lot for us to do,' she continued, 'and I for one mean to be useful for many years yet.'

Ellen gave herself a shake, and sat up as straight as her bent shoulders would allow.

'Another piece of cake, Ivy,' she said, 'would go down a treat.'

Ivy cut a wedge of sponge for Ellen and another for Doris, and, as the conversation seemed in danger of drying up, went to stand by the window, looking out across the Green, hoping for a subject for comment.

Heavy clouds lowered over the village, and the air was thick with moisture. It was like a big greenhouse, thought Ivy, all the colours so bright, and everything growing so fast you could almost see it happening. Her small front garden was full of flowers: pansies and forget-me-nots and sweet-scented wallflowers, all planted in neat, orderly rows.

'What's Bill Turner doing to that tree?' she said, pulling back the lace curtain. Doris and Ellen got up and the three women stood staring at the big chestnut on the school corner of the Green.

'There's a dead branch needs lopping,' said Doris. 'Doreen Price was telling me, Bill and her Tom are doing it.'

The Prices were farmers, and had lived in the village for generations. Tom was Chairman of the Parish Council, and his wife Vice-President of the WI. Tradition kept the President's job in the gift of the squire's lady, but Doreen Price was the one who got things done. Tom and Bill were good friends, and could cope with most of the parish jobs needing a

13

couple of strong men and a ladder. As the women watched, ropes were slung over branches and the chainsaw's earsplitting whine started up.

'There she goes, trust her not to be left out if Bill Turner's anywhere about,' said Ivy tartly.

Peggy Palmer, neat and quick, walked across the road from the shop and stood watching as the men took off the dead branch and lowered it gently to the ground.

'Don't you never leave off, our Ivy?' said old Ellen. 'Ain't that poor man got trouble enough at 'ome, without you addin' to it?'

'Trouble of his own making, if you ask me,' said Ivy Beasley.

'Nobody is asking you, Ivy,' said Doris Ashbourne, 'and Peggy Palmer can do with a little charity after all she's been through, and not your everlasting sniping.'

Ivy sniffed and shrugged her shoulders.

'As my dear mother used to say,' she pronounced firmly, 'charity begins at home.'

CHAPTER FOUR

Peggy Palmer watched Bill and Tom cut the big branch into shorter, manageable pieces and load them into the trailer. They brushed up twigs brought down by the amputation, and climbed into the Land Rover. Tom leaned out of the window and smiled.

'Right-o then, Peggy,' he said, 'I'll tell Doreen, another six dozen eggs if possible. You ready, then, Bill?'

Peggy looked at Bill, and he nodded to her without speaking, as if affirming something secret, and the Land Rover drove off, Tom's old sheep dog barking wildly from her usual place in the trailer.

Peggy returned to the shop, and was quickly followed by a tall, red-complexioned man, a lock of hair falling over his face as he stooped in the low doorway.

'Could have helped myself, Mrs Palmer,' he said. 'You must be careful when you leave the shop unattended.'

Mind your own business, thought Peggy, but smiled at him dutifully.

He was not, anyway, likely to be a big spender. Richard Standing was Ringford's hereditary squire, living in the Hall with his languid wife Susan, in a style which would have horrified his parents. By making do with a part-time cleaner and simplifying the grounds and gardens, the Standings held on to the estate which had been in their family for hundreds of years. It was a struggle, but Richard Standing could not imagine living anywhere else.

'What can I get for you?' Peggy straightened a display of birthday cards, askew from the last customer.

'Just a packet of envelopes, please,' said Richard Standing.

I might have known it, thought Peggy, and sighed. Although a small weekly order went up to the Hall, she knew that, like most of the families in the village, the bulk of their supplies came from the SupaShop at Tresham.

'Very sad about Reverend Collins,' she said, 'it will be difficult to replace such a popular man.'

'Such a good fellow,' agreed Richard Standing. 'Who could be better?'

'I think a family would be nice,' said Peggy. 'At least they'd fill up some of those rooms, warm the place up a bit.'

'Not the first duty of the incumbent, though, Mrs Palmer, to fill the vicarage with children,' said Richard.

'Incumbent?' said old Ellen, looming up behind him. She had left Ivy Beasley's and come directly into the shop for a tin of cocoa for her bedtime drink. 'Incumbent?' she repeated, making much of the word. 'Swallowed a dictionary, 'ave you, young Richard?'

This excess of familiarity was allowed old Ellen, because she had known Richard Standing since he first squawled into the world, and had been his favourite companion in the kitchens during the long, boring school holidays.

'Come on, Ellen,' he said, 'get your shopping and I'll give you a lift back to the Lodge.'

' 'E's not a bad bloke,' said Ellen, as Mr Richard left the shop and waited outside for her in his big silver car. 'Bin 'appy as a san'boy since his Susan came back – taught him a lesson he won't forget, I reckon.'

'It was a storm in a teacup, Ellen, nothing more. Anything else today?'

'That's it, my dear,' said Ellen, 'soon be time to put up the shutters and 'ave a nice cuppa. You look tired, and no wonder. Get yer feet up and watch the telly for a couple of hours, that's what I recommend.'

But Peggy had other plans for refreshing her soul and body after the long day in the shop. She locked up, fed her she-cat Gilbert, and pulled on boots and anorak. 'Back soon, Gilbertiney,' she said, and let herself out of the side gate next to the shop.

Bagley Woods were damp and cool, and the undergrowth soon made dark wet patches on Peggy's light-coloured skirt. 'God, these nettles have grown inches overnight!' she muttered, picking up a piece of stick and thrashing her way through waist-high stingers. As she lashed out fiercely at the tough, hairy stems, they seemed to fight back, and she gasped in alarm as a frightened young rabbit started up from under her feet and ran crazily through the underbrush. From beech and ash trees all around her, wood pigeons, disturbed by the noisy intruder, clattered into flight, and low, twiggy branches left bits of leaf in her hair as she ducked underneath.

Coming out with relief into a clear path bordering the wood, she saw pink-tipped shoots of wild honeysuckle in the hedge, and felt calmed and delighted at the delicate colour and the promise of scented summer days. Her mood lightening, she struck off into the wood again, across a carpet of bluebells, the heavenly colour shimmering through the trees. Her boots flattened the shiny leaves, and she looked back to see her own trail clearly marked. She emerged into a clearing where an old oak had been felled, leaving a broad stump surrounded by smooth, sandy greensward, dotted with tiny white woodruff flowers.

Warm from the climb up Bagley Hill and her struggle with the nettles, she took off her anorak, spreading it over the stump to give her a dry place to sit down. She shaded her eyes from the evening sun, brilliant again after a heavy shower of rain. The village lay before her in its protected hollow, and she could identify every feature.

'Poor old Cyril,' she said, 'all by himself all those years in that gloomy vicarage . . .'

'Talking to yourself again, Peg?' Bill Turner came up

17

behind her and planted a kiss on the top of her tangled hair. She turned, smiling, and he kissed her again. Then she shifted to one side, and he sat down close to her, taking her small hand in his, squeezing it gently.

'How's my Peg today?' he said. 'No more broadsides from Old Beasley?'

'Not directed at me,' said Peggy, leaning her head against Bill's shoulder. 'She and old Ellen had their usual barney. Keeps them going, the two of them.'

'Wicked old tabs,' said Bill absently, carefully pulling pieces of twig from Peggy's hair.

'And Joyce?' said Peggy tentatively. 'Has she been playing up?'

'No more than usual,' said Bill, sighing, 'but I couldn't get her to eat at dinnertime. Sometimes she eats it after I've gone out again, but not today. There was cold bacon and egg still on the plate when I looked in.'

'Oh Bill, I'm so sorry,' said Peggy, touching his cheek with a warm, loving hand. He turned and put his arms round her, holding her tight, kissing her softly at first.

'Peggy, oh Peggy,' he muttered, 'it isn't easy . . .' He released her and sat, hunched and defeated, his head bowed.

Peggy smoothed his hair, kissed him and tasted salt on his closed eyelids. 'Don't Bill, don't . . . I wish I could help . . . but . . . oh, I don't know . . .'

Bill kissed her again, and she pushed him gently away. Smiling shakily, she opened his waterproof jacket, and smoothed her hands over his broad chest, feeling the solid strength of him through his thin shirt. She slid her arms tightly around him under the jacket, drawing him close until she could feel his warmth hard against her, enclosing her.

'What now, then?' said Bill, fuzzily into her ear.

And then it was Frank, laughingly turning her over towards him in their marital bed, and she shook her head, pulling away and frowning.

'Oh Lord, I'm sorry, Bill,' she said, 'sod it all . . .'

Bill took a deep breath and stood back. 'We'd better walk, then, gel,' he said, 'I'm not made of wood.'

They wandered off through the trees, hand in hand, Bill pulling aside brambles for Peggy to walk safely, like young lovers oblivious of the world.

But the world in the shape of Ivy Beasley was far from oblivious of them. Her eagle eye was trained on the street, watching for their return. Bill had anticipated this, and he and Peggy parted in the trees, Bill going back past the new houses and along the footpath behind the cricket pavilion, straight home to Macmillan Gardens, while Peggy continued on down the road into the main street, and up the path at the side of the shop.

Doreen Price, large and solid, very much the farmer's wife, driving slowly with her trays of eggs for the shop, saw Peggy in her muddy boots and knew exactly where she had been. And it's none of my business, she thought, though I hope to God she knows what she's doing.

'You had a run on eggs, then, Peggy?' said Doreen. She was a broad-hipped, cheerful woman, and Peggy's best friend.

'Everybody's baking today,' said Peggy. 'Thanks for bringing them down.'

Doreen put the eggs on Peggy's kitchen table and settled herself on to a chair. Her solid figure was reassuring, comfortably at ease.

'Going to WI tonight?' she said.

Peggy nodded. She appreciated the companionship of the village women, and had been borne up by their kindness after Frank died. Ringford Women's Institute was one of the oldest in the county, and, though perhaps a bit slow to take on new ideas, maintained the comforting strength of a long-established rural institution.

'I've found the very first Minute Book, nineteen twenty-six,' said Doreen, 'thought I'd pass it round for members to see how it all started.'

'Any names we'd know?' said Peggy, filling the kettle and putting it to boil on the Rayburn.

'Mr Richard's grandmother was founding President, and old Mrs Beasley served as Honorary Secretary for years. They used to meet in the orangery up at the Hall.'

'Mrs Beasley was Ivy's mum, I presume?' said Peggy.

'She was a very strict woman,' said Doreen, 'kept a firm hand on Ivy and a sharp tongue for anybody she disapproved of. Caused a lot of trouble, one way and another, Granny Price used to say. She was not a popular woman, and folks were afraid of her. She had an all-seeing eye.'

'Are you trying to tell me something, Doreen?' said Peggy, looking straight at her friend.'

'Maybe,' said Doreen, 'you'll know yourself well enough, I dare say.'

Nothing more was said, but Peggy went to bed that night feeling frustrated and guilty. Her husband, her only companion for so many years, was still as real to her as when they moved to Ringford with such high hopes, and yet up there in the woods she had wanted Bill with an urgency she had never once felt with Frank.

What am I to do, my poor love? she said to the photograph smiling at her from the bedside table. It would be a lot easier if Bill were unattached, she thought, but not only is there Frank still popping unannounced into my mind, but the real live problem presence of Joyce, always there and always a threat of infinite complication.

Peggy moved over to Frank's side of the bed, trying and failing to gain some comfort from the ever-smiling face, and waited for sleep to come.

CHAPTER FIVE

'And where were you last evening?' said Joyce Turner, from her chair in the corner of the sitting room. 'Everybody else's husband was home to tea, but not Bill Turner, oh no, he was out with his fancy woman up Bagley Woods, like some randy little teenager!' The last words were loud and thrown at him like a weapon.

The Turners lived in Macmillan Gardens, a cluster of council houses set back from the main street. Across the far end, with a good view of the Green, were the old persons' bungalows, with tiny gardens where retired people, used to their own produce, could still grow a few potatoes and peas to eat as a treat with their small Sunday joints of spring lamb.

Bill Turner's house was distinguished by a high privet hedge, and windows perpetually blanked off by layers of drawn curtains.

He had found Joyce in bed with the door locked against him when he returned home, his head still full of thoughts of Peggy. He'd made a sandwich and watched television, and then retired to the hard little bed in the spare room, where he slept fitfully.

This morning, Joyce was still wearing yesterday's grubby pink dressing-gown and down-at-heel slippers, and her uncombed hair fell forward over her pale, discontented face.

'You promised to get washed and dressed today,' Bill said, ignoring her uncanny gift for guessing right. 'Why don't you go and smarten up now, while I'm getting breakfast? Ivy will be in later, with your magazines.'

'Not feeling well enough,' she said, with a pout and a little-girl voice that used to work with Bill, but no longer had any effect.

'There's nothing wrong with you, Joyce,' said Bill wearily. 'You know what the doctor said – try and get out and take your mind off yourself for a bit.'

Joyce got slowly to her feet, an unattractive, slovenly figure, wincing as she put her feet to the ground. 'What does he know?' she said. 'Stupid old fool in his dotage. He don't know what I've suffered all these years, nobody does.'

Bill wondered whether to tell her exactly what he thought of all of it – the dreadful miscarriage, the long years of blame and mourning and reclusion, the sluttishness and vindictive revenge, the jealousy and recriminations – how tired he was of her and everything to do with their travesty of a marriage. Or should he humour and pacify her as usual, buying a few more days of uneasy truce?

'Joycey,' he said, 'couldn't you just try, just this once? I'll get a nice piece of fish from Len's van, and we could have a proper tea, sitting up at the table. You could make yourself look decent – there's still plenty of clothes up there in your cupboard, and you . . .'

He dodged automatically, from long practice, as she threw one of her slippers at him. It flew straight into a picture on the wall, smashing the glass, which fell in shards on to the carpet.

Without speaking, Bill went out to the kitchen and fetched dustpan and brush. It was an almost daily task, brushing up after Joyce's wilful destruction of their home. Not much left now, he thought. I shall soon have to start buying stuff from the jumble sale just to give her something to break. He no longer felt compassion, and only seldom allowed anger to rise to the surface, but increasingly he longed to ditch the whole thing, get out and start again.

'Did you tumble her in the daisies, then?' shouted Joyce from her bedroom, where she had retreated, opening and shutting doors and drawers violently, working herself up into a frenzy of jealousy and rage.

'I'll be out with the rabbits,' called Bill. 'See if you can calm down by the time I come back.'

He went quietly out of the back door and walked down the concrete garden path, disappearing into the big shed where he kept his beautiful long-haired angora rabbits.

'Hello, my pretties,' he said, 'breakfast time . . .'

He put rabbit mix into the troughs, and changed the water, talking to each rabbit as he worked. 'There, my beauty, just you eat it up and grow big and strong. No need to be scared – Bill won't let any harm come to you.'

He did not see the shadow at the door, nor hear the back door of the house slam shut. He was deep in his own thoughts, feeling again the softness of Peggy's skin, and the warmth of her in his arms. He checked the cage doors, and set off back to the house.

'Hello Bill!' his neighbour, Jean Jenkins, called across rows of green vegetables and raspberry canes. 'Everything all right?' And then, because she knew it wasn't, she changed the subject. 'Sad about Reverend Collins, wasn't it? I was up there on Tuesday, and thought he looked very peaky.'

The Jenkins family lived next door to Bill and Joyce, and had grown used to Joyce's screams of rage coming through the thin dividing wall between the two houses. Jean and her husband Foxy, and their five children – three boys and twin girls – squeezed into their council house in Macmillan Gardens with surprising contentment, considering their lack of space. Jean was a big girl, tall and comfortably overweight, and Foxy's gingery head came happily up to her shoulder.

Bill was fond of Jean, grateful for her unsuccessful attempts to persuade Joyce to live a normal life.

He smiled at her and said, 'Poor old sod's probably worried himself to death, wonderin' what to do when he retired.'

'No, it were his heart, apparently,' said Jean. 'If only he'd said, we could all have helped a bit more.'

A sudden eruption of screaming came from the house, and

Jean rushed back in yelling. 'Gemma! Amy! Just cut it out, both of you, or I shall tell your dad when he comes home.'

CHAPTER SIX

'So matters are rather accelerated,' said Richard Standing to his wife. They were sitting after dinner in their cool, high-ceilinged drawing room at the Hall, discussing the ramifications of Cyril Collins's recent and unexpected death.

It was dusk, and one pink-shaded lamp barely kept the dark at bay in the room. Dimly visible ancestors with protruding eyes stared down at them from ornate gilt frames, and the scent from a silver vase of delicate freesias, grown by Bill Turner in the Hall greenhouse, combined with fragrant beeswax polish vigorously applied by Jean Jenkins each week, to give the room a pleasant, lived-in character.

'I suppose the Bishop will have taken charge of things?' said Susan, smoothing her cream linen skirt and crossing one slim leg over the other. She set a fragile coffee cup down on the little table by her chair. 'What is there for you to do, my darling? It's all a mystery to me.'

'Well, for a start I am one of the patrons, and have the right to present the incumbent to the benefice . . . at least, that's how things are at the moment, but there are changes afoot.'

'You've lost me, Richard,' said Susan.

'Just means it is my turn to choose the next vicar, along with parish approval, of course.' Richard turned the pages of *The Times* to see if the passing of Cyril Collins had been registered in print.

A companionable silence fell whilst they pondered the

strangeness of it all. Richard and Susan had had a choppy passage over the years of their marriage, but at present were in calm waters, and the departure of the kindly old man who had presided so sunnily over their wedding day made them think of those times and look affectionately upon one another.

'Difficult,' said Richard, after a while. 'It is difficult to know just what sort of a man would do the job well.'

'Does it really matter these days?' said Susan, turning the pages of *Country Life*, looking for faces she recognised, events she wished she had been seen at. 'After all,' she ventured, 'so few people go to church, and half of them are asleep by the time the sermon's preached.'

'Not necessarily, Susan, in town churches they have full congregations every week.'

'Well, they don't in Round Ringford, and I think it will be more important to get a really nice family who will fit in, than an academic clergyman who preaches above everybody's head. I mean, face it, Richard, Ivy Beasley is not desperately concerned with a philosophical proof of the existence of God.'

Richard, who had been summoned to the vicarage by Ivy Beasley on the day of Cyril Collins's death, had been moved by her dignity and self-composure, and found Susan's flippancy unacceptable.

'Maybe not,' he said stiffly, 'but that's because she has never doubted, and never would.'

Susan stood up and walked across to draw long, silver-grey curtains, shutting out the still, dark terrace outside.

'Fine, Richard,' she said, 'just a little joke, that's all. You do what you think best, you've always made the right decision for Ringford, anyway. Doreen Price is the one to talk to, she's the leader of the village opinion, the old guard, certainly.'

Tom and Doreen Price sat over their coffee at the farm kitchen table, listening to the weather forecast and thinking about Cyril Collins. Doreen was a big-boned woman, but well-proportioned, her muscles firm from constant use. She worked hard on the farm, her husband's traditional right hand, knowing how to do most things and happy to run errands to the agricultural engineers or to the big farm suppliers in Tresham. Her round, pink face was usually broadened with a cheerful smile, and she had her neatly permed brown hair cut short for convenience.

Two village families were united when Tom and Doreen married. Doreen's family farmed up the Bagley Road, and the Prices at Home Farm had been tenants of the Standing estate for as long as anyone could remember.

At lambing time, Doreen Price bloomed into a foster-mother for the orphan lambs, proud that she seldom lost even the most tiny and frail little creature. It was a passing sadness that their only child, a daughter, had married outside the village and lived in Manchester.

'Mr Richard's asked me to go up to the Hall this evening,' said Doreen. 'We have to advertise for a new vicar and the poor man's a bit lost, I think. It is a big responsibility for him. If we get the wrong man after years of Cyril being so right for the village, everybody'll blame him.'

'Then you must tell him, Doreen, tell him what we need is a youngish family and a good straightforward chap who won't try any fancy new rubbish.'

Doreen sighed. 'I'm very glad you're not on the church council,' she said, 'we've got enough old fogies as it is.'

'What about that nephew of Bateses, old Jim Bates's son, he went off to be a vicar of some sort. He'd be all right, fit in with what the village needs. Why don't we ask him? He's married now and got a couple of kids.'

Tom got up from the table, a tall, thick-set man with wavy, nearly white hair and a pleasant, outdoor face. He picked up a letter from his big roll-top desk, and opened the back door, lifting its black iron latch with a snap.

'Better get this in the post,' he said, 'don't want the bailiffs in.'

Like all farmers, Tom paid the bills at the last possible date, and would have thought it very foolish to do otherwise. Bills were paid, but discounts were bargained for, and favours to farming friends were rewarded by other favours in return. The golden age of fortunes to be made in farming was over, and Tom and Doreen watched the pennies like anyone else.

'I expect you'll be calling in at the Arms on the way back?' said Doreen, taking the coffee mugs to the sink. 'See you at bedtime, then, Tom. Mind that slurry in the road, you'd best clear that tomorrow, stinks the place out.'

The Standing Arms was an old ale house, recently smartened up and extended under the direction of the new landlord, Don Cutt, a boorish, tough character from Birmingham, who knew what kind of pub he wanted to run and had set out to make sure he got it. The locals felt ill at ease with the new furniture and the strange beers Don Cutt had brought in. But they admired his ability to deal firmly with trouble, and kept their heads over their dominoes when the smart set from Tresham came pub-crawling on Saturday nights.

Tom had negotiated his way through the offending slurry with reasonable success, and arrived at the pub with the comfortable feeling of good things to come. He joined old Fred in the usual corner, and settled down over his pint.

Doreen tidied up and went upstairs to change into something suitable for a visit to the Hall. As she walked up the long avenue, under the fine chestnut trees, she thought about Cyril Collins and how much he would be missed. 'End of an era,' she said aloud. 'Who knows what we might get next?'

Ringford Hall was an eighteenth-century manor house of pleasing proportions, surrounded by parkland where spreading oaks and chestnuts sheltered herds of sheep and cattle. From a distance, the green park, its grazing animals, and the elegant, long-windowed façade of the Hall, seemed little changed from the delicate watercolours executed by talented Standing daughters of two hundred years ago. Their paintings still hung in seldom-used guest rooms, and the colours had faded with the years, as had their leisured, privileged way of life.

Doreen Price and Richard Standing, fellow churchwardens, sat in the oak-panelled room that had been his father's study and was now his, where he used the same desk and books, and looked out over the same parkland. He loved it as his father had done, and now, talking to Doreen Price, he felt at ease, knowing that she and her forebears were part of it all.

'I was thinking,' Doreen said, 'it's true nobody much goes to church, not to the services, but most folk in this village are christened or married or buried through the church – or their children are – and it is still a very important part of our lives here, don't you think?

Richard nodded. 'There'd be a riot if we decided to close it down, I do know that, Doreen,' he said.

CHAPTER SEVEN

Robert Bates, son of the farmer at Bates's End, opened the shop door and looked in.

'Boots are muddy, Mrs P,' he said. 'Could you hand me out a jar of coffee for Mother? She's run out, and we're all gasping up there.'

Peggy smiled. Robert was one of her favourite customers, a nice, quiet lad in his twenties, who was consistently polite and considerate. It was Robert who had found Frank in his crumpled car after the accident.

'It's a lovely morning,' she said. 'The village looks as if nothing bad could ever happen here. I keep thinking of poor Reverend Collins, and how he loved Ringford. He'd have been wandering down here for his ham and tomatoes this morning, taking his time in the sun, sitting on the seat under the tree and talking to the old boys . . .' Peggy felt her eyes prickle, and a lump in her throat.

It's not just Reverend Collins she's thinking about, Robert thought, and smiled kindly at her.

'Best not to dwell on it, Mrs P.' He looked over his shoulder down the street. 'Oh Lord,' he said, 'could you take the money quickly? I can see Octavia Jones coming, and you know what that means!'

The whole village knew that Octavia had a long-standing crush on Robert Bates. He had given her absolutely no encouragement – ran like a frightened rabbit every time he set eyes on her – but this seemed to intensify her passion. She wandered up and down the village when not at school, hoping to catch a glimpse of Robert, and if all else failed she would borrow the Jenkins's terrier to take for a walk, then spend most of the time lurking outside the farm.

Nobody much minded this, except the Jenkins's terrier, who was used to patrolling the village on his own, and certainly not on the end of a piece of string.

Robert clumped down the steps from the shop, and made a dash for his tractor, which he'd left with the engine idling by the pavement.

'Robert! Robert!' shouted Octavia, running along with blonde hair flying, past Victoria Villa, where her speedy progress was duly monitored. 'Wait, Robert! I want to ask you something . . .' But Robert jerked his tractor into gear, stood hard on the accelerator and was off with a racing start, swerving across the road and heading for home.

Ivy Beasley shook her head, and said to her silent sitting room, That girl will come to no good, mark my words, Mother. She sat down in her watching chair, and took up her knitting. She was making gloves, big, men's gloves in strong grey wool. They were for Robert Bates, who was the nearest Ivy had come to a child of her own.

After a difficult time with Robert's birth, Mrs Bates had accepted Ivy's help in looking after the baby. He had been a bit seedy, but under the tender loving care of Bates and Beasley women he had flourished, and become the mainstay of his ageing father's farm. Ivy had loved him dearly, and could scarcely bear it when she was no longer needed to help with him. But tiny Robert did not forget her, and toddled towards her with his little arms open. Now he called to see her regularly each week for a cup of tea and a chat, and Ivy's heart beat a little faster on Monday afternoons.

She knitted on, skilfully managing to look out of the window at the same time, and saw Warren Jenkins and his troublesome friend, William Roberts, kicking a football idly round the Green. Something small and grey streaked across where they were playing, heading for the chestnut tree, and William turning like lightning, chasing it at full pelt, until it leapt at the trunk of the tree, fell back, and then leapt again, this time shooting up the tree and disappearing into the leafy branches and safety.

Squirrels still in that tree, Mother, said Ivy conversationally, remembering how the boys used to chase them right up into the top when she was a girl. Never caught them, mind. Not once, to my knowledge, she said.

Doreen Price's muddy blue estate car drew up outside, and Ivy watched her get out. Into the shop for something quick and easy for the men's dinner, no doubt, she thought. But Doreen opened Ivy's little iron front gate and walked up the path.

'Morning, Mrs Price,' said Ivy Beasley, 'are you comin' in?'

'Thank you,' said Doreen, 'I'd just like a word, Ivy, about Mr Collins's funeral and one or two other matters.'

Doreen followed Ivy into the front room, though she would have been happier in the kitchen.

'Will you take a glass of elderflower wine?' said Ivy Beasley. 'There's a nice cool bottle down in the cellar.'

'Your own making, Ivy? Then I certainly won't say no,' said Doreen, sitting on a stern, upright chair by the bookcase. 'I've come straight from cleaning out the hen house,' she said, looking round the immaculate room. 'It's thirsty work!'

'And smelly work, too, if I remember rightly,' said Ivy, wrinkling her nose. 'Nothing worse than the smell of chicken muck.'

Doreen Price agreed uncomfortably, thinking that only Ivy Beasley could make chicken muck sound like the work of the Devil.

Ivy fetched glasses and a bottle of elderflower wine, expertly poured out a large glass for Doreen, and a smaller one for herself. She looked expectantly at Doreen, who began to talk about the old vicar.

Cyril Collins had apparently had few relations, and some of

those that were still alive were old and living in South Africa, and were reluctant to make the journey for the funeral. He had told Doreen many times that he wanted to be buried in Ringford, his home for so many years.

'We don't want him to go without honouring him with the proper rites,' said Ivy.

'His friend from Tresham is coming to take the service,' said Doreen, 'and there should be quite a few folk from the three parishes, enough to make a decent show, anyway.'

'You can leave it to Doris and myself to see that the church looks nice,' Ivy said confidently. 'He was a good man, Reverend Collins, always did his duty by this village.'

'Ah,' said Doreen, 'well, that brings me to the other thing. You keep your ear to the ground, Ivy, what sort of man do you think is wanted to take Cyril's place?'

Ivy was not too keen on the 'ear to the ground' bit, but she got up and refilled Doreen's glass from the tall green bottle. She walked over to the window, from habit rather than wanting to see out, and was silent for a minute or two. Doreen sipped the delicious cool wine and felt her head beginning to buzz. Watch it, she said to herself, Ivy's wines are known for their strength.

'What we don't want,' said Ivy, turning round and looking at Doreen with a stern expression, 'is a smart young know-all who wants to change everything and bring in all kinds of unnecessaries.'

'Well,' said Doreen expansively, 'you're in full agreement with Tom there, Ivy, but what do you think about a family man?'

'Could be a good idea,' said Ivy, 'but it depends on the wife. If she's one that fits in and likes to work in the parish, it could work well. But again, you could get a flibbertigibbet with no interest in the village. Pity we can't choose on our own, I say.'

'Mr Richardsdoin' his best,' said Doreen. 'Wants to getit right.'

No head for a real good drink, thought Ivy, filling up

Doreen's glass with the sparkling elderflower. What's coming next, I wonder.

'Mr Richard did say he had a cousin who might be interested,' said Doreen with dutch courage, 'but he wasn't sure the parish would approve.'

'Why shouldn't we?' said Ivy, suspicion growing.

'Because, well . . . because the cousin is a woman,' said Doreen, and took a deep, defensive gulp of wine.

'A WOMAN!' said Ivy, putting the cork firmly in the bottle. 'I trust you are not serious, Mrs Price, that wine is quite strong, you know.'

Doreen stood up, and felt the room swim. She hung on to the back of the chair, and, trying hard to collect her balance and her dignity, she made for the door. 'I'm perfectly serious, Ivy,' she said, 'it will have to be consdidered.'

On a bright, sunny day, with the wind fresh and lively, and the Ringle high and in a hurry, the Reverend Cyril Collins was laid to rest in the little cemetery across the road from the churchyard.

Gabriella played a cheerful piece by Handel, one of Cyril's favourites, as the congregation gathered, and Tom Price and Richard Standing stood by the door, welcoming a small, self-consciously sombre group of distant relations. The many villagers who came to make their farewells smiled and chatted, as they knew their old vicar would have wanted.

From her seat at the organ, Gabriella saw the sunlight streaming in through the stained glass, making coloured patterns on the pale stone floor in the chancel. She thought how many times Cyril Collins must have seen this, and thanked his God for all the natural beauties of the world. None of us knew him very well, she reflected, but he always seemed happy and content. His private time was spent amongst books and papers, and once or twice he had mentioned writing articles for learned journals. But nobody she knew had ever read them, and they were put away modestly in his desk drawer, with old photographs and yellowing letters from Oxford and Cambridge colleagues.

With endless patience and understanding, he had gone about his parish, listening and ministering, always making time for families in trouble, never discriminating between those who came to his church and those who didn't.

The undertakers carried his simple coffin down the little path, slippery and dangerous in winter, but now dry and safe for the people following slowly, crossing the narrow lane and grouping around the freshly dug grave.

The wind blew strongly, billowing the surplice of Cyril's rector friend as he pronounced the final blessing. Ivy Beasley clutched her hat, and Doreen Price grabbed at her service sheet as it blew out of her hands and landed against the mossy tombstone marking the grave of Tom's long dead great-grandmother Price.

'End of an era,' said Doreen, as she walked down the road with Tom, back to the farm and the routine of jobs which must be done, animals fed and made safe for the night.

'He was a good old boy,' said Tom, 'we shall not find it easy to replace him.'

'You'd best get those clothes off as soon as we get back,' said Doreen, quickening her step. 'Cyril wouldn't have wanted your best suit going to the cleaners after one afternoon's wearing.'

Tom looked at her in surprise, but, seeing that she was perfectly serious, he nodded, and they walked back in silence over the bridge, along the Green and up the quiet street to the farm, each thinking of Cyril Collins and the indelible place he had earned for himself in the history of Round Ringford.

CHAPTER EIGHT

'We can't have a woman parson, surely,' said Foxy to Jean Jenkins, who had just heard the news from Peggy in the shop. 'It wouldn't do for Ringford.'

'Well, Mr Richard seems to think so,' said Jean. She got up from the table, took an apple from the draining board, and began to peel it. 'You're right, of course, Fox, but you can't help wonderin' if it wouldn't be a bit of a lark.' She cut the apple into small pieces and put it on a saucer in front of Eddie.

Gemma and Amy finished their dinner at the same moment, and said in unison, 'Please can we get down,' being half off their seats before they got to the end of the sentence. Mark, a solid lad, overweight like his mother, chewed on, always a slow eater, but in any case anxious to hear how this conversation of his parents developed. Eddie, in his high chair, dropped half-chewed lumps of apple to the terrier waiting beneath, who obligingly ate them. Then he dropped the saucer, and it shattered noisily. After calm was restored, Foxy returned to the subject.

'I still think it should be a family man,' he said. 'They were having it over in the pub last night, and Tom Price were laying down the law about no new fancy ways and suchlike. Mind you, I agree . . .'

'When did you last go to church, Foxy my lad?' said Jean Jenkins, thumping him affectionately on the shoulder. 'You wouldn't know one end of a hymn book from the other.'

'Nor would you, come to that,' said Fox defensively, 'but that ain't the point. The church belongs to the village, and that means the vicar has to do what's right for the village. Always was like that in Cyril's day, and should continue, if you ask me.'

'I don't know,' said Jean, 'Reverend Collins told me one morning when we were havin' our coffee – he used to love to talk, poor old Cyril – he said that when he first come here, he was full of new ideas and plans for what he would do in the village – wake 'em up and get lots of new young people in the church. But them old biddies on the PCC and doin' the brasses and that, they took the heart out of him, gradually, he said, and in the end he just did what they wanted.'

'But he did it his way,' said Fox, 'so he won in the end.'

A sharp clacking of heels shifted their minds to the present, and Fox's head jerked to one side, listening, just like his namesake.

'Fox, come here and look at those two,' said Jean, smiling and looking out of the window into the garden. Gemma and Amy, each pushing a doll's pram with doll neatly tucked up inside, stalked unsteadily down the concrete path between the neat rows of lettuces and peas, each wearing a pair of Jean's best high-heeled shoes.

'It'll be smack bums for those two,' said Fox, 'if they don't ask first before taking your shoes.'

'And lipstick,' said Jean happily. 'Look at their faces!'

The normally pale faces of the twins shone with cream liberally applied and scarlet lipstick inexpertly smudged with a speedy and furtive hand.

Jean opened the window and called out in a loud and angry voice, 'Gemma! Amy! Just you get in 'ere and see what I've got to say!'

The twins looked at each other and smiled. They turned their prams and tottered obediently back up towards the house, knowing in their telepathic way that their mother was not all that cross, not really.

*

37

Bill walked over the river bridge, and stopped to look into the water, his watchful eye noting that the water-weed was getting too thick again under the stone arches and would need sorting out. He looked back at the church, the weathercock shining in the morning sun, and thought for the hundredth time that anybody but his Joyce would be happy to live in such a village.

He had come across the fields from a spinney far over towards Fletching, where he and Mr Richard planned to make a hide for Susan Standing to pursue her new enthusiasm for bird-watching.

The hedgerows were full of flowers, the result of Mr Richard's ordering a stop to blanket spraying of fertiliser and insecticides. Bill had seen misty-blue scabious and scarlet poppies, shining yellow buttercups and great white heads of cow mumble, all blowing in the wind amongst feathery grasses in every shade of green and purple. There had been a time when he and Joyce had walked hand in hand down the lanes, and she had known the names of all the flowers and grasses, laughing at Bill for his ignorance. 'Call yourself a country boy,' she said, 'you might just as well have been born in Tresham . . .'

But he knew them now, because he had learned from Joyce, admiring her quick brain and her wiry strength. What a sodding shame, he thought, blaming himself for not knowing how to cope with her when she needed him most. He walked slowly across the sunlit Green to the shop, and climbed the steps.

'Morning Bill,' said Peggy, looking down at the order book from the Hall. Ellen Biggs was in the shop, examining closely every gooseberry she put into a brown paper bag. It was pension morning, and Mary York sat in the Post Office cubicle counting out notes for old Fred Mills.

Mary York lived up the Bagley Road in an ugly bungalow, happily and tidily married to Graham, who worked in the Inland Revenue office at Tresham. They had no children, never talked about having any, and kept themselves to themselves. Mary was a pleasant, helpful girl, plain and honest, and had worked in the shop since the days when Doris Ashbourne trained her straight from school. Peggy could not afford to employ her full-time, but on very busy days, Mary came in and efficiently and quietly got on with the job.

'Morning Peggy,' said Bill, and Peggy felt her colour rise. This is ridiculous, she thought, anybody would think I was a young chit of a girl, instead of a middle-aged widow woman. She had lately become self-conscious about looking directly at Bill when other people were around. She was sure her feelings must show in her face, and she was equally sure the echoing warmth in his eyes and smile were glaring evidence of deepening affection between them.

Bill hung back, looking at things on shelves that he was never likely to buy, and when Ellen and Fred Mills had gone he came forward to the counter.

'Must see you alone, Peggy,' he said very quietly, so that Mary York, apparently occupied counting stamps, did not hear.

Peggy looked at him, startled at the urgency in his voice. She straightened the pile of postcards of Ringford Green, and looked across at Mary.

'Just going to get Bill to look at that drain in the yard,' she said. 'I've tried unblocking it, but the water is still not going down.'

Mary York nodded. It wasn't easy for Peggy, she thought innocently, being without a man in the house. Just as well Bill Turner was one who could turn his hand to anything.

Bill followed Peggy into the kitchen and then out into the back yard. Conscious of the Beasley look-out next door, Peggy said in a loud voice, 'There it is, Bill, still blocked, though I've tried my best to clear it.'

They bent their heads together over the drain, and Bill whispered, 'Somebody's telling Joyce tales about us, Peggy. We shall have to be very careful, gel. Not that I mind about the village – the old tabs will make a meal out of the smallest morsel – but if Joyce gets really upset she might do anything.

She's always threatening to do away with herself, and she just might . . .'

'Oh God,' said Peggy, 'Well, there can be only one person gossiping to Joyce and that's Poison Ivy next door. Joyce doesn't see anyone else, does she?'

Bill nodded, glancing over the fence at Victoria Villa. 'Ivy's a wicked woman, but not stupid, and doesn't often get caught out,' he said.

The yard was full of the scent of honeysuckle, climbing over the washhouse and intermingling with a crimson rose which had rambled over its trellis arch and ventured up the washhouse roof. It was warm in the full sun, and Peggy stood up straight, wishing she and Bill could sit on the old bench by the back door and have a cup of coffee and savour the scents and the warmth of the day. She sighed, and she too looked across at Ivy Beasley's woodpile.

'So it'll need drain rods, you think, Bill?' she said in a carrying voice. 'I'd be glad if you could fit the job in some time when you're not busy.'

'Be down Saturday afternoon,' said Bill, 'and don't worry if you need to go into Tresham, I can manage perfectly well on my own. Just leave the side gate unlocked . . .'

They went back into the shop, Bill buying bacon and baked beans, and Peggy taking the money and avoiding the bleak look in his eyes.

The bent figure of Ivy Beasley, pulling weeds behind the woodpile, slowly straightened up and pushed her springy grey hair back from her eyes. Well, Mother, she said, that was interesting.

CHAPTER NINE

One hundred and fifty miles away from Round Ringford, in a newly built vicarage in a medium-sized Welsh town, the Reverend Nigel Brooks, tall, greying at the temples, handsome in a crinkly, old-fashioned, Hollywood way, was talking to his wife Sophie over a sizeable breakfast of bacon, sausage, tomatoes and fried bread.

'There's one here, Sophie,' said Nigel, 'shall I read it to you?'

He looked across the table at his wife, who had a magazine propped up against her coffee mug. 'Mmm . . . what, dear?' she said, not looking up.

'This sounds a possible,' said Nigel, pushing away his empty plate and opening out the *Church Times* on the table. ' "Diocese of Tresham," ' he read, 'that's in the Midlands somewhere, isn't it? "Round Ringford, Fletching and Waltonby, three churches, twelve hundred population. Full details and application forms from The Patron, The Hon. Richard Standing, Ringford Hall, Tresham." What do you think, Soph?'

'The Midlands?' said Sophie, opening her dark brown eyes wide. 'That's a bit off our patch isn't it, Nigel?'

'Well, at least we'd have only one language to cope with. You'd be happy about that, wouldn't you, Soph?'

Nigel Brooks was the son of an English vicar and a Welsh girl from Carmarthen. His mother had insisted that he spoke

Welsh alongside English from the minute he could talk, and as a result he was usefully bilingual.

His father had hidden his disappointment when Nigel had opted for a career in the law, not reacting against his father's faith, but wanting complete independence from parental influence. He had practised successfully as a solicitor, and married his secretary, Sophie Fothergill, a small, red-haired Yorkshire girl. She came from a well-heeled rural family and had the fine features of an aristocratic greyhound, warmed by a burst of freckles over her nose and cheeks. Nigel and Sophie had raised two daughters and a son and lived in quiet affluence.

At forty-five Nigel had had an unexpected challenge. Not particularly disillusioned with the legal world, not wanting to retreat into the comfort of organised religion, he nevertheless knew without doubt that God required him to work for Him.

This was quite embarrassing to explain to partners and clients. The strict logic of the law was a million miles from Nigel's emotional decision. He felt quite sure that he should become a parson with a flock to tend, and he was pretty sure he would be good at it.

This lack of humility was tackled during his training, which he completed with honour, and after serving his curacy he had gone to a vacancy in the Church in Wales, to a town where his Welsh blood and his charming manner had made him the success he had hoped for.

Sophie was a different matter. She could not settle into the narrow, confined life of many of the housewives in her husband's parish. She hated housework, did not consider herself her husband's chattel, and loved to roam around an open landscape, not caring what she looked like and happy not to be speaking to anyone.

She did what she considered was required of her as the minister's wife, and expected his parishioners to respect her right to be herself. This they did not always do, and after three years a kind of uneasy compromise had settled on the parish. She agreed to take part where she could be useful and interested, and Nigel agreed to defend her against any criticism of being stand-offish and English.

'Worth finding out more, anyway,' said Sophie, beginning to think that the Midlands were not so very far from Yorkshire, and when she and Nigel found Tresham on the map, she saw the the M1 was quite handy for a quick dash up to see her elderly parents.

'Round Ringford's not marked,' said Nigel, looking up the gazetteer, 'so it must be pretty small.'

'Population's only twelve hundred for the three parishes,' said Sophie. 'Which one has the vicarage?'

'Doesn't say,' said Richard, reading the advertisement again, 'but my guess is that if the patron lives at Ringford Hall the vicarage will be in Round Ringford. It all sounds very feudal, Soph, do you think I could cope?'

'Very well, Nigel,' said Sophie wryly, 'you'd be in your element – sherry at the Hall, striding about the village in your canonicals, wowing the old ladies, absolutely in your element.'

'You're right,' said Nigel, accepting this with enthusiasm. 'I shall write off straight away.'

CHAPTER TEN

Ellen Biggs and Ivy Beasley were walking slowly down the avenue from the Hall, shaded from the hot sun by the cool, dark green canopy of branches above them. As they emerged into the heat of the full sun, they stopped as always on the stone bridge to look at the clear, rippling water, and the village shimmered around them. A group of children, specks of bright colour, livened up the yellowing grass as they played in vivid summer clothes on freshly painted climbing frames and swings, their play area fenced off from the likes of the Jenkins terrier.

'Things have come to a pretty pass, Ellen,' said Ivy Beasley, 'if Mr Richard is about to foist a woman vicar on us. Poor Reverend Collins would turn in his grave.'

'Don't believe a word of it,' said Ellen, shaking her head. 'Where'd you get that from, anyway?'

Ivy Beasley tightened her lips, signifying a vow of silence on sources, and reluctantly began to take off her grey cardigan. 'It's enough to fry you alive today, Ellen Biggs,' she said. 'Do you want to come in for a cool glass?'

Ellen looked at Ivy, stern-faced and devoid of any colour in her grey skirt and strict white blouse. Ellen herself was carefully dressed in a striped skirt of many colours and a blue and white flowery open-necked blouse, with cool, wide flapping sleeves and an odd assortment of brass buttons. 'To cheer it up a bit,' Ellen had said to an astonished Ivy. 'With your scraggy old neck,' Ivy had said, 'you'd do better with a decent high collar, Ellen Biggs.'

The two women crossed over to the Green and continued their stroll, following the footpath, which led almost directly to Victoria Villa. A single car moved slowly through the village, otherwise there was nothing much happening. All the silage had been gathered in, shiny black plastic bags of concentrated goodness for the winter cattle, and it was too early for harvest machinery to grind into action with its attendant dust and noise.

'That's a skylark, ain't it?' said Ellen, as they trod their measured way through the short dry grass. She leaned back, shading her old eyes from the glaring sun. 'You can hear it, but you can't see it,' she said. 'Must be a lesson to be learned there, Ivy.'

'Don't know what you . . . ouch!' yelled Ivy, jumping to one side with a sudden hop and skip.

'What's the matter with you, Ivy?' said Ellen, unmoved. 'Got a flea in yer knickers?'

'I been stung, that's what's the matter,' said Ivy, leaning down and rubbing her leg through her stocking.

'Prob'ly a horse fly,' said Ellen. 'Them things'll bite anything, they ain't fussy.'

Crossing the road, they came to the gate outside Victoria Villa. 'You offerin' me a glass, then, Ivy?' said Ellen.

'Certainly not,' said Ivy. 'I'm going to get something on this bite, it's driving me crazy. Go next door and get yourself a drink of orange – Pushy Peg'll take pity on you.' And she marched smartly up her path and into the house, shutting the door firmly behind her. Ellen Biggs shrugged. There wasn't nothin' nice to be said about old Ivy, she thought, try as you would, nothin' nice at all.

She struggled up the steps and into the shop. Peggy had drawn the blinds, and it was cool and airy, a flow of air coming in through the open kitchen door.

'You couldn't oblige me with a drink of water – perhaps a splash of squash in it, could you, dear?' Ellen said to Peggy.

45

My goodness, she thought, she's looking better, lost all that peaky look what came on after her Frank died.

Peggy smiled, and went off to make a drink for Ellen. She put two tinkling cubes of ice in the glass, and returned to the shop. 'Why don't you sit down on that stool and have a bit of a rest before you go back home?' she said kindly. Frank had put a stool by the Post Office window for the pensioners who had to wait for a few minutes for their money.

' 'Ave you 'eard about the woman vicar, then, Peggy?' Ellen said, comfortably settled. 'Our Ivy was full of it, but you can't always go by what she says. A grain of truth turns into a large loaf of gospel with our Ivy.'

'I did hear that some distant female relation of Mr Richard's had gone into the church,' said Peggy. 'But even if she does apply, there'll be probably be others, and the decision is not just Mr Richard's. There'll be a meeting in the village, I'm sure, so everybody can sum up the hopefuls.'

'What if the Standing woman is the only one?' said Ellen gloomily, but then she brightened. 'Still, it wouldn't 'alf make our Ivy mad,' she continued, 'that'd be something to witness!'

'Ellen Biggs,' said Peggy, 'you're a wicked woman.' She nodded to Colin Osman, who had just sprung athletically up the steps and into the shop. With one bound, she thought, Colin leapt clear. 'Morning, Mr Osman,' she said, 'lovely morning.'

Colin Osman was a tall, sporty young man. His fair, springy hair was cut short and his greenish eyes were lively against tanned skin. He and his young wife had recently moved into the village, and he was very anxious to enter into local activities in a big way. He had wanted to buy the shop when Peggy thought of selling after Frank's accident, but now he had transferred his enthusiasm for village life to schemes for resurrecting the cricket team and for forming a youth club to, as he put it, 'keep the young people off the streets'.

'Having a well-earned rest, Mrs Biggs?' he said, with an all-embracing smile. Ellen stared at him over the top of her glass. 'When you get to my age, young man . . .' she muttered.

'What can I get you, Mr Osman,' said Peggy. 'I expect you're in a rush as usual!'

Colin Osman was not a sensitive young man, and he nodded brightly. 'Just a couple of bars of soap, please, Peggy,' he said.

'She's Mrs Palmer to you, young sprig,' said Ellen under her breath. She'd nearly finished the squash, and swirled a sliver of ice round the bottom of the glass, making it last.

'Wonder if you'd put up this notice of the cricket meeting for me' Colin Osman said, unrolling a piece of paper and spreading it out in front of Peggy. 'There's quite a lot of interest already, and I do want to get things moving with a few practice games this season, if possible.'

'I remember times when it weren't a summer Saturday if there weren't a game o' cricket on the Green,' said Ellen. 'Then it got took over by that man at the pub . . . 'im that was there before Cutt . . . and 'e wouldn't let nobody play if they weren't regulars in the pub. Ran it into the ground, 'e did.'

'Perhaps,' said Peggy, fixing the notice to the board Frank had put up for the purpose, 'perhaps we should make it a condition of the vicar job that any applicant must be a good cricketer?'

'Good idea, Peggy!' said Colin Osman, impervious to irony, and, putting a bar of soap into each trouser pocket, he bounded down the steps and disappeared.

'Well, Susan darling,' said Richard Standing, 'that makes two applicants so far.' He had just opened a letter delivered by postlady Maureen, whose brown legs and chubby knees had distracted him for a moment or two.

'Beginning to think we wouldn't get any,' he said, unfolding several sheets of paper, 'and then we could encourage Sylvia to apply.'

'Darling, not frumpy cousin Sylvia!' said Susan. 'Though I suppose not even she would be frumpy enough to please the Beasleys and Biggses of Ringford.'

'Well, look at this!' said Richard, reading the letter. 'He's

47

actually put a love of cricket as his hobby – young Osman will be all for him, for a start.'

'Young Osman never goes to church,' said Susan, 'nor his chirpy little wife, so I don't see that he has much to say in the matter.'

'Oh, he'll be there if we have a general parish meeting to meet the applicants, sure to be,' said Richard, reading on.

'In a parish in Wales at the moment, wife comes from Yorkshire. Grown-up kids, and . . . oh, a latecomer to the cloth. Not so sure about that, probably full of bright modern ideas. Might not go down too well with Tom and his lot.

'Oh, but this is rather jolly,' he added. 'His family is now reduced to three living at home, he and his wife Sophie, and Ricky, an aged black labrador spaniel cross. That says a lot for him, don't you think?'

Susan did not answer, but picked up her small Yorkshire terrier, busily snuffling around her feet. 'We don't want any nasty old cross-breeds in Ringford, do we, Georgie darling,' she said in a silly voice, and kissed the top of his silky head. The dog turned and snapped at her ungratefully, and she put him down sharply. He wandered to the other side of the room and began to make advances to an upholstered footstool by the fireplace.

'Don't do that, George,' said Susan automatically, and reached out a hand towards Richard. 'May I have a look?' she said. 'He does sound just possible.'

CHAPTER ELEVEN

'I should be glad if you could spread the word, Mrs Palmer,' said Richard Standing, poking his head round the shop door. 'We shall be meeting at seven thirty in the church on Tuesday and Wednesday, one applicant each evening. I've put a notice on the church door with all the details.'

Sometimes he looks quite presentable, thought Peggy. Richard Standing was on his way to a meeting with his accountant, and his crisp white shirt, well-cut grey suit, and worn but well-polished shoes flattered his florid colouring and gave a kind of comfortable distinction to his incipient paunch.

Ivy Beasley turned round from inspecting a new line in chocolate biscuits, and stared at Mr Richard's Range Rover disappearing down to Bates's End.

'Two applicants, eh?' she said. 'And is one of them a woman?'

Peggy perched on the edge of a tall stool she kept behind the counter for times when her legs ached. It was another warm day, and she had been working hard in the garden all the previous evening, anchoring tall hollyhocks, heavy with dark red and pink frilly flowers, to the garden wall.

'Not necessarily, Miss Beasley,' she said patiently. 'Mr Richard has never mentioned a woman applicant. I know it's all round the village, but Mrs Price hasn't said anything either, and she's a churchwarden.'

'She's welcome to that job,' said Ivy, who had been very

annoyed that she had not been asked to fill the vacancy when old grandad Bates had died. 'Those two churchwardens have had to run the parish since Reverend Collins went . . . oh yes, and I can see from your face, Mrs Palmer, that you think it must be a cushy enough job in such a small village. But let me tell you, it is not. There is a great deal to do, fixing services and dealing with the paperwork and all that.'

'Of course,' said Peggy placatingly, wishing her neighbour would make up her mind about biscuits and get going. Then she could leave the shop for a minute or two and make a cup of tea.

'Well, I hope these haven't melted in this heat,' said Ivy, picking up a packet of chocolate creams. 'I shall be there, and not afraid to speak up either,' she added.

'I'm sure that's what the meeting is for, Miss Beasley,' said Peggy. 'I hope to be there myself.'

'*By* yourself?' said Ivy Beasley with a horrid smile, handing Peggy the exact money.

'What do you mean?' said Peggy, frowning, but Miss Beasley had pushed the biscuits into her basket and with quick steps disappeared into the street.

It was a big day for Nigel Brooks, and he had left Wales with the sudden feeling of panic that strikes when there's no going back. Of course, the job was not yet his, but he knew that even if Round Ringford did not appoint him, he would continue to look for another living. Sophie had been increasingly excited at the prospect of moving, and had given him a big hug and waved him off as he accelerated down the busy street and out into the Welsh countryside at the start of his important journey.

He reached Ringford at lunchtime and drove slowly down the street, past the shop and up Bates's End, unaware of the turning eyes that followed him all the way. Richard and Susan Standing had invited him for lunch, and they all sat, rather too far apart for a convivial atmosphere, around the big, polished mahogany dining table. Conversation centred on Nigel's ideas for the parish, with Richard and Susan feeding in loaded questions and bits of local knowledge which would help Nigel when he faced the parish later that afternoon. The Standing woman cousin had not after all applied for the job, and the other candidate had been the previous evening. Nigel had gathered that Richard and Susan had not been all that impressed with this first interviewee.

With some relief, after what seemed like a very long afternoon, Nigel left the Hall, saying he would like to walk down to the church on his own, to meet the waiting people. Richard Standing hesitated, feeling that protocol required him to introduce Nigel Brooks to the village, but something determined in Nigel's eye made him agree, saying he would pick him up later and bring him back to collect his car.

Round Ringford was looking its magical best. After the heat of the day, a cool breeze had sprung up and set the willow branches swinging over the rippling water of the Ringle, and the old stone houses glowed in the evening sun. The river path had tempted out Mr and Mrs Ross, a retired, shy couple from up the Bagley Road, with their little black and white dog; and Colin and Pat Osman, both back from a day spent in hot cars, strolled along behind the Rosses, gratefully drinking in the cool, grass-scented air. They nodded to Nigel as he passed, knowing exactly who he was.

He looked across the Green and could see a small group of young people. He felt glad that it wouldn't be all old ducks and charming aristocrats, and quickened his step, raising a hand to the slim, blonde girl who had left the others and was slowly cycling towards him.

It was Octavia Jones, who had been talking to her friends, Tanya and Tim Bright, at their modern house next to the Village Hall. The girls had offered desultorily to help polish Tim Bright's already gleaming red sports car, but he had refused.

That's a pretty girl, thought Nigel, as she came closer. He couldn't know that she had barely noticed him, but was keeping a weather eye open for Robert Bates, as usual.

'Hello,' she said absently to Nigel, her eyes on the gate leading from Bates's Farm. Nigel smiled, and walked on.

Tom and Doreen Price stood inside the church door, welcoming a trickle of parishioners who had come to meet the next applicant for the benefice of Round Ringford. The interior of the ancient church was wonderfully cool, and scented with sweetpeas arranged by Doris Ashbourne in brass vases on the altar that morning.

Doris was once again manning the tea urn over by the font, pouring strong, tan-coloured tea, and filling plastic beakers with orange squash for those who wanted a cold drink.

Nigel Brooks's footsteps sounded sharply on the stone paving, and everyone looked at the door as he arrived at the church porch and shook Tom's hand. The Prices were a bit taken aback, expecting Richard Standing to usher in the second candidate for their approval.

'I walked down from the Hall,' said Nigel, in explanation. 'Such a lovely evening, and the village looking so marvellous.' His warm smile took in the ladies at the urn, the group chatting by the pulpit and the little knot of children giggling in the Lady Chapel.

Doris Ashbourne, thinking already that here was a very nice man, broke the ice by filling the cup with steaming tea, and walked with it over to Nigel and the Prices.

'You must be thirsty after your walk, Reverend Brooks,' she said. 'Welcome to Ringford church.'

'A biscuit, Reverend Brooks?' said old Ellen, coming up behind Doris, not to be outdone.

'Thank you so much, Mrs er . . .' Nigel helped himself to a ginger nut, and took a small bite, knowing from long practice that it is difficult to answer questions with a mouth full of biscuit.

'Ashbourne,' said Doris, elbowing Ellen Biggs to one side, 'Doris Ashbourne, formerly of Round Ringford Post Office and General Stores.'

'Ah!' said Nigel. 'Then who has now taken over the most important position in the village?' He glanced round, still smiling, acknowledging his own secondary standing.

Peggy, standing pressed up against a pew-end by the group which had gathered round, said, 'I have, but I haven't been here very long. Peggy Palmer, pleased to meet you. Doris still gives me a hand, you know, and very useful she is too.'

Ah ha, Mrs Palmer is a diplomat, thought Nigel. An ally there, I hope.

'Takes a long time to settle in to Ringford properly,' said Ivy Beasley, pushing her way through to introduce herself. 'As, no doubt, you will find out for yourself, Vicar, should you come amongst us.'

'Don't take no notice of 'er,' said old Ellen, who, though not a regular worshipper, was not going to pass up the chance of a squint at the new parson – well, possible new parson. 'Ivy don't mean no 'arm,' she said. ' 'Er bark's worse'n 'er bite.'

'That's a whopper,' muttered Peggy to Doreen, who had come to stand next to her, handing her a cup of tea, 'I should have thought they were equally lethal. No thanks, Doreen, I must be getting home, Gilbert hasn't been fed.'

Nigel Brooks saw her go out of the corner of his eye, and made a mental note to call on her. She looked very pleasant, and a possible chum for Sophie, who did not make friends easily. He turned to Ivy Beasley with practised charm.

'My dear lady,' he said, smiling his crinkly smile, 'it is right and proper that any newcomer to such an ancient and lovely parish as yours should take a humble part for many a long month before presuming to lead his flock.'

'*Feed* his flock, I think you'll find the Good Book says,' said Ivy, and stretched out her hand. 'Another cup, Vicar?'

'I have had a most enjoyable day, Mr Standing,' said Nigel, getting into Richard's car outside the church. 'Everyone has been most kind. I cannot think of a lovelier setting for a village, and shall count myself most fortunate if I should be selected. My wife will, of course, want to come and have a look around, but I am sure I can include her in my enthusiasm.'

Doreen Price locked up the church and walked down to the

53

shop, now closed and shuttered, to chew over the day's events with Peggy. The back door stood open, and she could hear voices inside. One of the voices was Bill Turner's, and she hesitated, then turned on her heel and made her way back to the farm with a worried frown.

'You couldn't blame the poor bugger,' said Tom, as they sat in their cool sitting room, watching the news. 'That Joyce has asked for everything she gets. Just hope Peggy has the sense to know that nothing's secret in Ringford . . . specially if Ivy Beasley lives next door.'

'And speaking of old Ivy,' said Doreen, 'I just hope she didn't put off that nice Reverend Brooks. He made a good impression on me, turning up like that without Mr Richard, showing he was his own man, and that.'

'Ah,' said Tom, switching channels to watch the cricket, 'he certainly took charge of things straight away. Well, we shall see.'

CHAPTER TWELVE

'Mandy,' said Robert Bates, as they sat in his car outside his girlfriend's semi-detached house in the suburbs of Tresham. The film has been violent and noisy, and Mandy had held Robert's hand in a tight, tense grip for a couple of hours. Neither of them had enjoyed the evening much, and Robert wished it had been a romantic film, a love story to put Mandy in the right mood.

'Yes, Robert?' said Mandy, a slender, quick-moving girl with olive skin and a nose like a lump of putty stuck more or less in the middle of her face. Her smile was wide, and her teeth attractively crooked, and she had worshipped Robert Bates since they were at Tresham Comprehensive together.

'I love you, Mandy,' said Robert.'

'I love you too, Robert,' said Mandy, staring straight ahead through the fly-spattered windscreen.

'Will you marry me, Mandy?' said Robert, with a dopey smile.

'Yes please, Robert,' said Mandy, and they both burst out laughing, turning and kissing each other in delight.

They calmed down, and Mandy took Robert's hand. 'Come on,' she said, 'might as well get it over. Dad's at home this evening.'

'Oh Gawd,' said Robert. 'Must I?'

'Yep,' said Mandy. 'We're going to do this thing properly, or not at all.'

'Oh no, not the full white wedding and penguin suit?' said Robert, groaning.

'That's it,' said Mandy, opening the car door. 'Come on, Robert, he'll not bite you. He's probably expecting something of the sort anyway.'

Mandy Butler's father and mother sat in front of the television set, Mrs Butler completely immersed in an old film and Mr Butler fast asleep with his head back and his mouth open.

'Mother, we're back,' said Mandy.

'Good film, dear?' said Mrs Butler, without taking her eyes off the screen.

'Not bad,' said Robert. 'Um, I wonder if we could wake Mr Butler? I've something to ask him.'

Mrs Butler's attention was immediately redirected. She'd watched so many television soaps that her antennae were well tuned to the signs of an important development. 'Reg,' she said. 'Reg, wake up!'

He awoke with some snorting and choking, and denied hotly that he had been asleep. 'Just resting my eyes for a minute or two,' he said.

'Mr Butler,' said Robert, anxious to get the whole thing over. 'I – that is, me and Mandy – um, well, we'd like to get wed if that's all right with you . . . and Mrs Butler, of course.'

Mandy's mother rose with a shriek and flung her arms round Mandy, while Mr Butler got slowly to his feet. Robert wondered nervously whether he was going to eject him by the scruff of his neck.

'Well done, Robert,' Mr Butler said, extending his hand. 'Me and Mother was wondering when you'd get around to it.'

They all laughed with the release of tension, and Mrs Butler went happily out to the kitchen to fetch a bottle of wine put by for just such a special occasion.

'Mother,' said Mandy, as they toasted each other with glasses of the sweet, yellow wine, 'you might as well know that I want the wedding to be in Ringford.' She looked at her mother, dreading the wobbly chin and eyes filling with tears.

Her mother was a very emotional person, and it was not easy to know which way she would take things.

'Oh, I do agree, dear,' she said to her only daughter. 'A village wedding, white dress with a long train, your little cousins for bridesmaids, and Robert in one of those lovely suits. I can see it now . . .' She had a dreamy look on her face, and Mandy knew that all was well.

'It is the most beautiful village,' said Nigel to Sophie. He had returned very late the night before absolutely exhausted, but so cheerful that Sophie knew it had gone well. She made him go straight to bed, promising to listen to a full account the following morning. 'Seems the other applicant was only two years off retiring, and the churchwardens sensibly thought it would be mad to have to go through the whole thing all over again so soon.'

'Tell me about the village, and the house,' said Sophie.

'Ah,' said Nigel, 'yes, the house. Well, it is a lovely eighteenth-century, three-storey stone house. It has five bedrooms and attic rooms, and a wonderful drawing room and a huge dining room, and big kitchen, scullery, walk-in larder, tiled hall the size of this room, and big garden with paddock behind.' He waited anxiously, trying to read Sophie's expression.

A slow smile spread over her face. 'Let's go, then,' she said.

They talked about the village, and Nigel described the wide Green and the chestnut trees leading to the Hall. 'It was a beautiful evening, and I had the feeling I was stepping back in time. The village lies in the Ringle valley, and with wooded hills all round it's like a forgotten hamlet. One of the last to get main sewerage, I was told! Of course, it is an illusion. They are firmly in the twentieth century, and the folk I met were straightforward, practical people, and very kind and welcoming.'

He paused, decided not to mention Miss Beasley, and continued. 'Richard Standing seemed a nice enough chap – bit feudal, as we thought, but very approachable – and Mrs Price, the farmer's wife, was a very comfortable sort of soul. Kindness itself, I should imagine.'

'Anybody I would like?' said Sophie, already beginning to think of a donkey in the paddock, and summer walks by the Ringle.

'A very nice woman called Peggy Palmer keeps the shop. She didn't stay long at the meeting, but said some very sensible things and had a good sense of humour. Seems her husband died last year, and she works hard keeping the shop going.'

'So when do we start?' said Sophie, with a big smile.

The Welsh parish had already got wind of Nigel's intentions, and with unseemly haste had got a new incumbent in mind. He was young, known for his youth work, and one hundred per cent Welsh. He could come as soon as needed, and nothing stood in the way of a quick handover.

'End of August, I should think,' said Nigel.

'Right in the middle of harvest,' said Sophie happily. 'Round Ringford, here we come,' she said, and gave Nigel a big, impulsive kiss on his handsome face.

There was general agreement in Ringford that the Reverend Nigel Brooks seemed a decent sort of chap. One or two of the men in the pub, led by Tom Price and backed up by Foxy Jenkins, who had been bullied along to the meeting by his insistent wife, said they thought he was 'a bit smarmy', but Colin Osman had whooped at the news that Nigel was a cricketer and already had plans for the opening match on Ringford Green.

'And anyroad,' said old Fred Mills from his dominoes corner, 'that other chap was one of Them, if you ask me. Bachelor all his life, hobby was makin' lace . . . well, what more d'you need to know?'

The Honourable Richard and Mrs Standing were perfectly happy with Nigel Brooks, although Richard said he could not imagine why such an all-round good sort of man should want to come to a tiny living like Round Ringford, and the village should count itself very lucky.

'Perhaps you'd want a complete change if you had been holed up in a frightful little Welsh town,' said Susan. 'I can quite see Ringford must have looked like paradise to him.'

'I think Pa knew his wife's people up in Yorkshire,' said Richard. 'I do remember him talking about some northern Fothergills quite a lot at one time.'

'That clinches it, then,' said Susan, with a quiet smile. 'If Pa knew her people, the whole thing looks absolutely meant to be.'

Warren Jenkins and William Roberts wandered idly across the Green, dribbling a football over the bridge and down past the church and Ellen Biggs's little Lodge house at the entrance to the Hall avenue. There were heavy black clouds massing over the hills on the Bagley Road, and the sunlight had a sharp edge to it, presaging a storm.

William and Warren had formed their own opinion of the vicar presumptive from their hiding place in the bell tower, overlooking Wednesday evening's meeting. Both of them were learning to ring the bells, and knew about the narrow oak door in the vestry, which led up to where thl-ropes hung, never still, always gently swaying in the draughty chamber. The ropes were looped up for safety, and William and Warren had sat cross-legged by a crack in the floorboards, listening to the conversation which had floated up from the meeting below.

'He'll be a pushover,' said William, and Warren had nodded. 'A right softie, if you ask me,' he said. 'What you bet he tries to get the choir goin' again?' 'We'll be ready for him if he does,' said William, with a sinister leer. 'It worked last time, didn't it?' They had clambered down after most people had gone, and slipped out of the church unnoticed.

No thoughts of vicars troubled their minds now as they stopped opposite the Lodge gate, staring in.

'There's the three witches of Ringford,' said Warren, seeing

Ellen's front door open and three dark shapes inside. 'Come on, William!' he yelled. 'They're gettin' the broomsticks out!' They shot off at great speed, whooping with what they imagined were witch-noises, and expertly passing the football from one to another, all the way up the avenue until they came within sight of the Hall. There they turned off through a much-used hole in the hedge and disappeared.

'If I catch that Warren Jenkins,' said Ivy Beasley, 'I'll give him something to remember me by.'

Ivy and Doris Ashbourne had walked down to Ellen Biggs's house for tea. It was Ellen's turn, and she had covered a rickety little three-legged cane table with a cloth, the embroidery faded and rusty spots on the creases.

'I remember that cloth, don't I, Ellen?' said Ivy Beasley. 'Used to be on the side table in the dining room at the Hall?'

'They done with it,' said Ellen dismissively. 'Too old and faded for them.'

She set out three cups, two matching saucers and the other very nearly the same. There were hairline cracks and the odd chip, but the china was delicate, and these too had seen better days on the Standing tea tray.

'There you are, Ivy,' said Ellen grandly, bringing in an iced sponge with walnuts on top. 'Slaved all morning in a hot kitchen makin' that for your tea.'

Ivy Beasley leaned forward and took a small piece of cellophane from the side of the cake. 'How come it says "Mr Kip . . ." on this scrap o' paper, then, Ellen Biggs you old liar?' she said.

The sky had darkened, and one or two spots of rain spattered on Ellen's mullioned windows. It was dim at the best of times in the Lodge, and now it seemed like twilight in the little sitting room.

Ellen poured cups of strong tea from a big brown pot, slopping a little into the saucers as her hand shook with the weight.

'Gettin' old,' she said. 'That's what, we're all gettin' old.'

'Speak for yourself,' said Ivy Beasley. 'You're as young as you feel, Mother always used to say.'

'Yes, well,' said Ellen Biggs tartly, 'your mother was old from the day she was born.'

'Could we change the subject?' said Doris the peacemaker. 'What did we all think of the Reverend Nigel Brooks?'

'All the same, these vicars,' said Ellen, with an evil chuckle, 'lazy men, ridin' on the backs of the churchwardens, most of 'em.' She poured second cups all round.

'Rubbish, Ellen Biggs!' said Ivy hotly. 'It's not a job I'd say thank you for, and I reckoned that Reverend Brooks was very pleasant, considering.'

'Considering what?' said Doris, licking the sticky white icing from her fingertips and making a mental note to give Ellen some paper napkins for Christmas.

'Considering he'd been listening to all kinds of nonsense from people who never go to church, except to gawp at the new man,' said Ivy, sending a poisonous dart at old Ellen, who deflected it with the ease of long practice.

'All the parish were invited,' she said, 'and Reverend Brooks said to me that he would think of himself as the pastor of the whole village, not just the churchgoers.'

'He addressed no more than two words to you, Ellen Biggs,' said Ivy Beasley, flushing with annoyance, 'you having been a fixture at the coffee table all evening, eating your way through refreshments provided by someone else!'

Doris Ashbourne stood up, brushing crumbs from her smooth navy skirt. 'If you two are going to bicker all afternoon, I'm going home,' she said. 'I've got better things to do.'

Ivy and Ellen were silent for a moment, then Ellen said, 'Oh, all right, Ivy, he never said it to me. But you do provoke on purpose, don't yer?'

Ivy's face was set. She continued to sit in silence, and the other two chatted of gardens and the price of vegetables at the shop and why they weren't fresher, considering they were surrounded by good growing land, and then Ivy put down her plate with a clatter.

'Well, if you want to know what I think of the new parson,' she said, 'I think we'll be very lucky if he decides to come. Course, we don't know what his wife's like, but I thought he was a very nice man.'

Praise such as this from Ivy Beasley was so unexpected that Ellen sat down with a bump in her chair, widening the split in the threadbare upholstery.

'What 'as come over you, our Ivy?' she said, but Doris chimed in quickly, 'I quite agree, Ivy, a very nice man indeed. He seemed to get to know everybody at once, and listened to what you had to say.'

'Well, I don't know I'm sure,' said Ellen Biggs. ' 'Ow much is it to join the Reverend Brooks's fan club?'

A clap of thunder drowned Ivy Beasley's reply, and old Ellen struggled to her feet. 'You'd best be off 'ome,' she said, 'else I'm goin' to be stuck with the pair of you for hours.'

They hurriedly took the tea things out to Ellen's tiny kitchen, and then Ivy and Doris, glancing apprehensively at the lowering sky, began to walk quickly back towards the Green. The rain was heavier, and streaks of lightning flashed over the Hall, lighting up the village with an eerie electricity.

'Need a lift, ladies?' said a voice. With the rumbling thunder in their ears, Doris and Ivy had not noticed Bill Turner's old van drawing up behind them. 'Hop in the back quick,' he said, 'you won't be there for more 'n a minute.'

It was no time to argue, and the women scrambled into the back of the van, pulling the doors shut behind them. The rain beat harder down on the roof of the van, and Doris said, 'You came along just in time, Bill, we'd have got soaked to the skin.'

Ivy Beasley sat on a paper sack of rabbit mix and stared at the floor of the van. As it drew up outside Victoria Villa, she leaned forward and carefully picked up something from the floor. 'What you got there, Ivy?' said Doris, but Ivy Beasley shook her head. 'It's nothing,' she said. 'Just thought I saw a coin down there, but it was only a stone.'

Why, then, wondered Doris Ashbourne, did you pick it up and put it in your pocket, Ivy Beasley, answer me that . . .

CHAPTER THIRTEEN

'I saw Joyce Turner in the garden after dinner,' said Jean Jenkins to her husband as they sat having their tea. 'She were still in that scruffy dressing-gown – I don't know how she has the nerve . . . anybody could see her over the fences.'

'Shouldn't think anybody would want to look,' said Foxy, wiping little Eddie's face with a wet flannel. 'Come on, my duck, let the dog see the rabbit . . . I'll get that chocolate off . . . watch out, here it comes!'

Eddie fought him off bravely, but in the end his face was wiped and he was lifted down to go and play. 'C'mon Eddie,' called Mark, 'there's a good programme on – lots of cars . . . cars, Eddie!' The magic word did the trick and Eddie disappeared into the front room, where the assembled Jenkins children sat relaxing in front of the television screen.

'Suppose we shouldn't let them watch so much,' said Jean comfortably, pouring Fox another cup of tea, 'but they can't go outside in this rain.'

'What was Joyce Turner doing, anyway?' said Foxy. 'She don't usually come out of the house in daylight.'

'Dunno,' said Jean. 'She went into Bill's shed for a few minutes, and next thing I saw her goin' back into her kitchen and banging the door behind her.'

Sounds of dissension from the front room brought Jean to her feet. 'Mark! Warren! Stop it at once, whatever it is!' she said, and went through to give them a good sort out.

Bill drove home through the storm after dropping first Ivy at Victoria Villa, and then Doris a few doors away from his own house in Macmillan Gardens. Miniature rivers were flowing importantly down the Gardens, swelling the water in the main street when they emerged, only to disappear in a dramatic swirl down the big drain.

'It's chucking it down out there, black as night over Bagley Woods,' he said to Joyce, who greeted him with a blank stare as he came into the sitting room. The television was on as usual, and Joyce sat on the sofa, her feet up on a stool in front of her. But there was one good sign. She had changed out of the old dressing-gown and slippers, and had put on a loose dress and a pair of white, old-fashioned sandals. Then Bill realised with disquiet that the dress was a maternity one, bought all those years ago in anticipation of the longed-for baby.

Joyce rocked herself from side to side, and Bill saw that she had a cushion in her arms, and that she was humming. It was the same lullaby as always, the words varied to suit her mood. 'Wee baby bunting,' she sang, 'Daddy's gone a-hunting, Mummy's got a rabbit skin to wrap wee baby bunting in.'

The word 'rabbit' rang alarm bells, and Bill turned and dashed out into the back garden, down the path and into his shed. He went rapidly from one cage to another, checking on each to make sure they were all alive and untouched. All seemed as usual, and Bill sighed with relief.

'Might as well feed you now, my beauties,' he said, and filled up each trough from the sack of rabbit mixture in the corner of the shed. He checked their water, talking to each one as he worked. 'Better be seeing to Joyce now,' he said to them. 'I'll be back later to say goodnight.'

I don't know, he thought, as he went back up the path, Joyce cuddles a cushion, and I talk to rabbits as if they're my kids. Not much to choose between us, some would say.

He got the tea ready and took a tray into Joyce in the sitting room. She shook her head at him. 'Not hungry,' she said, pushing the tray away.

'Try a little bit, Joycey,' Bill said, 'you got to eat, keep up your strength.' He realised he was playing along with her fantasies and despised himself. But it was no good crossing her or trying to bring her back to reality. Her screams and tantrums over the years had weakened his resolve, and now he humoured her most of the time. His only defence was to leave the house, to get out of earshot . . . but then it all had to be faced when he returned.

'I'll just have a bite in the kitchen,' he said, gently putting the tray down on a table beside her, 'then I'd better get out there and tackle them weeds.'

Macmillan Gardens formed three sides of a square, the fourth being the main street. A rectangle of grass, designed as a play space for the children, was maintained by the Council, but old Fred Mills had taken to caring for the flower beds in the centre and mounted guard over them from his front gate, seeing off any charging children with threats and curses.

The Turners lived on one side of the square, and the Roberts family almost opposite. Michael and Renata Roberts had produced four children, two of whom had now left home, leaving William and Andrew to cope with the untidy relationship of their parents. Michael Roberts was a violent man. His wife Renata, named after her Italian grandmother, had been an attractive, dark-haired girl who fell for Michael's blustering ways. She was a weak woman, and gave in on all issues, never daring to disagree or venture an opinion of her own. This seemed to her the best course for her to take, since Michael Roberts's idea of an argument was to answer with a blow. All the children had grown up with a keen ability to dodge.

Michael Roberts was coming back from the pub late in the evening. The moon was full, and in his befuddled state he walked up the wrong side of the Gardens, passing first the Jenkins's house and then the Turners', where a light showed through a crack in the thick curtains.

'Turner's up late,' Michael Roberts said to himself. He and Bill had a wary relationship, Michael Roberts knowing that

Bill disapproved of him, and he in turn despising Bill for not being able to handle a silly woman. He started on a short cut across the grass, swearing as he stepped into one of Fred's precious flower beds, and paused to regain his balance.

It was then that he heard the scream.

'Christ Almighty!' he said, looking back to the Turners' house. 'What's that woman done now!'

Sobered up by the awfulness of the scream, he reluctantly went back and pushed open the Turners' gate. He could see a light on in Bill's shed, and the back door of the house stood open. Sounds of crying and jumbled words came from the kitchen, but Michael was not up to facing Joyce. He went on down the path to the shed and opened the door.

He couldn't see anyone at first, then noticed a crouching shape in the far corner. He could see it was Bill, and then realised with horror that he too was crying. 'Bill?' he said. 'What the hell's goin' on?'

There was no reply, but Bill straightened up and wiped his face with a grubby handkerchief. He tried to say something, choked, and then indicated the rabbit cages with a hopeless wave of his hand. Michael Roberts saw that all the doors were open, and he peered inside.

'Oh God, no . . .' he said. 'Oh, good God, no.'

Each cage contained a small, stiff corpse. Protruding eyes stared lifelessly out at Michael as he went round the shed, unable to believe what he saw. Bill sat down heavily on an old chair, and put his head in his hands.

'I never thought she'd do it,' he said in a muffled voice. 'She threatened often enough, but I never thought she'd do it.'

'What a bloody nightmare,' said Michael Roberts, quite sober now. 'They bin poisoned?'

Bill nodded. 'My fault,' he said. 'I got the stuff to deal with rats eating the feed.' He looked up at his neighbour, and said, 'What am I going to do?'

'Beat the livin' daylights out of her,' said Michael Roberts. 'I'll do it myself if you're squeamish.' He patted Bill awkwardly on the shoulder and said, 'Come on, Bill, let's go and see to 'er.'

Bill shook his head. 'Won't do any good,' he said. 'Even if I agreed with you, which I don't. Violence doesn't answer violence. Better go now, Michael, and leave me to deal with her. She's screaming the place down now out of fright, scared of what I'll do.'

'You sure?' said Michael Roberts, beginning to wish he was back home where he knew how to act when retribution was needed.

'Yep,' said Bill. 'I'll just clear up in here, calm down a bit. If I go back in there now I shall kill her. You could just shut the back door, Michael, as you go by. Thanks for coming over.'

He began to pull out the dead rabbits and put them in an empty sack, stroking each one for the last time before they fell with a dull thud into the growing pile.

'That's it, then, Joyce,' he said.

CHAPTER FOURTEEN

Ivy Beasley sat in her kitchen, her damp coat hanging over the back of a chair in front of the range, steaming gently. She looked speculatively at a small enamelled brooch, shaped like a violet flower, which she had taken from her pocket and placed on the table.

'Now, my little beauty,' she said, 'who do you belong to, and how did you get on the floor of Bill Turner's van?'

Who do you think it belongs to? said the voice in her head. You'll not have far to go to find the owner of that.

Ivy got up and fetched a little box from the table drawer. It had a few drawing pins rattling around inside, and she emptied these on to the table. She fitted the brooch carefully inside, and tucked in the flap, sealing it with a small rubber band.

Just the right size, she said. Now, I think that will be safest in your desk, Mother, and she took it through to her sitting room, tucking the little box neatly inside a shallow drawer her mother had used for pens and pencils.

She looked out of her window, across the Green where children had come out to play as soon as the rain had stopped. Mark and the twins were jumping in puddles, seeing how much muddy water they could splash into each other's boots. They were all laughing and shouting, and Ivy Beasley felt a stab of loneliness, catching her unawares.

Why was I an only one, Mother?' she said. But this time there was no answering voice in her head. In death as in life,

69

her mother backed away when Ivy ventured a question bordering on intimacy.

Ivy sighed, and went to fetch her raincoat. She did not trust the sky, which still glowered and threatened more showers, in spite of weak sunlight striking wet roofs and leaves. Picking up a bunch of roses cut earlier in the day from her garden, she walked out into the glistening evening to pay homage to her mother's grave.

It was quiet in the graveyard, and Ivy fetched a bucket of water and pulled a scrubbing brush and bar of strong green soap from her basket. She knelt down, and began to scrub the white marble headstone. Not much dirt had collected since Ivy last scrubbed, and when she was satisfied that the stone was sparkling clean, she arranged the roses in a glass vase and stood back to admire the effect.

'Good evening,' said a pleasant, man's voice. She looked round, startled, and saw Richard Standing, dressed in his town clothes, leaning against the old pump and smiling at her.

'Mr Richard!' she said. 'You gave me a fright!'

'So sorry,' said Richard. 'I just saw you from the road and thought I'd catch you for a quick word. It's about the new vicar.'

'A word with me?' said Ivy Beasley, wondering why she should be consulted at this late stage, when her opinion had not been sought before. Richard Standing was aware of this, of course, and, knowing Ivy's influence in the village, decided on the spur of the moment to make her feel she was part of a decision which was, in fact, already made.

'I'd like very much to know what you thought of Nigel Brooks,' he said. 'Your family have been in Ringford very nearly as long as mine, and your comments would be most valuable.' Don't overdo it, Richard, he said to himself, old Ivy's not stupid.

She flushed with pleasure, however, and said, 'I'm not one for making hasty judgements, Mr Richard, but on first meeting he did seem a very nice man, and quite suitable for the village. That's not to say his wife will be the same, o' course.'

Her mouth closed tightly, as if surprised that such favourable sentiments could be expressed by Ivy Beasley.

'Oh good,' said Richard Standing. 'We all liked him very much, and I'm so glad you agree. And as to his wife, they are both coming next week to spend a couple of days looking round. They'll stay at the pub – good sign, I thought, when Nigel suggested it!'

So it's 'Nigel' already, is it, thought Ivy Beasley, well, that must mean he's the one. She felt a little frisson of excitement at the thought, and subdued it instantly. Many a slip, my girl, she told herself, better wait and see what his wife's like.

Peggy sat at her dressing-table in her nightdress brushing her hair and looking absently at herself in the looking glass. She had watched a film on television and gone up to bed later than usual. Just as she pulled the covers back on the lonely double bed the telephone rang.

She stood stock-still in alarm. Who on earth would be ringing her at this time of night? She considered not answering it, but then thought perhaps it might be an emergency and, pulling on her dressing-gown, ran downstairs to the sitting room.

The last voice she was expecting was Bill's. 'Peggy?' he said, and he sounded stiff and strange. She had seldom spoken to him on the telephone, and certainly not in the middle of the night.

'Bill!' she said. 'What's wrong, where are you?'

'In the box up by the village hall,' he said. 'I must see you.'

'Don't be ridiculous,' Peggy said, beginning to feel frightened, sensing something awful. 'It's nearly midnight!'

'If I wait outside in the van, will you slip out and we can go somewhere Ivy won't see us?'

'Bill, this is really silly, why can't it wait until morning?'

'Please, Peggy,' he said, 'please come.'

'But I'm ready for bed,' she said, 'I can't see . . .' There was a click as Bill's money ran out, and then the dialling tone. Peggy put down the telephone and stood frowning. I wish I could ask Frank what to do, she thought, and then realised what a stupid thought it was.

She went back upstairs and looked out of the window. The road was empty in the moonlight, and the village asleep. She sighed with relief, thinking that Bill must have gone home. Then she saw a shadow moving along opposite the school, and knew that it was Bill's old white van. It stopped short of the Stores, out of sight of Victoria Villa, and she heard the engine cut out.

Peggy slowly took off her nightdress, and began to put on the day's clothes still in a heap on a chair. She combed her hair roughly, collected her anorak from a peg in the hall, and quietly let herself out of the back door, going down the path at the side of the Stores and through the little gate on to the pavement outside.

Bill leaned over and opened the passenger door for her, and she got in. He said nothing, but started the engine, and began to back slowly until he could turn up the Bagley Road, then they climbed up the hill and were out of the village.

Neither of them spoke until Bill turned the van off the road into a clearing in the woods and switched off the engine. He put his arms round Peggy and held her so tightly that she could not breathe. He did not kiss her, and she knew something really bad had happened.

'What is it, Bill?' she said, when he finally released her.

Hesitantly, and with his voice breaking from time to time, he told her about Joyce and the rabbits. Peggy listened in growing horror. Nobody would do such a dreadful thing unless they were very sick, or very full of hate.

'Where is she now?' she asked, stroking Bill's hand comfortingly.

'Gone to bed,' he said. 'Sleeping like a baby when I came out. She always does after one of her storms.' He turned and looked at Peggy in the shadowy moonlight under the trees.

'Can I come home with you, Peggy?' he said. 'I could leave before folks are up. I can't go back there tonight.'

Peggy did not answer for a long while, and Bill just sat and looked at her, drawing comfort from her presence, holding her hand. Finally she took a deep breath and said, 'No, Bill, not like this. Not when we're both shocked by your Joyce. And then you having to creep out like some criminal at first light. I couldn't bear it, Bill, not like that.' She did not say that Frank's photograph was by the bed, and she could never turn his face to the wall.

Bill silently shook his head, and his face was so beaten that Peggy reached out and touched his mouth with her fingers, inviting a kiss.

'Bill,' she said, 'I think I love you . . .'

He took her hand and kissed the palm, folding her fingers over and squeezing her fist very gently.

'Could've bin worth it, then,' he said, 'to hear you say that.'

They sat in silence, looking at the woods and the silhouetted tree-tops where the bright moon shone through. An owl hooted, and they saw it swoop, a whitish floating shadow, absorbed in its nightly hunt, unaware of intruders. Bill reached out and turned the key, and the engine was loud and alien. He backed the van round, and coasted down the hill into Ringford. The village was still and sharply outlined in the moonlight, like an abandoned toy, all life gone out of it.

'I'd better get back and face it,' he said, his voice now firm and more his own. 'I'll do some cleanin' up while she's asleep. And don't forget,' he whispered, as he drew up just before the Stores, 'I know I love you, Peggy Palmer.'

CHAPTER FIFTEEN

Nigel and Sophie Brooks drove over the brow of Bagley Hill and marvelled at the view. It was a calm, brilliant day, and the village smiled, all its green and golden colours heightened in the bright sun. The Ringle glinted through the willows and the white flag pole in the school yard stood out like a marker post for travellers across the wilderness.

'Slow down, Nigel,' said Sophie, 'there's something in the road down there.'

The something was a herd of black and white cows being driven to new pasture by Foxy Jenkins, and they were taking their time. At last the final cow lumbered by, and Foxy followed, waving his thank you to the car. When he saw who was in it, his smile broadened, and he shouted, 'Mornin', vicar! Mornin', missus!' and went on his gingery way, calling instructions to the cows who took no notice at all but wandered where impulse took them.

'Looked a nice chap,' said Sophie, her spirits rising. It had been a grey, misty morning when they left Wales, and she and Nigel had travelled in silence for most of the first hour or so. Then, as the sun began to break through, Nigel talked about Round Ringford, telling Sophie details which were coming back to him as he drove nearer to the village.

He was at that church meeting,' said Nigel. 'Can't remember his name, but he had a fat and jolly wife.'

Nigel had had a telephone call from Richard Standing, who

said that of course it all had to be finalised by the Bishop and a number of formalities gone through, but assured him that if he still wanted the living of Round Ringford, Fletching and Waltonby, it was his. Nigel and Sophie had celebrated with a half-bottle of good champagne, and toasted each other over a delicious supper enthusiastically prepared by Sophie.

'Are we to go straight to the pub?' said Sophie, turning her head this way and that, not wanting to miss anything as they drove down the main street past the Green and came to a halt outside the Standing Arms.

'Yes, Richard Standing will find us later on, he said.'

'Come on, then, Nigel,' said Sophie, 'let's go and check in. I can't wait to get out into the village and see the church and the vicarage and . . . oh, come on Nigel, quickly!'

Their progress had been observed from Victoria Villa, and Ivy Beasley felt her heart flutter in an unaccustomed way as she caught sight of a handsome greying head, and knew it was Nigel Brooks. For the moment, Ivy had only a swift impression of the red hair and fine features of Sophie sitting beside him.

She got out of her chair and watched the car pull up outside the pub. The passenger door opened first, and a small, slender woman got out, stretching and turning round in a complete circle, taking in the whole village in a long, slow look.

Looks a bit of a titch, Mother, said Ivy Beasley, and pulled the lace curtain a little to one side to get a better view. The driver's door opened, and the familiar figure of Nigel Brooks emerged. Ivy thrust tightly closed hands into her cardigan pockets and watched Nigel say something to Sophie, and then both of them disappeared into the Standing Arms.

Ivy walked back into the kitchen and looked at herself in the small mirror over the sink. She saw a long face, the skin red and coarsened by lack of care, and a short bush of grey hair cut relentlessly without shape. Her eyes stared back at her, grey, with flecks of black, and short, straight lashes. Not much to look at there, Mother. Never was, said her mother's voice, looks aren't everything. Ivy tried a smile at the face in the mirror, and was comforted by her white, even teeth. Pity there's not much to smile about, said Ivy. Stop feeling sorry for yourself, said the answering voice, get on and do something useful.

But Ivy felt restless. She didn't want to bake, or work in the garden, or knit. Even the prospect of seeing Bill Turner going yet again into the shop could not tempt her back to the window. I think I'll nip up and see Doris, she thought, take her a few peas. Not for one moment would she admit to herself that she might just bump into the Reverend Nigel Brooks.

'That's very nice of you, Ivy,' said a surprised Doris, taking the little basket full of fresh pea pods and two small lettuces from the garden of Victoria Villa. 'Have you had your dinner, or do you want a sandwich with me?'

Ivy would usually have spurned such an offer, rejecting a quick sandwich as part of the general decline in standards, but today she needed company and so nodded stiffly. 'If you've got some spare, Doris, I wouldn't say no,' she said.

It was very pleasant in Doris's little sitting room, with the sunshine warming it, and the two women sat eating and drinking tea, chatting idly and watching the Roberts and Jenkins children with their bikes and dolls' prams and footballs.

'You got company here, anyway, Doris,' said Ivy. 'You could've been lonely after all them years in the shop with folks in and out all the time.'

'Quite right, Ivy,' said Doris, 'it's almost as good a look-out as your front room.'

Ivy looked at her suspiciously, but Doris's face was bland. 'Do you fancy a bit of ice-cream, Ivy?'

'Turning into quite a party!' said Ivy Beasley, and at that moment caught sight of Nigel and Sophie Brooks walking hand in hand across the end of the Gardens.

'No thanks, Doris,' she called out to the kitchen, 'better be off now – thanks for the sandwiches.' She was out of the door and halfway down Macmillan Gardens before the ice-cream was dished out, and Doris stared at her retreating back in amazement.

'Might have known something was behind Ivy callin' like that,' she said to old Ellen as they met later outside the shop.

'What's she schemin' now?' said Ellen. 'God 'elp some poor soul.'

Sophie sat with Nigel in Ivy's front room wondering how they could get away. Ivy had nabbed them as they stood looking across the Green, and asked them if they'd like a glass of elderflower wine to quench their thirst.

'It is most delicious,' said Nigel appreciatively. 'Have you always made wine, Miss Beasley?'

'Oh, indeed, Reverend Brooks,' said Ivy, 'and my mother before me, and generations of Beasleys before that. We've lived in this village for hundreds of years, you know, though not in this particular house.'

Ivy's voice had a strangulated posh edge, and the voice in her head said warning things to her as she poured herself another glass of the cool, clear wine. Ivy ignored them.

'We are very much looking forward to you coming to Ringford,' she said, remembering to include Sophie in her smile. 'When do you think you will be with us? In time for Open Gardens Sunday?'

'Unfortunately not, but it should be by the end of August with any luck,' said Nigel, returning her smile with his customary twinkle. 'There seem to be no obstacles, and we can't wait, can we, Sophie?'

Sophie nodded, and tried to signal with her eyes to Nigel that she wanted to go. There was something not quite right about this Beasley woman, something lurking under the surface that Sophie did not like. She stood up, draining her glass.

'Well, Nigel, if we are to see the rest of the village, we must be moving.'

Nigel took the hint, and stretched out his hand to Ivy Beasley. She took it and he shook hands warmly.

'Thank you so much for your warm welcome, Miss Beasley,' he said. 'No doubt we shall soon be firm friends!'

Ivy watched them walking slowly along the street, stopping to read the stone tablet on the school commemorating its benefactor, the Hon. Charles William Standing. Reverend Brooks is a lovely man, she thought, hoping Mother wasn't listening, but her ghostly parent was never far away. Be your age, Ivy, the voice said, that wife of his is a very attractive woman. Ivy looked at the hand that had been shaken so warmly, and reflected that it was the first time anybody had touched her since Mother died, apart from Robert's quick peck on the cheek.

Be your age, do, repeated the voice, and there was a tinge of unkind amusement.

Ivy slammed the tray of glasses down on the draining-board and turned on the tap until the water ran violently into the bowl, splashing up round the sink and on to her skirt.

Why don't you just leave me alone, Mother, she said, just leave me alone and go away! She swished the glasses through the water and stood them to drain, then went to fetch a drying-up cloth from the range. Halfway across the kitchen she stood still, frowning, her mouth pursed. She sat down suddenly on a chair by the table, bowed her head, and cried bitterly into a white handkerchief with exquisite drawn-thread work that had been her mother's.

CHAPTER SIXTEEN

Open Gardens Sunday was the one day of the year when the whole village prayed for fine weather. Eight gardens were to be opened to a well-behaved, meandering crowd who came from the ends of the county to praise and criticise, to make notes of interesting plants, and to have a surreptitious snoop into open windows of houses which they wouldn't otherwise have reason to visit.

From steady, thorough hard work throughout the winter and spring, clearing and trimming, sowing and planting, the nervous owners of gardens on the list reached a frenzy of last-minute clipping and tweaking as the Open Day dawned.

Fred Mills was up at six thirty in Macmillan Gardens, pulling scarcely visible weeds out of his immaculate circular flower bed, positioned exactly in the centre of a smooth, knife-edge trimmed lawn of velvety green grass.

At the Hall, Bill Turner had a last conference with Mr Richard about how to route the crowds round the rose gardens and the shrubbery, so that they would get the full impact of the lavender walk down to the exquisite stone shepherd boy, eternally merry as he blew on his silent pipes.

Bill's garden was to be open, too, by special request from the Parish Council. Everyone knew that the Turners' flowers and vegetables were well-nigh perfect, and in spite of all the spring rain, Bill had a display of dahlias and snapdragons, asters and delphiniums, golden rod and montbretia, rivalling the grandest garden in the district. His orderly rows of vegetables, and rich, shiny clusters of red and yellow tomatoes, were a delight to the eye as well as the stomach. But he never put his name forward, and everyone knew that it was because of Joyce.

'Don't you dare let all those bloody strangers in our garden!' she had screamed, when he tentatively mentioned the idea. But in the pub one night Tom Price had persuaded him over a couple of pints to add his garden to the list. 'She'll never know, boy,' Tom had said, 'with all them curtains constantly drawn. And if she does peep out, it'll be too late for her to do anything about it.'

'I shall pay for it later, though,' Bill had said gloomily, but allowed his garden to be listed nevertheless. He was proud of it, knew it was worth seeing, and he still had just enough fight left in him to risk a confrontation with Joyce.

'Best get back now, Mr Richard,' he said, 'make sure everything's tidy for the visitors.'

'Well done, Turner,' said Mr Richard, 'and best of luck.'

Mr Ross, in his neo-Tudor house up the Bagley Road, nervously tied up a stray rambler and called to his wife to set up the card-table at the gate. Each open garden had its entry manned by one or two locals, who checked tickets and handed out the sheets of closely typed script giving histories and details of the gardens.

For many years, in his geometrically arranged garden, Mr Ross had mown and edged, and planted French marigolds, salvia and alyssum at exact intervals, all in quiet isolation from the rest of the village. But now he had neighbours, the new development in Walnuts Farm Close, and although he and his wife had hated the thought of their privacy being disturbed, Mr Ross had gradually become a friend and adviser to the young couples starting their gardens from patches of builders' rubble. One of his protégés had joined the list of open gardens, and Mr Ross felt a glow of pride.

Pat and Colin Osman had inherited a tightly controlled garden from their predecessors at Casa Pera, and had maintained it in much the same way. Planting had been organised for colour all the year round, and fruit trees were bullied into tortuous shapes, taking up the minimum space but producing the maximum harvest. Beyond their garden, in sharp contrast, was the Hall parkland, widely spreading and free from constraint. But, as Colin had pointed out knowledgeably to his wife, the park itself had been just as artificially designed in the first place. Only time had given it the illusion of Nature wild and free.

Colin Osman was a member of the Gardens Committee which organised the event, and had tackled it with customary enthusiasm. He was up at the crack of dawn, sorting and stacking leaflets, and telephoning people who had not yet stirred from their beds.

Refreshments were being served at Doreen Price's farm, and she and fellow WI members had spent a whole day scrubbing out an old stable, setting up an attractive tea-shop with red and white gingham cloths and posies of flowers on each table. Doreen's green and generous garden was open to visitors, too, and Tom had grumbled that she'd have no time left to collect eggs or feed the chickens in the top field. Doreen had just smiled and blown him a kiss as she passed by with a box full of crockery from the Village Hall.

'Looks like we're going to be lucky with the weather,' she said. 'There's not a cloud in the sky.'

At two o'clock precisely, Ivy Beasley stepped out of her front door and locked it carefully behind her. She walked up towards Macmillan Gardens, and joined Doris Ashbourne who was waiting for her on the corner.

'Where's Ellen Biggs, then?' she said, looking back across the Green. 'Late as usual, the old slug.'

'Don't you ever stop to think what you say, Ivy?' said Doris. 'Ellen could be ill, or held up for a good reason.'

'Not her,' said Ivy, 'strong as an ox, that one. There she is, look, just coming over the bridge, and taking her time about it.'

They watched Ellen silently, and the old woman quickened her pace, shouting a greeting to Don Cutt in the pub yard, and finally catching up, her chest heaving with the effort of hurrying.

'Where shall we go first, then?' she said, hoarsely, but with a cheerful smile. Gardens Open Day was a treat for Ellen, as she was incurably nosy, and the influx of strangers was a welcome source of novelty and speculation. She had dressed appropriately, in a full-skirted white cotton dress, printed with tiny sprays of forget-me-nots, and unashamedly feminine with big puff-sleeves and a heart-shaped neckline. The white ankle socks and large men's plimsolls rather spoiled the effect, but Ellen had sacrificed looks for comfort.

'I remember Doreen Price's daughter in that dress,' said Ivy. 'She was about sixteen at the time, and just the right age for such a garment. You do look a right fool, Ellen, but there's no telling you, is there?'

'Now, now, that's enough,' said Doris quickly. 'I suggest we go to Fred's garden first, and Standings' last, and the others in between.'

The gardens had been open since eleven o'clock in the morning, and cars were parked nose to nose around the Green. Local people mixed with visitors from Tresham and around, and there was a pleasant hum of conversation as the three women approached Fred Mills's house in Macmillan Gardens.

Fred was in his element, his pipe tucked in the pocket of a grubby linen jacket that could have done with a visit to the cleaners. He lived with his old, bed-ridden sister, and they did well enough. But niceties like taking clothes to the cleaners had been given up long since.

Fred hadn't stopped talking since the first visitor arrived, and his rheumy eyes shone behind a pair of spectacles as he read aloud the details of his own garden from the dog-eared sheet he kept firmly clenched in his hand.

'Noted for a fine collection of brassicas,' he read, peering over the top of the sheet at Ivy, Ellen and Doris.

'Don't be such an old fool,' said Ivy, 'we know you've got

some decent cabbages coming on. You don't have to put on a show for us.'

'Nasty Black Spot on them roses, Fred,' said Ellen, pulling off a disfigured leaf.

'It's everywhere this year,' said Fred defensively, leaving the trio to get on with it, and going back to the gate to welcome strangers who were hovering uncertainly on his concrete path, and could be trusted not to make snide remarks.

'It is nice and neat, though,' said Doris. 'Considering his age, old Fred does very well.'

'No better than mine,' said Ivy, 'and I've nobody to help with the heavy work.'

'Better ask your beloved Robert to do some digging this autumn,' said Ellen. 'If he can spare the time, that is, from courtin' his Mandy.'

A ripple of excitement passed through all three women as they approached Bill Turner's garden on the opposite side of Macmillan Gardens. It being Bill's first year, curiosity had drawn most of the village to file through the narrow passage by the house and marvel at the rich productiveness of Bill's garden. The shed, they noticed, was shut firmly, and its windows were whitewashed, blind and forbidding.

'That's where 'e kept them rabbits,' whispered Ellen, 'them what Joyce . . . you know, Doris.'

'I do know,' said Doris, 'and so does everybody else. It's a wonder Bill didn't do for her right there and . . .' Her voice tailed away as she turned to look back at the house, and at the same moment a silence fell on the sunlit garden.

At the front gate, Bill was trying to persuade a reluctant Peggy to come in.

'I'll pick you some parsley, gel,' he said, 'you said yours was no good.' She followed him nervously through the passage and round to the patch of lush green herbs by the water-butt, aware that nobody was talking and convinced that they were all looking at her. Bill bent down, and was beginning to pick the parsley when he heard Peggy gasp.

He straightened up and was rooted to the spot, staring with

her and every other visitor at the bedroom window over-looking the garden.

'Oh my God,' he said. 'Oh, dear God, she's done it now.'

Joyce had drawn back the curtains, and those who saw her do it reported a mad theatricality in the act. There she stood, posed like Botticelli's vision of the birth of Venus, except that there were no long tresses to hide her nakedness, and confinement and lack of exercise had loosened her body so that it sagged and bulged in a way that would have disgraced the goddess of love.

She looked down at where Bill stood beside Peggy, and her face was full so full of hate that Peggy winced.

'Bill,' she said quietly, 'Bill, dear, you'd better go in and sort her out. I'll see you later.'

In the shocked stillness in the garden, Bill made his way to the back door, his head bent and his face scarlet. He disappeared inside, and seconds later could be seen pushing his way in front of Joyce and drawing the curtains once more.

'Show's over,' said Peggy in a cracked voice, and turned to leave. As she passed Ivy Beasley, the spinster put out a hand, barring Peggy's way.

'Satisfied, are we, Mrs Palmer?' she said. 'A person can be driven only so far, you know. But no doubt you think you know best.'

Ivy turned on her heel, and proceeded past the lettuces and marrow bed, and on down to the compost heap at the bottom of the garden. She stayed there, looking out over the quiet fields, until Ellen and Doris joined her, and then without speaking they continued on their way.

Peggy fumbled with her back-door key and almost fell into the kitchen. She collapsed on to a chair and thumped at her temples with clenched fists.

'What the bloody hell are you doing to that woman?' she yelled, and Gilbert shot out of her basket and through the cat flap in alarm.

A long time went by and Peggy did not move. The kitchen

84

was silent and still, and then Gilbert returned, rubbing against Peggy's leg and miaowing softly for her supper. At last Peggy stood up and went wearily to the fridge, taking out a half-full tin of cat food and spooning the strong-smelling meat into a yellow plastic dish.

'It's no good,' said Peggy. 'What I'm doing is wicked, and there are no excuses. I shall have to explain to Bill, and he'll have to accept it.' She shivered. I have to get out of here, she thought, get some fresh air. I feel dirty.

She pulled on a cardigan and went out of the back door again, latching the side gate and setting off in the direction of the church. It was after closing time for the gardens, but a few people still lingered, sitting on the bench on the Green in the evening sunlight, and strolling in groups by the river.

One by one the cars drove off, people staring out at Peggy as she crossed the road without looking, causing a big grey Mercedes to stop with a jolt and hoot angrily.

She came to the bridge and for once did not stop to look at the water. Her mind was blank, and her eyes saw only the road beneath her.

Finally she stopped, and realised where she was. There was the headstone, so sadly new and clean. 'FRANK ARTHUR PALMER – Died 6.12.1992. aged 53 years. Beloved husband of MARGARET. "Tomorrow to fresh woods, and pastures new." '

Peggy stood looking at it for several minutes, and then sat down on the warm grass by the gentle mound. 'It's a mess, Frank,' she said. 'You would be ashamed of me. Come to that, I'm ashamed of myself. But I'm so afraid that I can't stop it. Bill means too much to me now, and he is so unhappy, always will be unhappy with that woman, whatever I do or say. It isn't fair, Frank, it isn't fair at all.

A blackbird sitting high above her on the church roof began his liquid, magical evening song, and she looked up. The sky was pale and limpid, and the breeze too slight to stir the heavy black yews. She looked down at Frank's grave, and put her hands on the short grass, digging her nails into the turf, deeper and deeper. 'Frank,' she said, and repeated his name desperately as her fingers grew black with earth and became entangled in the mat of roots.

'Don't do that, Peggy,' said a woman's voice, 'you'll do yourself no good, my dear. Come away now, come away.'

It was Doreen Price, large and comforting, and Peggy allowed herself to be led out of the churchyard to where Doreen had parked her car.

'Hop in,' Doreen said. 'We'll go back to the farm and have a nice cup of tea.'

CHAPTER SEVENTEEN

She's had one husband and lost him, and now she's well on the way to snatching somebody else's, said Ivy Beasley to her empty front room. For once there was no answering voice in her head, and Ivy felt a moment of panic.

Mother? I said Pushy Peg's driving that poor Joyce round the bend . . .

Nothing. No sharp rejoinder, no goad to urge her on.

Ivy walked into the kitchen and began to fill the kettle. After the drama at the Turners', she and Doris and Ellen had continued round the other gardens, their enthusiasm dampened by Bill's humiliation. Even old Ellen was subdued, and after they had walked round the Hall terraces and gravel paths, she had said she was tired and disappeared into her Lodge without suggesting a cup of tea. Doris, too, had gone straight home, saying she had some jobs to see to, and left Ivy standing at her gate. There's a funny feeling in the village, Ivy thought, looking round, seeing nothing amiss, everything as usual, but able to sense intangible shock waves.

Now the sky was pink with the setting sun, and long shadows stretched across Ivy's garden, like pointing fingers. She banged her hand on the window and a flock of sharp-suited starlings flew off. As she watched, Gilbert sauntered through the fence and began to dig a hole in Ivy's vegetable patch. She knocked on the window again, and the cat looked up, startled. Ivy went to the back door and called, 'Here, kitty, here . . .'

She had been feeding the little cat for months, hoping it would prefer her quiet home and leave the haphazard life of the shop next door. But Gilbert knew when she was on to a good thing, and lived in both camps, growing fat and glossy, distributing her favours equally.

'Hello, Tiddles,' she said, picking up the tabby and stroking the soft fur. 'You mustn't dig holes in my garden, you know, best to do that next door.'

She sat down on a kitchen chair, the cat curled comfortably in her lap. 'Do you know, pussy,' Ivy said, 'I think Mother's gone and left me.' Her voice trembled as she realised the enormity of this, the possibility of freedom at last.

Gilbert mewed and dug her claws into the thick material of Ivy's skirt.

'Shall we have something to eat?' said Ivy. 'There's a bit of fish for you, and a nice chop for me.'

Ivy got up, the cat jumping down and settling on the mat in front of the old range. Taking a saucepan from the cupboard, Ivy put the fish to stew in milk, and placed her chop in a pan, sprinkling it with thyme and salt and sliding the dish carefully into the oven.

'There we are, won't be long,' she said.

Ivy reached for a book, neatly covered in brown paper, from the mantelshelf, and opened it where a bookmark of brown leather, embossed with the Tresham town crest, marked her place. She sat back in the spindle-back kitchen chair and began to read. It was very peaceful, and Ivy at last had a feeling of complete solitude, of being alone without observation or comment. She adjusted a cushion in the small of her back, rested her feet in their sensible brown shoes on the brass fender, and began to read.

The brown paper cover concealed a picture of a young woman with nut-brown hair and blue eyes gazing raptly up at a stone pulpit, where a handsome cleric in surplice and dog-collar directed his lop-sided smile at the congregation, but his eyes were for the girl in the front pew.

' "You see how difficult it is for me, Amanda," ' Ivy read.

' "My poor invalid wife never stirs from her chair, but I am bound to her with my vows before God, and . . ." '

A sizzling on the stove and the rank smell of burning fishy milk brought Ivy to her feet in alarm. She was full of the usual fear of criticism and reprimand, but in her head there was silence. Are you there, Mother, are you watching? No answer. Then it's of no account, thought Ivy. I can let the milk boil over and the chop sizzle to a bit of old leather, and there's only me to care. She began to hum in her cracked, tuneless voice, as she mopped up the spilt milk. The little cat looked up at her in surprise.

'I shall have a glass of elderflower,' Ivy said, 'and you can have the top of the milk, Tiddles. A small celebration is called for, I think.'

The tall green bottle was broached, and Ivy settled again with a sparkling glass and her book. She began to read on, but then put down her glass and carefully pulled the brown wrapper from the cover, screwing it up and throwing it from her chair into the glowing coals. It burst into a triumphant flame and Ivy laughed aloud.

'There we are, Tiddles,' she said, 'that's a start. And tomorrow . . .'

Tomorrow, Ivy Dorothy Beasley? And just what are you going to do tomorrow?

Ivy whipped round as if to catch the ghostly form of her mother, cruelly returned to shatter her liberation.

Very nasty this afternoon, wasn't it, the voice continued. You were quite restrained, Ivy. You'll have to do better than that, you know, if you're going to put a stop to it. Who knows what that Joyce Turner will do next?

Ivy's face had fallen into an expression of disappointment and despair, and she did not bother to reply. She hid her book in the folds of her apron, and stood up wearily to dish up the food.

CHAPTER EIGHTEEN

The summer advanced with more sunshine than rain, and even the farmers were forced to admit that the prospects for the harvest were good. Every day the combine harvesters roared through the village, and great grain trailers shook the foundations of the old houses. Elderly people mourned once more the passing of the horse and cart and the old threshing machine that had once caused such a stir in the village when it arrived to service each farm. Each year these memories receded further into the distance, and young Mark Jenkins scoffed when his gran told him about picnics in the harvest fields, and gleaning for straw to make dollies and hats.

'Vicar's settled in, then,' said Ellen Biggs, coming into the shop in an outfit Peggy had not seen before.

'Where did you get that lovely dress?' said Peggy, thinking that Ellen never failed to surprise with her extraordinary flair for getting it wrong. She had on a long, Indian cotton skirt, rich with the colours of the East, and with a few bright beads still clinging to it; and over it, worn as a tunic, Ellen had put a deep purple mini-dress of generous proportions. Round her neck, remembering Ivy's strictures, she had tied a yellow chiffon scarf. A bow at the front, she had said to herself, will be a nice touch.

' 'Arrods of course,' said Ellen, laughing loudly. 'No, my dear, I do all my shoppin' at the jumble sale. Get some lovely bargains there, if you're quick.'

Peggy laughed with Ellen, vowed to be the first in the queue when the time came, and then reverted to the subject of the vicar.

'Did you see the Brookses, then, Ellen? Most of the village walked by yesterday to watch them arrive. Not so many offered to help, I noticed.'

'No, well, they wouldn't, would they?' said Ellen. 'No good gettin' too friendly and then wishin' you 'adn't. Can I take one o' them chocolate cake mixes, dear, that'll do nicely for the next time Ivy and Doris come down.'

Peggy handed the packet to Ellen, and said, 'We shall be glad, anyway Ellen, to have a vicar in the village again. It's not the same in church, is it, with lay readers and visiting parsons?'

Ellen was not much seen in church, but she agreed wholeheartedly. 'You got to 'ave somebody over you,' she said, 'somebody you can look up to. Reverend Collins were just right for that, God rest 'is soul.'

'We've got a couple of weeks before we take up duties, Sophie,' said Nigel. 'You don't have to get everything done in twenty-four hours. Come on, sit down for a minute and have a cup of coffee. I'll make it.'

Sophie wiped her face with a dirty hand, leaving a smear across her freckled nose. Her hair, once so flaming red and now a little faded and speckled with grey, was protected by a clean duster, and she was wearing an old boiler suit several sizes too large for her, and covered in paint splashes. With its sleeves rolled up she looked like an exploited factory child, and Nigel put his arms round her as she leaned on her broom.

'Happy, Soph?' he said.

'It's wonderful,' she said, 'all this lovely dirt and dust. Just what I've always wanted.'

'You're not sorry . . . ?' He looked anxiously at her.

She shoved him with a dirty hand, leaving a smudge on his fresh linen jacket. 'You know I'm not, Nigel,' she said. 'As long as no one speaks to me in the Celtic tongue I shall be perfectly content.'

Nigel made the coffee and took it into the drawing room, newly decorated on the instructions of the churchwardens, and called Sophie. Why she has to turn out attics when there's so much clean space elsewhere, I do not know, thought Nigel. Women were a never-ending source of puzzlement to him. He knew how to charm them into compliance when he wanted a job done, but they always reverted to unpredictability when he least expected it.

They sat happily drinking coffee and looking out into the garden which had been licked into shape by Michael Roberts and his old father. Roberts father and son worked on Price's farm and had for generations been the village's gravediggers. It was a rough job, and there was tacit agreement that Michael Roberts was the best man to do it. And anyway, he's got the right, they said, his family's been digging graves in this village for donkey's years. He could be worse, they said.

The vicarage doorbell rang once, touched lightly and briefly.

'I'll go,' said Nigel, and walked through to the hall, his leather-soled shoes tapping neatly on the tiled floor.

'Mrs Jones,' he said, 'how nice! Come in, my dear.'

Gabriella Jones, slender and sun-tanned, wearing jeans and a simple white cotton T-shirt, walked into the sitting room and smiled at Sophie, who looked down at her boiler suit and apologised for her appearance.

'Such a lot to do, I know,' said Gabriella, 'when you move house. It's not so long since we did it ourselves.'

'What can we do for you?' said Nigel, indicating a chair. Gabriella perched on the edge, shook back her blonde hair, and said she did hope she wasn't interrupting anything.

'I was wondering,' she said, 'if you would like to choose the hymns for this Sunday? I know you're not officially in charge for a week or so, but it would be nice for us, and perhaps help to make you feel at home . . .'

'What a perfectly lovely idea!' said Nigel, and immediately fetched a hymn book and pen and paper, and sat discussing tunes and words with Gabriella.

'We are so lucky, Sophie,' he said, after Gabriella had left with precise details of what Nigel wanted, 'to have a smashing girl like that to play the organ. It's usually some old tab who plays everything at the pace of a funeral march, and sulks if you suggest anything new.'

'Don't count your chickens, Nigel,' said Sophie. 'We've been disillusioned before, don't forget.'

'Oh, I don't think so this time,' said Nigel, picking up the coffee tray and starting out on the long trek to the kitchen. 'I've had an idea for Christmas. What do you think about a concert in the church? I'm sure that nice Gabriella would help.'

Sophie frowned. 'It doesn't matter what I think,' she said. 'There are a number of others who will have very strong opinions, no doubt, and Miss Beasley is well up there in the front line.'

She took up her broom, and climbed several flights of stairs to the attic, where she sat on the floor and looked with delight through tiny dormer windows across the village and down the shining valley of the Ringle.

Gabriella walked down the lane, picking off dried heads of hogweed and rubbing the seeds through her fingers. She heard the church clock chiming twelve noon and quickened her pace. What a pleasant couple the Brookses are, she thought, so relaxed, and, well, ordinary. Cyril had been a dear old man, but he was always very much the priest, and she never dared to suggest anything new.

She stopped and leaned on the old stone bridge to look into the water. Sooner or later, she thought, I suppose I shall have to get a job. She felt no burning ambition to go back to teaching, and loved the slow of life in the village. But Greg had dropped one or two hints about the expense of keeping a lively young daughter on his meagre salary. It wasn't meagre, she knew, but Octavia's demands were more and more ambitious, and she was in such a hurry to grow up.

A car approached the bridge, and Gabriella saw it was Robert Bates. She flattened herself against the side of the bridge and waved as he went slowly by. He didn't wave back, and only half smiled at her in return.

Oh dear, she thought, is Octavia still being a nuisance?

She had tried to talk to her daughter about her all-consuming passion for Robert Bates, tried to tell her about her own teenage crushes on her brother's friends, all of whom had regarded the young Gabriella as beneath their notice. She'd tried laughing it into proportion with a sullen Octavia, who barely listened, and rushed off the minute the one-sided conversation approached an end.

Gabriella turned away from the water and walked on by the side of the Green. Greg refused to take any of it seriously, but Gabriella knew that, foolish as it was, it was very real to Octavia. She'd had so many brief enthusiasms – riding, roller skating, theatricals, playing the trumpet – and none of them had lasted long. But her obsession with Robert Bates was undimmed. Sometimes it frightened Gabriella, but Greg laughed at her fears, and said it was perfectly normal. He'd been the victim of schoolgirl crushes on many occasions himself, he'd said, it was quite normal.

'Good morning, Mrs Jones.' It was Ivy Beasley, marching purposefully along the Green, heading for the bridge. She stopped and shifted a bulging carrier bag from one hand to the other.

'Morning,' said Gabriella. 'Lovely morning, Miss Beasley.' She felt trapped, and edged slowly away. But Ivy Beasley had a reason for stopping.

'Glad I met you, Mrs Jones,' she said. 'I've wanted a word.'

Gabriella's heart sank. She waited, and Ivy Beasley crossed the road and stood in front of her, her dark eyes fixed accusingly on Gabriella.

'Your daughter, Mrs Jones,' she said, 'is making a fool of herself and our Robert. I'm not one for mincing my words, and someone should tell you.'

Gabriella sighed. 'I am perfectly aware of Octavia's crush on Robert Bates, Miss Beasley,' she said, and added to herself that it was nothing to do with the old bat, anyway.

But Ivy had not finished. 'I had a word with your daughter at the bus stop,' she said. 'Our Robert is too shy. I've told her that he's getting engaged to Mandy Butler any minute now, and she'd better stop her silly tricks.'

Gabriella frowned, angry that Ivy Beasley should have taken it upon herself to speak to Octavia.

'I am not at all pleased to hear this, Miss Beasley,' she said. Ivy smirked, thinking that at least she had got her point home to this silly woman.

'I mean,' said Gabriella, warming up, 'that I think it extremely wrong of you to have talked to a young girl without first speaking to her parents. Girls of that age are extremely impressionable, and need careful guidance. Which, you may rest assured, Miss Beasley,' she added fiercely, 'Octavia's father and myself are quite capable of handling.'

'Needs a good smack bottom,' said Ivy tartly, and before Gabriella could reply she crossed the road again and went swiftly on her way.

Gabriella walked home, her peace of mind shattered, cursing Ivy Beasley for not minding her own business. She opened her garden gate and was surprised to see Greg standing at the open front door. He had just started back at school for the autumn term, and had no reason to be home at midday.

'Greg! What's up?' she said. 'Why are you back? Are you ill?'

'No, Gabbie, not me, it's Octavia. Her form teacher asked me if she was ill, as she was not at school. She did get the bus this morning, didn't she?'

Octavia Jones refused to travel to school with her father. It was difficult enough having a parent who was also a teacher, without having to arrive in his car and be laughed at by the other kids.

Gabriella thought immediately of abduction and worse, and her heart began to thump. She rushed indoors, pushing Greg to one side and yelling, ' 'Tavie! . . . 'Tavie!'

'I've done that,' said Greg reasonably. 'That's all I have done, so far, I haven't been home many minutes.'

Gabriella continued to call, dashing from room to room, and then upstairs. She tried Octavia's door and found it locked. ' 'Tavie! Are you in there? Open up at once!' There was no reply, and Gabriella shot downstairs again.

'Greg! She's in her room, and the door's locked and it's completely quiet in there! What are we going to do?'

They both ran upstairs once more, and tried knocking and shouting and cajoling. Absolute silence greeted their efforts.

'She couldn't have got out of the window and left her door locked, just to frighten us?' said Gabriella. Greg shook his head. 'Her windows are shut,' he said. 'I looked.'

He took a deep breath and got hold of Gabriella by both arms. 'She's in there,' he said, 'and either she's doing this deliberately, or . . .' He hesitated, trying to find moderate words. '. . . or she can't hear us.'

Gabriella began to cry, and Greg shook her. 'Stop it, Gabbie, stop it,' he said. 'We have to get in there, and quickly.'

He stepped back and took a run at the door, but he was a slight man, and made little impact, only hurting his shoulder. 'We need help,' he said, and started off downstairs.

The Joneses' house was opposite Macmillan Gardens, and as Greg ran out, not really sure where he was going, he saw Bill Turner coming down the Gardens on his bike.

'Bill!' he yelled. 'Bill, can you give us a hand!' His relief in seeing Bill's tall, solid figure was great. He opened his garden gate and pulled Bill inside, rapidly filling him in on the situation.

'Right-o, boy,' said Bill, 'we'll get in there, don't you worry. I've had plenty of practice with locked doors.'

They joined Gabriella, who still stood rooted to the spot outside Octavia's door. Her hands were tightly clenched by her sides, and she seemed to have gone into a trance. 'Shock,' said Bill. 'Don't worry, Mrs Jones, we'll soon have her out safe and sound.'

Bill gathered himself together, and heaved his bulk at the modern, flimsy door. It gave way at first shove, and Gabriella came to life. She rushed into the room and flung herself at the prone figure of her daughter, childlike and vulnerable, curled up on the bed, her blonde hair over her face and her thumb in her mouth.

' 'Tavie!' she shouted, and shook the girl by her shoulder. ' 'Tavie, darling, wake up, it's Mummy!'

But there was no movement, no flickering of eyelids, no yawning awakening, no smile of recognition for her mother.

Bill came forward and put his fingers to the girl's narrow neck. 'There's a pulse,' he said. 'Go and phone the doctor and the ambulance, Mr Jones, and be quick about it. She's taken something.'

Gabriella sat by the hospital bed watching over her only daughter. Octavia's eyes were big dark shadows in her pale face, but she slept apparently peacefully. Gabriella wished they would take away the angular drip apparatus, with its snaking tube. It was alien, forbidding, separating her from her child.

A close vigil was maintained by the nursing staff, and Gabriella was reassured, but she had been upset by the Sister's callous remark as she looked at Octavia's notes. 'Don't worry, Mrs Jones,' she had said cheerfully, 'she took just enough to give you a good scare.'

It had been a nightmare of empty aspirin bottles and the stomach pump, and Octavia being sick until Gabriella thought the girl would die of exhaustion. Bill Turner had been steady as a rock, seemed to know exactly what to do. Poor Greg looked just about as ill as Octavia, until Gabbie had packed him off to buy some tissues and squash from the hospital shop.

'But why?' said Greg, over and over again. He seemed reluctant to believe that Octavia might be in real trouble, stressing to Gabriella that their daughter had a core of good common sense. He clung on to the Sister's words. 'Just meant to give us a scare, Gabbie,' he said.

Several times Gabriella had started to tell him about her conversation with Ivy Beasley, but each time she hesitated, hearing again the derisive 'needs a good smack bottom'. I

97

expect it's my fault, thought Gabriella. She is a bit spoilt, I suppose.

'We shall just have to wait until she's well enough to tell us,' Greg had said.

'There may be just one clue,' said Gabriella tentatively. 'When she was conscious and between bouts of vomiting, she said something, and I thought it sounded like "Robert, how could you." I know, I know,' she added quickly, before Greg could scoff, 'it does sound stupid, but teenage crushes are very strong. I remember . . .'

'Gabbie dear,' said Greg, 'I doubt it, I really do.'

But in her feverish dreams, Octavia was walking down the aisle of Ringford church, a floating vision in white, on the arm of Robert Bates, her newly wedded husband.

CHAPTER NINETEEN

Nigel Brooks walked smartly down Bates's End, his black cloak protecting him from the rain, his four-cornered hat set flatteringly over his wavy grey hair.

He obeyed the unwritten Ringford rule, and stopped on the bridge to look into the water. Through the clear swirls he could see shoals of small fish darting through the weed. Raindrops fell in concentric circles on the surface, and Nigel thought once more what a good job the Lord had made of His creation. I will make you fishers of men, he reminded himself, and set off again with renewed vigour to widen his acquaintance with his parishioners. His official induction service had yet to take place, but Nigel was not one for wasting time, and he was confident that the parish was as anxious to get to know him as he was to become one of them.

The shop was first on his list of visits. 'Morning, Mrs Palmer,' he said, and Peggy answered him politely, but without her usual smile.

'You're looking worried, my dear,' said Nigel, chancing a personal remark, pretty sure that Peggy would not retreat.

'Yes, well,' said Peggy, sighing, 'it's been a nasty twenty-four hours in Ringford. I expect you've heard about Octavia Jones?'

'Gabriella's daughter?' said Nigel, feeling stupidly uninformed.

Peggy told him briefly the details of Octavia's botched attempt to do away with herself.

'But she's more or less all right?' he said.

'Physically, yes,' said Peggy, 'but it's not something a normal, happy girl would do without good reason, is it?'

'Love,' said Nigel confidently. 'It's usually love at that age. I've seen it once or twice before. Hope that's it, anyway,' he added with a reassuring smile. 'Love at that age is infinitely transferable . . .'

Peggy looked at his handsome face and kindly smile, and thought what a nice man he seemed to be. It was a funny hat, though, she'd never seen one of those before.

'Can I get you anything, Mr Brooks,' she said, 'or is this just a pastoral call?'

Nigel had not intended to buy anything, just pop in for a few words, but there was something in the way Peggy had asked him that made him fumble in his pocket for loose coins. 'Have you any butter mints?' he asked. 'Sophie's still slaving away at the vicarage . . . needs some sweeties to keep her going.'

'Would she like a hand?' said Peggy, remembering her own total exhaustion when she and Frank moved into the shop. 'I could look in this evening after closing time, maybe help with curtains and things?' She handed him the packet of mints and took his money, counting out his change.

Nigel shook his head. 'You have far too much to do here on your own,' he said, 'but I am most grateful for the offer. Why don't you come round anyway, and have a cup of coffee with us? I know Sophie would be delighted.'

The shop door opened quietly, and Ivy Beasley stepped inside without her usual flourish. Peggy looked across the counter at her and knew there was something different about her neighbour. She's changed her hair-do, she thought, well I never. Looks quite nice, curled under like that.

'Good morning, Miss Beasley,' said Nigel, turning round to greet her with his usual welcome. 'What a wet morning! Still, good for the gardens, I'm sure.'

'Morning, Vicar,' said Ivy. 'Yes, indeed, we needed the

rain.' She said nothing more, and turned away to hide a faint blush which scarcely deepened her high colour.

'We'll see you this evening, then Mrs Palmer,' said Nigel. Good morning again, Miss Beasley.' And he gathered his cloak around him and left the shop in a swirl of bonhomie.

So, thought Ivy Beasley, trust pushy Peg to get in with them already. She resumed her usual scowl, and pushed a half-eaten loaf of bread across the counter. 'Look at this,' she said, pulling a small stone out of the dough. 'That's where it was, right in the middle there, nearly broke my tooth on it. Please make a complaint to the bakers. I shall expect my money back.'

Peggy took the loaf and looked at it, and at the small white stone. How could she possibly argue? She hadn't the courage to suggest that Ivy might have put the stone there herself to make trouble.

'I am so sorry, Miss Beasley,' she said. 'Of course I shall complain. It could have been really dangerous. Would you like the money back, or a fresh loaf?'

'Money,' said Ivy tersely. 'In future I shall obtain my bread elsewhere. Or make it myself,' she added, glaring at Peggy.

'I hear you are an extremely good baker,' said Peggy, despising herself for creeping.

'You hear a lot of things, I don't doubt,' said Ivy, 'but then, so do I, living so close to the shop. I heard that stupid Jones child has been worrying her parents again. No telling some people, is there.'

She took the money for the loaf, and marched out, banging the door behind her.

Peggy walked out of her side gate and crossed the road. She took the short cut across the Green, making for the bridge and the vicarage. The heavy rain had slackened off to a hanging mist, edging the leaves with shiny beads of water, and covering Peggy's hair with a moist veil, tightening her curls and dampening her fresh, pink face.

The door opened as she walked up the sandy path of the

vicarage. Peggy noticed two big tubs of geraniums had been placed on either side of the porch, colourful and welcoming. Sophie stood in the open doorway, a small figure in blue skirt and white fine lawn shirt, holding back a big old black dog by his collar. She held out her free hand in welcome.

'Mrs Palmer,' she said, 'how nice of you to come round.'

Peggy warmed to her at once. 'Please call me Peggy,' she said, 'most people do.' Except my charming neighbour, she thought, and reflected on the impossibility of ever saying, 'Good morning, Ivy.'

'And we're Nigel and Sophie,' said the vicar, rising from his chair and shaking her warmly by the hand. 'Come and sit down . . . I've forbidden any more work today.'

'Not that that would stop me,' said Sophie, grinning at him, 'but I am tired now, so delighted to see you and glad of the excuse to take a break.'

From this good beginning, the three sat in the big drawing room amiably chatting about the village and Nigel's idea for a Christmas concert in the church, until the grandfather clock in the hall struck seven, and Peggy jumped up. 'Gracious!' she said. 'I must be off, you will be wanting your supper. It has been nice, and you must come round and have coffee with me soon.' She reached the door, and then turned back. 'Oh, and by the way,' she said, 'you were right, Nigel, about Octavia Jones. Seems she had just heard about Robert Bates's engagement, and her heart was broken. She's always been a bit of a drama queen, but this time she really scared her parents, poor things.'

'Poor lass,' said Nigel. 'She'll need comfort and understanding from us all. I must call on Gabriella tomorrow.'

What a very nice man, thought Peggy, walking back along the twilit street, I do hope they'll be happy here. I must get Doreen to invite Sophie along to WI. Still, she's probably done that already.

Feeling completely at one with her village, not even bothering to glance at Victoria Villa, Peggy crossed the road and let herself into the back door of the shop. 'Hello,

Gilbertiney,' she said to the little tabby rubbing herself round her legs. 'Mummy's home.'

CHAPTER TWENTY

The induction ceremony for the new vicar had been a splendid and moving occasion, with a full church and much ritual and dignity as befitted the occasion. Richard Standing had felt a glow of satisfaction, as Nigel Brooks went elegantly through the service, with just the right mixture of humility and confidence.

'Seems to be doing well,' Richard said to Susan over breakfast.

'Who is, darling?' she said. 'You do have a habit of starting sentences midway through a thought.'

'Nigel – who else?' said Richard.

'Well, yes, but it's early days yet. One or two of the old tabs have complained about new tunes and tiny changes in the services. Still, in a couple of months he seems to have won quite a few hearts . . . including Ivy Beasley's, so I hear.'

'Good gracious!' said Richard. 'Is there a heart there to be won?'

'And now he's got this concert idea, and quite a few people are keen.'

'Thank God I can't sing a note. And neither can you, Susan, so don't get any ideas . . .'

'Since you are completely tone deaf,' said Susan, 'I don't see how you can judge.'

She walked through to the drawing room, followed by Richard, and sat down at the grand piano, which, though not often played, was kept regularly tuned.

'Ear – ly one mor – hor – ning, just as the sun was ri – hi – sing,' she sang, and stopped.

'Ah well,' she said, getting up from the piano stool, 'maybe you're right, Richard darling,' and went off to the kitchen to set Jean Jenkins to work. I must be nice to Jean Jenkins, she chanted like a schoolchild, I must be nice to Jean Jenkins. After Jean had handed in her duster in a huff, and Susan was without help for some time, Richard had tempted her back with a rise in wages, and Susan promised him she would be nice and not step on Jean's touchy pride.

Nigel Brooks had persuaded a number of men and women to form the nucleus of a choir, having gently suggested to Gabriella that getting together the Christmas concert might help to prevent her dwelling too much on past horrors. Octavia had returned to school, apparently healed, and the family had been given more advice and analysis than was perhaps helpful. Robert Bates had been very upset when he heard the full circumstances, and kept out of Octavia's way even more than before.

Gabriella continued to have dreadful dreams about Octavia, still and lifeless on a mortuary slab, and when she awoke, sweating and crying, Greg put his arms round her and confided that he too was unfairly tormented in his sleep.

'If you feel you can take charge, Gabriella,' Nigel Brooks had said, 'Sophie and I will give you all possible help and support. With your musical training and lovely singing voice, you will be able to do the job standing on your head . . . but only if you feel up to it.' His charming smile warmed Gabriella, and she agreed to take it on.

'Morning, Peggy,' said Doreen Price, coming into the shop with a tower of egg trays, which she carefully set down on the counter. 'Now, then,' she said in a businesslike fashion, 'are we going to sing? You sound all right in *Jerusalem*, so I don't see why you shouldn't. Not so sure about me, though Nigel won't hear a word of doubt.'

'First rehearsal tonight, isn't it?' said Peggy.

'I mean t' be there,' said a voice from behind the display units.

Ellen Biggs emerged with a small packet of All-Bran. 'This should keep me goin',' she said with a wicked smile. 'I reckon I can sing as good as ol' Ivy, and Reverend Brooks said all comers would be welcome.'

Peggy widened her eyes at Doreen, who said, 'Well, you won't have far to go, Ellen, though don't forget you'll have to turn out on winter evenings in wind and rain, no slacking.'

Ellen shrugged. 'If I'm singin' for the Almighty, surely he'll keep the rain off?' She muttered to herself something about being old and unwanted, and struggled down the shop steps and along to Victoria Villa.

There was an unmistakable scent of autumn in the air, a smell of bonfire smoke floating over the allotments. Fields of oil-seed rape had been harvested, and tough, fibrous stalks were left standing, leafless and harmful to foraging animals. The Jenkinses' terrier came home with his face skinned and bleeding from chasing rabbits through the unyielding jungle.

Ellen stood and stared over the Green, feeling the changing season in her bones with a sinking dread of cold, damp weather to come. Yesterday, lured by a sunny afternoon, she had plodded off along the old railway line to collect sticks for the fire, swearing at the low, fiercely stinging nettles and taking handfuls of dock leaves to rub on her smarting ankles. The small white flowers of mayweed, still sturdy and cheerful, caught her eye, and she hurt her hands and her back trying to pick a small bunch. There'll soon come a time, she thought, when I shall 'ave to give up collectin' sticks and everythin' else. Old age is a devil, nothin' surer. She knocked on Ivy's door and stood dejectedly on the scrubbed white step.

'What's eating you, Ellen Biggs?' said Ivy, setting a cup of steaming coffee in front of the old woman. Ellen had slumped down on to a kitchen chair and lapsed into silence.

'Nuthin',' she grunted.

' "There's always something in nothing." my mother used to say.' Ivy folded her arms and waited.

Ellen shifted in her chair and drank her coffee noisily. She looked up speculatively and said, 'I suppose you won't be singin' in this concert thing, Ivy?' She knew perfectly well that Ivy fully intended to sing.

'I might go along to see what it's all about,' said Ivy defensively.

'Better get yer curlers out, then,' said Ellen, with pinpoint cruelty.

'Do you want to come, is that it, Ellen Biggs?'

'Wouldn't be seen dead,' said Ellen, with a shrug.

'I'll call for you at a quarter past seven,' said Ivy, 'and you'd better be ready. And for goodness sake, dress in something suitable for churchgoing. None of your gypsy costumes, else you can go by yourself.'

'It won't be easy to get away,' said Bill, sitting in Peggy's kitchen after the shop closed. 'I can't see Joyce believing that I want to sing in a choir.'

Bill had brought in a load of logs from the estate farm, and chanced a quick cup of tea before going home. He laughed ruefully, and put his arm round Peggy's waist as she stood washing up teacups in the sink. 'It'd just be a chance to be in the same place as my true love for a couple of hours, maybe hold hands in the vestry? He kissed the soft hair on the back of her neck, and she wriggled.

'Well, I've promised Doreen I'll give it a go,' she said, 'though I haven't done any singing since Frank and I were in the chorus of *Pirates of Penzance* in Coventry.'

'There you are, then!' said Bill, still uncomfortable at the mention of Frank's name when he had his arms round his friend's widow.

'Bill,' said Peggy.

'Mmm,' said Bill.

'You know you said Mr Richard was making a hide for Susan to watch birds?'

'Yep,' said Bill.

'Does she go there much?'

'Not at all yet, it's not finished. I've got a fair bit to do to it yet.'

'Well,' said Peggy, moving away from him and looking out of the window at her cherry tree ablaze in the sun, 'I was thinking, maybe when it's finished . . .'

Bill was not slow to see where this was leading. He turned her round to face him, and held both her hands. '. . . when it's finished,' he said, 'it might be a good hiding place for more than just bird-watching? Is that what you were thinking, Peg?'

She looked at him and nodded. 'Is it a silly idea?' she said.

'No central heating,' said Bill, 'but there's other ways of keeping warm.'

'Why can't I go?' said Jean Jenkins.

'Because you'll make a fool of yourself,' said Foxy, switching channels on television to get the local weather forecast.

'I can sing,' said Jean huffily. 'I remember singing a solo at school, "All Things Bright and Beautiful" it were, and Miss Layton put me on a chair so's I could be seen.'

'They won't need to do that now,' said Foxy, laughing and dodging the deserved blow.

'All right, then, I won't go,' she said, and started clattering dishes and throwing knives and forks into the kitchen sink.

'For God's sake, woman,' shouted Foxy, 'go, if you want to, otherwise we shan't have nothing left to eat off!'

Jean smiled quietly into the sudsy water, and planned what she would wear.

'I wonder who else will be there,' she said. 'Reverend Brooks has been very busy drummin' up support. Old Poison Ivy is bound to turn up, just to see her precious Nigel, and Mrs Price and Peggy Palmer are great mates with Sophie Brooks now, so they'll be there. Can't see Mr Richard and Madam lowerin' themselves, can you, Fox?'

'Mm,' said Foxy, deep in the racing results.

'That Colin and Pat Osman are bound to join, him bein' so keen on "village activities".' Jean's imitation of Colin Osman was deadly.

'You'd best get on with that and stop chatterin',' said Foxy. 'It'll soon be time to go. You can leave Eddie and the kids to me. I'll see them into bed.'

'You mustn't be too hard on them, Fox,' said Jean, wiping her hands on the towel behind the kitchen door. 'They always moan if I don't see to them.'

'Don't worry,' said Foxy. 'Now, where did I put that strap?'

A steady trickle of people climbed up the narrow path through the black yews to the church door, where Nigel stood waiting to welcome his potential choir, some hesitant, some bouncy and full of enthusiasm. The heaters had been on in the church for half an hour, but there was still a chill from the stone floor, and draughts whistled round Gabriella's neck as she stood shuffling her music. The old piano had been pushed out from the wall so that she could play and look at the singers at the same time.

It was odd, she thought, the church at night, with no service going on, no ethereal organ music, the chancel dark and shadowy. It was as if the laughing voices of people coming in and standing about, backs to the altar, had frightened God away.

She looked at the octagonal stone font, its Victorian cover like a miniature steeple, shutting it off. The blue light burning steadily in the Lady Chapel, symbolic of the continual presence of the Holy Spirit, was just a flickering light. It was an empty stone building, draughty and in need of restoration, with damp, peeling patches on its whitewashed walls. Was it all really a confidence trick, as Greg sometimes maintained, in the hands of a decreasing number of inept magicians?

Well, thought Gabriella, seeing Nigel approaching, let's see what kind of tricks you can perform with this bunch.

'Good!' said Nigel, looking round at twenty or so people

standing in attentive groups. 'Wonderful! Welcome everybody to Ringford Concert Choir! Allow me to introduce,' he said, with an appropriate flourish, 'our charming choirmistress, Gabriella Jones, who will guide us through the mysteries of major and minor keys in praise of the Lord! Over to you, my dear.' He bowed slightly to Gabriella, who smiled obediently.

'Silly bugger,' said Bill, standing behind his own true love. 'Why don't he just get on with it?'

CHAPTER TWENTY-ONE

Gabriella looked round at the assembled group of villagers, some she knew well, others she knew only in passing. She felt a moment of panic, wishing Greg had come to give her confidence. But after Octavia's botched suicide attempt they had never once left her alone in the house. Nothing had been said, but Gabriella and Greg had a tacit understanding that if one went out, the other stayed in. Both knew it couldn't go on for ever, but for the moment they were playing safe.

Even if he had come, thought Gabriella, he might have been a liability. He could never resist being sir, and in charge.

It was so long since Gabriella had stood in front of a class of any kind, let alone assorted adults, that she did not quite know where to begin. Then the old heady feeling of being in control came back, and she banged her hand on the top of the piano.

'Right,' she said, 'let's make a start.'

The sound of authority in her voice quietened the chatterers, and they looked expectantly at her. They were mostly on her side, anyway, wanting to do well for her, cheer her up after the terrible time she had had with that daughter of hers.

'We shall try some four-part singing,' she said, and smiled at the groans. 'Just decide whether you can sing high or low, and get into groups accordingly, two men's and two women's. Then we can shift people around later if they sing better in sopranos than altos and so on.'

'Ere,' said Ellen Biggs, soberly dressed in her best black coat and a squashed felt hat to match, 'what's she on about? I'm off home, Ivy, this ain't for me.'

'Mrs Biggs?' said Gabriella. 'You're not leaving us already?'

'Made a mistake, dear,' said Ellen, 'I'll just wish you all the best.'

'Oh, please, just stay for a while,' said Gabriella, 'give it a try, please . . .'

Gabriella had a stupid feeling that if she failed with Ellen Biggs, the whole thing would founder in disaster.

Ellen hesitated, then tut-tutted and returned to stand by Peggy Palmer in the altos. Peggy smiled reassuringly at her, and said, 'Wait till you hear me, Ellen!'

'A few la-las to start, then,' said Gabriella, playing arpeggios loudly on the piano. Crumbs, she thought, I shall have to get this tuned. 'Come on then, everybody, start softly, then louder at the top and back down softly again.'

After a shaky start, the choir gathered confidence and produced quite a respectable sound. Gabriella was startled to hear a lovely alto voice, true and rounded, and even more surprised to discover it was coming from old Ellen.

Unfortunately, another sound was coming through equally clearly, and Gabriella knew she had a growler. In her days as an infant teacher there were always growlers, and she loved them and forgave them, hoping they wouldn't shout. But in an adult choir it was a different matter. She looked hard at the singers, earnestly belting out 'While Shepherds Watched', and tried to isolate the gravelly voice. Oh no, she thought, oh, please God no, not Ivy Beasley.

By the end of the evening, the singers were feeling a lot happier, exchanging views about pieces for the concert, and reassuring one another on their singing.

'You'll be here next week, Mrs Biggs, I hope?' said Gabriella. 'You've got a lovely voice, you know, we wouldn't be the same without you!'

Ellen nodded. She knew quite well that she could sing. She had always sung at the top of her voice in the kitchen at the

Hall, keeping her spirits up over the bubbling saucepans, banishing the creeping fatigue as the long working day wore on. It was talk of sopranos and altos, and the idea of reading music, that frightened her, but others were clearly just as much at sea.

She had been particularly cheered by hearing Ivy Beasley grating her way through the music, and her heart had glowed. She ain't no good at all, crowed Ellen to herself. Old Ivy can't sing a note.

Nigel Brooks was happy, too, and looked round with forgivable pride at the little crowd of people chatting and laughing together after the practice. He walked over to Peggy Palmer, who was trying not to stand next to Bill Turner for too long, and said, 'What do you think, then, Peggy, shall we make a go of it?'

Peggy smiled at him warmly, anxious to be seen sharing her favours. 'It was great fun, Nigel, and Gabriella made a terrific start. She certainly knows what she's doing. It was a really good idea of yours,' she added, overdoing the enthusiasm in her attempt at impartiality.

'Pushy Peg at work again,' said Ivy Beasley to Ellen, as they stood a little apart from the rest. 'She doesn't care, does she. Not satisfied with enticing one woman's husband, now she's after another.'

'Don't be s' daft, Ivy,' said Ellen impatiently, 'you're just jealous, you and your precious Reverend Nigel. Go and speak to 'im yerself, say somethin' nice to somebody for a change.'

But Ivy Beasley gathered up her umbrella and the sheets of music Gabriella had handed round, and marched out of the church, her stout heels clacking disapprovingly on the stone floor as she went.

'She might've waited for me,' muttered Ellen, and went to smile nicely at Bill Turner, who obligingly offered to see her to her door.

It was late when Peggy turned the key and switched on the light in the warm, welcoming kitchen. She had gone back with Doreen to the farm for a cup of coffee, and sat gossiping until Tom came back from the pub.

'Poor Gilbertiney,' said Peggy, 'are you starving, kitty?' She opened a tin of cat food and spooned out a generous helping into Gilbert's feeding bowl. She slipped off her anorak and scarf and went out to hang them up in the hall. A white envelope on the door mat caught her eye.

She picked it up and returned to the kitchen, slitting it open with a knife. 'What's this, pussy, I wonder?' she said, and pulled out a folded sheet of paper and something small and hard wrapped in a scrap of tissue.

Funny, she thought, not recognising the handwriting, and then a fearful chill grabbed her as she began to read. The note was not signed, and capital letters had been used to prevent identification. The language was direct and message clear. Peggy Palmer would do well to keep her brazen ways a secret, and not leave bits of her apparel all over the village. A thinly-veiled threat of divine vengeance ended the note.

With trembling fingers, Peggy pulled at the tissue, and a small bright object fell on to the kitchen table. It was her enamelled violet brooch, and she knew she last wore it when her own car was being serviced and Bill gave her a lift back from Tresham.

CHAPTER TWENTY-TWO

'There's only one person who could have put it through the letterbox at that time,' said Peggy.

'And we both know who that is,' said Bill. 'The miserable old bag has finally lost her wits. Doesn't she know that she could get in real trouble for sending anonymous letters?'

Peggy and Bill were trudging through the wood along their now familiar path to the clearing. The fierce growth of nettles had fallen away with the arrival of autumn, and the spongy ground under the trees was soggy and treacherous. All the tiny woodland flowers had gone, and the smell of decaying wood and parasitic fungi was strong.

Misty air blurred the edges of Round Ringford as Bill and Peggy stood in their clearing, looking down on the village. It seemed remote, removed from them, putting their troubles into perspective.

'Take my advice,' said Bill, 'and ignore the whole thing. She's only done it to hurt you. God knows why. She knows as well as anyone what a mess my marriage has been for years. If you don't let her see you're upset, she won't get any gratification from it.'

Peggy understood the sense of this, but she longed for a good sort out with Ivy Beasley.

'I wish I could just face her and give her a piece of my mind,' she said, 'but she's right, the fact is I am a scarlet woman, with not a leg to stand on.'

'Scarlet women wouldn't be much good without legs,' said Bill, and put a comforting arm round Peggy's shoulders. 'It'll pass, gel, you'll see. Ivy's not worth bothering with. If she hasn't scored with her latest poison arrow, she'll have a go somewhere else, with some other poor sod.'

Rain began to fall in earnest, and Peggy put up the hood of her anorak. 'We'd better be getting back, Bill,' she said. 'Winter's not going to be so easy for us, is it.'

'I know, Peg love, I know,' said Bill, 'meeting in secret, being ashamed and hiding our feelings. I hate it. I'd like to stand on Ringford Green and shout out that I love Peggy Palmer and don't care who knows it.'

'Bloody woman's spoilt it all, hasn't she?' said Peggy vehemently. She wrenched at a whippy elder sucker, which failed to break, hurting her hand.

Bill frowned and looked at her without speaking. Then he took her in his arms and kissed her consolingly. 'Don't let her win, Peg,' he said. 'Don't let the old devil win.'

Sophie Brooks wandered up Bagley Hill, delighting in the road through the woods, and the constant rustle of hedge sparrows and rabbits in the dying grass, and thought about Nigel. He was busy and cheerful, thrilled with the first rehearsal of the concert choir, and planning a gradual overhaul of church life in Ringford. 'Gently does it,' he said to Sophie, 'village people are slow to change, and rightly so. But I hope to bring in a few changes where change is for the better.'

Sophie had counselled him to make sure his parishioners thought the changes were justified before going ahead. 'There's a strong sense of continuity in villages, families have been here for hundreds of years,' she said, 'and all those rituals link them with their past.'

Nigel had taken her advice, and agreed to concentrate on the concert until after Christmas, making sure that this first innovation was a success. As a consequence, he was a frequent visitor to Barnstones, where he and Gabriella spent happy hours working out programmes, plotting solo performances from the best singers, and sending off for unusual music which could not be found in Tresham.

The rain began to penetrate through the trees, and Sophie decided to turn back. She stood on the road overlooking the valley, and could pick out quite clearly the bulk of the vicarage next to the church. How lucky we are, she thought, it has all turned out so well. But though she was a good and optimistic Christian, she could not help a quick stab of superstitious fear that such happiness could not last. There were bound to be a few clouds on the horizon, sooner or later.

'That's quite enough of that,' she said to herself, and set off down the road, looking round as she heard footsteps behind her.

'Peggy!' She stopped and waited for her friend to catch up. 'Where have you been, you look absolutely drenched!'

That's the first time I've seen Peggy Palmer blush, she thought. What has she been up to? Trespassing in the woods, I suppose, though nobody seems to mind.

The two women walked quickly down the hill, hurrying to get home out of the rain. The sound of thunder and a flash of lightning behind her, from Bagley direction, caused Sophie to look back. A hundred yards or so behind them, halfway down the hill, she saw the bulky figure of Bill Turner, and was about to point him out to Peggy . . . and then didn't. Surely not, she thought. Oh dear, was Ivy Beasley right?

The curtains twitched in Victoria Villa, and Ivy sat back in her chair, picking up her knitting. Robert would soon be needing the gloves, and her needles clicked rapidly.

Mind you, said her mother's voice, his young woman should be knitting for him now, no need for you to wear your fingers out on his behalf, Ivy.

Ivy ignored this. She was doing her best to forget Robert Bates's engagement, though she had tried hard to smile and say the right thing when he told her the news. Mustn't lose him altogether, she thought, and at the prospect of this possibility she felt a sense of desolation so strong that she put a hand to her chest to stem the pain.

That Peggy Palmer has no shame, Mother, she said, forcing her mind on to another subject. There she is, coming along the road with Mrs Brooks, when she was all over the woman's husband not twenty-four hours ago, and keeping Bill Turner dangling as well.

Your little trick hasn't worked, then, Ivy, said the voice maliciously. You'll have to think again.

Don't know what you're talking about, said Ivy. I must put the dinner on.

She got up to set the potatoes to boil, and began to cut up a cabbage into neat shreds. I suppose Sophie Brooks is taken in by that blue-eyed smile, she thought. Everybody is except me. Reverend Brooks should watch his step, somebody should tell him. He's too nice-lookin' for his own good.

With the dinner simmering and appetising smells rising from the kitchen, Ivy went up into the front bedroom that had been her mother's. It was like a shrine to the dead woman, everything just as she had left it, and, apart from careful dusting, never touched. It was not a frivolous room, but the furniture was good walnut, and a snowy white, thick cotton spread covered the bed.

Ivy pulled open a small drawer at the dressing table, and picked up a round gilt and black powder compact. Old Mrs Beasley had disapproved of make-up, said it made Ivy look like a tart, but Ivy had secretly watched her mother indulge with a few dabs of powder and a touch of scent for special nights at the WI.

She opened the compact and gently rubbed the little puff over the compressed powder. Holding it up so that the light from the window fell on her face, she shakily powdered her nose, and then the red, shiny cheeks. She turned, holding the compact so that she could see a reflection of her back view in the dressing-table mirror. She smoothed her hair, curling it under her fingers where it stuck out straight over her collar.

What a sight, Ivy Beasley! said the voice in her head. Shut up, Mother, said Ivy fiercely, and, putting the compact back in the little drawer, she went downstairs to take the potatoes off the boil.

'It did seem rather odd,' said Sophie, 'and Peggy was certainly uncomfortable about something.'

Sophie Brooks was standing squarely at the big kitchen table, slicing onions and mopping her eyes with her sleeve. Nigel wore his favourite apron, the butcher's one with blue and white strips, and with a lethally sharp knife was cutting stewing steak into small cubes, rolling them expertly in seasoned flour.

'Sophie darling,' he said, 'long before we came here, Richard Standing warned me about Ivy Beasley. She is a dreadful gossip and mischief-maker – every village has one – and it is very important not to give her any encouragement whatsoever. If Peggy Palmer and Bill Turner go for walks together in Bagley Woods, it is none of Ivy Beasley's business, and none of ours, either. They are grown-up, mature people, and they must take responsibility for their own actions . . .'

'Hey!' said Sophie. 'Spare me the sermon, Nigel. I know all about Poison Ivy, and you might just watch it yourself, or you'll be next on the hit list. Gabriella Jones is a very attractive young woman.'

Nigel stared at her, horrified. 'Don't be ridiculous, Soph,' he said. 'What can you mean?'

'Just that all those consultations at Barnstones, and little run-throughs on the organ in the church, do not go un-remarked by the three witches of Ringford.'

Sophie scooped the pile of sliced onions into a big sizzling pan, and turned to the stone sink, where she began to run hot water into the washing-up bowl. Nigel followed up the onions with the cubes of meat, and turned the mixture round with a wooden spoon. They had cooked amiably together since they were first married, when they had had few skills between them, and each learned from the other.

'You've been talking to William Roberts,' said Nigel. 'He and that Warren Jenkins are quite a pair.' He patted Sophie's neat bottom with a floury hand. 'Still,' he added, brightening, 'better keep in with those two young tearaways – I mean to have them in a regular choir after Christmas.'

He has a genius for sidestepping, thought Sophie, and then forgot all about it as she put the casserole in the oven and sat down to read once again the lovely three-page letter from their married daughter in Paris.

CHAPTER TWENTY-THREE

Bates's Farm was part of the Standing estate, and the Bates family had been tenants there for three generations before Robert. His mother and father, Olive and Ted Bates, had settled obediently, as was expected of them, into the work of the farm. After Grandfather died, Granny Bates moved to Barrow Cottage next to the pub, where she was handy for cups of tea with old Mrs Beasley, and the pair of them had sat in Victoria Villa's front window pronouncing acidly on the evil doings of the village. Granny Bates followed Ivy's mother quite soon to the graveyard, where they lay companionably next to one another.

The farmhouse was a pleasant old stone building, four-square and with the front door facing a small garden, where Robert kept the grass neat and tidy, and his father lovingly cultivated large, deep blue delphiniums and not much else. The vegetable garden was another matter, and the cornucopia of produce from the richly manured earth kept the family going summer and winter.

Olive Bates doted on Robert, her only son, especially since he had been a frail baby, and though she was reticent and not at all articulate, she showed her great love for him by cooking and cleaning, washing, ironing, knitting and sewing, making a warm, secure home for him all through his childhood and early years of being a man. Like Ivy Beasley, she had not been at all sure about his engagement to Mandy Butler, a town girl who knew nothing about farming, and so far showed no signs of wanting to learn.

'Why couldn't he have chosen from his own kind?' Olive said to her husband, who as usual grunted his reply. Ted Bates was a tall, thin man, already bent with years of physical strain on the farm, and with a big hook nose that glowed red after a good night out with the boys in the Standing Arms.

'It's not as if we had another son to take over the farm,' said Olive.

She stood by the window, looking out over fields full of sheep, green fields and greyish-white, woolly sheep, like a child's picture book. But Olive, a wiry woman with short, straight grey hair, saw only a tough, demanding farm, which had taken all the energy of herself and her husband, and in due course Robert too, to keep going in spite of weather and all kinds of unexpected diseases and economic pressures over the years.

'There is only Robert, and he'll need a proper wife to help him,' continued Olive, warming her roughened hands in front of the fire.

Ted Bates looked up at her over the top of his spectacles. He was sitting in their comfortable front room, where an unseasonal log fire insulated them from the dingy, damp day outside the small-paned windows. It was Sunday, and Robert and Mandy were due for tea. Olive had baked a large, golden fruit cake, and had placed it on Granny Bates's cut-glass stand next to a plateful of small, crustless sandwiches. The best china was set out on a crisp white embroidered tablecloth, waiting for the young couple to arrive.

'Good God, woman, I ain't dead yet,' said Ted Bates, and returned to the Sunday paper, his lips moving unashamedly as he read.

'You never do want to look to the future,' said Olive. 'So long as you got a pint in your hand and the weather's not too bad for the farm, that's all you care.' She disappeared from the room, banging about in the kitchen and filling the kettle noisily from the old brass tap.

'There ain't a girl livin' as you'd think right for our Robert,' said Ted under his breath.

The sound of a car set the old liver and white spaniel barking in joyful anticipation, and as Robert and Mandy came through the back door into the kitchen, bringing in a flurry of moist air and farmyard smells, the dog leapt up at Mandy, catching his claws in her long black jersey. Her shoulder-length silky brown hair was loose, and her pretty legs were shown off to advantage in their tight black leggings. Ted looked at his only son with envy.

'Charlie! Get down at once!' scolded Olive, apologising profusely. Mandy smiled bravely, and smoothed down the snags in her jersey. She was well aware of how unsuitable she must seem to the Bateses, and had made a private vow to be the best farmer's wife in the district. 'I'll show them snotty Young Farmers,' she had said to Robert, who said he didn't want her to change one bit, he loved her exactly the way she was.

'I thought we might settle a few things over tea, Mandy,' said Olive Bates. She had been delighted and flattered that the wedding was going to be in Ringford, and, whilst being very shy of offering help to Mandy's mother, she meant to have a reasonable hand in all the excitement of planning a village wedding. It would have been so much better if Mandy had been a village girl, but there it was. 'It is lovely for us,' she said. 'It was one of my sorrows at not having a little girl. Now we shall have a Ringford wedding after all.'

'Done something right, then,' Mandy said quietly to Robert, as his mother went to fill the pot. 'If I could dredge up some long-lost farmer cousin it would be almost perfect.'

But Robert saw only the lovely girl he had fancied since schooldays, who miraculously felt the same about him. All talk of townies and not knowing what hard work was passed over his besotted head.

'Reverend Brooks has booked the date in February, and we've to go and see him together,' said Robert, handing round the tea for his mother.

Mandy made a face. 'No embarrassing stuff about the facts of life, I hope!' she said.

'Bit late for that, I should say,' said Ted, and Olive frowned at him. Trust him to make a coarse remark, she thought. I hope Mandy won't be offended. Olive knew, of course, that young people all tried out what she would have had difficulty in finding words for. But that didn't mean you had to mention it, let alone make jokes about it. She changed the subject.

'I'm going to ask your mum and dad to come next Sunday,' she said, 'then we can have a real run through what's left to be done. A winter wedding is really unusual, isn't it.' It was another thing that didn't suit Olive. No Ringford girl would get married in mid-winter. Could be snowing, and none of the guests get through. And flowers will cost a fortune, and the Village Hall will have to be heated for hours before the reception. Still, thank God we're not paying for it, she thought. Ted had offered to buy the drink – typical of him, that – and the rest was up to the Butlers.

Ted went off into a deep, snoring sleep, and the evening advanced, Mandy helping Olive with the washing up and chatting desultorily about wedding plans. Olive found her future daughter-in-law difficult to talk to, having nothing in common with an attractive young hairdresser from town.

'We'll be off now, Mother,' Robert said, as soon as it was tactfully possible. 'See you later.' Olive nodded, and watched the lights of the car as they drove off towards Tresham.

'She'll not settle easily,' she said to Ted, who continued to snore. Olive sighed. Marriage to Ted had been hard work with few treats. He had expected her to carry on where his mother had left off, and she had done so unquestioningly. Now she saw in Robert and Mandy a different way altogether, more of a partnership, and in that partnership there was no room for her. She sniffed, and bent down to pick up the newspaper which had slid from Ted's lap.

He snuffled and choked, and surfaced enough to say something which Olive didn't catch.

'What did you say, Ted dear?'

He opened one eye and looked at her in surprise, the endearment having got through the barriers of sleep.

'You goin' deaf, Mother?' he muttered. 'I said to put another log on the fire, that's all.' And he rearranged the cushion behind his head and went back to sleep.

Robert and Mandy sat in silence for a few minutes, and then Mandy said, 'Your father and mine have one thing in common, anyway.' Robert looked sideways at her, his eyebrows raised.

'They both snore their horrible heads off,' said Mandy, all her pent-up resentment making it sound a deadly offence.

Robert laughed, and slowly cruised the car to a halt. He put his arm round her and kissed her until all the tension went out of her and she remembered it was Robert she was marrying, not his miserable father.

Unfortunately, Robert had stopped the car outside Barnstones, where the curtains were not yet drawn. Octavia Jones was standing morosely at the window, wishing something wonderful would happen, when she saw Robert's car draw up under the single street lamp at the bottom of Macmillan Gardens.

Her heartbeat quickened, but then she saw the two shadowy figures become one, and it was more than she could bear. 'I'm going out, might go to Tanya's,' she said to her parents who sat peacefully reading the Sunday papers. Before they could question her, Octavia had grabbed her jacket and disappeared, banging the front door as she went.

CHAPTER TWENTY-FOUR

Octavia shivered in the evening chill as she half ran out of her gate and turned into the dark street. The light outside the pub illuminated the pavement and road, and she made her way towards it without really thinking where she was going, or what she intended to do. A dog barked, frantically yapping from Macmillan Gardens as she passed, and she saw a white flash as the Jenkins terrier shot across the grass, in hot pursuit of something shadowy and terrified.

Hope it's not Mrs Palmer's cat, she thought, walking by the shop, closed off and unwelcoming with its white blind down over the big window.

A dark figure turned out of the Village Hall and approached. Octavia recognised the bulk of Mrs Jenkins, and immediately turned round and began to walk back towards home. 'Don't want that fat old cow asking questions,' she muttered.

She heard Mrs Jenkins's footsteps fade as she turned into the Gardens, and Octavia continued back along the main street. She had no intention of going to the Brights'. She knew Tanya was away, staying with her grandmother. Better go home, I suppose, she thought. They'll only give me another of their sympathy sessions if I don't.

But the thought of being smothered with parental concern was more than she could take, and she walked on, past Barnstones and Price's farm, and out of the village on the Tresham road. She just wanted to think about Robert, and without irritating distractions began to construct one of her favourite fantasies. In the darkness, walking steadily, she imagined the bathing pool, a wide stretch of the Ringle where children splashed and learned to swim by the shallow far bank. The sun shone from a clear blue sky, and she was alone in the pool, all by herself and naked. No need to be wearing a swimsuit if nobody was around.

She felt the thick mud beneath her feet as she tried to stand up in the deep part of the pool. Then her feet were sinking in, and she lost her balance. Fear made her shout, and, just as the water was closing over her head, Robert came dashing along the river bank. 'Hold on, Octavia, hold on, I'm coming!'

His strong arms were round her body, gently lifting her out of the water. She felt the warmth of his breath on her face, as she slowly opened her eyes. She saw her own slender, sun-tanned body stretched out on the warm grass, and Robert bending anxiously over her. 'Octavia! Are you all right?' She smiled at him, and saw the expression in his eyes change from concern to passion . . .

Dazzling lights jolted her back to the cold emptiness of the Tresham road, and she jumped on to the muddy verge for safety.

The car slowed and stopped, and Octavia could hardly believe that it was Robert's voice. 'Octavia! Are you all right?' he said, and came walking back towards her.

She smiled at him, but in the darkness he could see only the outline of a pale, young face. 'You silly girl,' he said, 'it isn't safe to be out here at night, walking along the edge of the road without a torch or anything. What are you doing, anyway? You ought to be back home with your mum and dad.'

'Give me a lift, then, Robert?' said Octavia, back in the real world. And without waiting for his answer, she climbed into the passenger seat of his car and fastened her seat belt.

They drove in silence for a minute, and then Robert said, 'Lucky I was coming back early. You never know who might have picked you up.'

'Nothing would have happened to me,' said Octavia. 'I was going to turn back just about then.'

'You've caused enough trouble lately, young lady,' said Robert. 'You ought to think of your parents a bit more. They must be worried sick by now, wondering where you've got to.'

He pulled up outside Barnstones, and Octavia got out, slamming the door shut and standing on the pavement looking resentfully at Robert's car. He wound down the window and shouted, 'Go on, I want to see you open that front door.'

Octavia shrugged and turned into her garden, slinking along the path and turning to blow Robert a mocking kiss as she opened the door and disappeared inside.

Greg, his overcoat buttoned up and scarf tied round his neck, stood by the fireplace, and Gabriella sat on the edge of her seat, rigid with tension. They were both listening to the door opening and the sound of a car starting off outside. Gabriella began to get up, but Greg motioned to her to sit down, and she sank back on to the sofa. They heard rustling sounds in the hall, and then after a few moments the sitting room door opened and Octavia came in.

'Octavia!' said Gabriella, shooting up from her seat. 'What on earth has happened to you!'

The silky blonde hair was wild, tangled and falling over Octavia's face, and her jacket had been twisted round, revealing one shoulder where her shirt was open down to her waist, her bra showing alarmingly white and exposed.

She rushed to her mother and began to cry, sobbing louder as she got going.

'Sit down, child,' said Greg, and then, to Gabriella, 'Don't panic, Gabbie, let's calm her down and hear what she has to say.'

He had an odd feeling. He had seen dramatic outbursts many times in his career as a teacher, and had grown to recognise the genuine from the carefully calculated. There was something about the speculative look in Octavia's eyes as she came into the room . . . but maybe he was wrong.

He got up and made a pot of tea, while Gabriella quietened down Octavia, straightened her hair and clothes. She held the smooth hands in a protective grasp. 'Hush, 'Tavie, Mother's here, you are quite safe now,' she crooned.

'It was a man, gave me a lift back into the village,' said Octavia, when she had emptied the mug of sweet tea and settled back among the cushions. 'I went to the Brights', but Tanya wasn't there, so I thought I'd go for a walk. I went up the Tresham road, but it was cold, and I'd just turned back when this car stopped and the driver offered me a lift. I got in, and he started off, but then he stopped again and began to pull me about, and then I screamed . . .' She stopped, her lips trembling, and put her hands to her face.

'Take it steady, girlie,' said Greg. 'Take your time.'

'Then I got out of the car and ran, ran and ran, until I was home and safe.'

'Thank God,' said Gabriella. 'And nothing else happened? He didn't try to . . .' She dried up, and Greg took over.

'That's all he did, just pulled your clothes about a bit?' said Greg, frowning.

Gabriella scowled at him. 'That must have been terrifying, darling,' she said to Octavia, and her voice began to rise, 'but why on earth did you accept a lift from a stranger in the dark? Did you recognise him, get a good look at him?'

Octavia was silent, staring at Gabriella with brimming eyes.

'Well?' said Greg. 'Who was it? Do you know who it was?'

Octavia answered in a muffled voice, and Gabriella reached out and put her arm round the girl's shoulders.

'What did you say, darling?' she said.

'It was Robert Bates.'

Tears began to fall again in the shocked silence, and Greg pulled a large handkerchief from his pocket and handed it to his daughter.

'Christ,' he said. 'What do we do now?'

CHAPTER TWENTY-FIVE

Half past ten, and the Stores was crowded with morning shoppers. It was a dull morning, and the children waiting at the bus stop for the school bus in the early autumn chill had been glad of anoraks. Most of them were still wearing their summer uniforms, except for Octavia, who ignored the rules and wore a mini-skirt and long sweater, so long that the skirt underneath looked like a frill round her bottom.

The harvest was safely gathered in, and a notice billing the Harvest Supper in the Village Hall flapped against its two remaining drawing pins on the noticeboard by the bus shelter.

'Did you see that wonderful sunset yesterday, Peggy?' Sophie Brooks said, as she packed her groceries into her basket. 'Thank God there's no more stubble-burning, now you can see the contours of the land.'

Sophie Brooks, standing chatting at the counter to Peggy, had for days been tramping round the footpaths, most of them overgrown from lack of use, and seen the few remaining stubble fields shining gold in the sun against nearby newly ploughed earth, had marvelled at great round bales of hay abandoned in a field where new grass was already thick. Some of the sweet-smelling hay hung in rebellious swathes from the end of the bales, like wisps of soft hair escaped from a plait.

'What's she on about?' said old Ellen to Ivy Beasley, as the two of them stood waiting to be served.

'Stuck up madam, if you ask me,' said Ivy, not bothering to lower her voice.

Peggy continued to wrap and add and count out change with efficient ease, asking the right questions and keeping an eye on Mark Jenkins, who was looking longingly at a display of boxed cars, brought from the warehouse by Bill.

'Had them when I was a lad,' he had said, holding them up in delight. 'My dad used to buy me a new one every birthday, and I kept them on the windowsill in my bedroom. Mum used to grumble about the dust, but she never put them away.'

'Have you still got them?' Peggy asked, remembering Frank's collection of cigarette cards, carefully stuck into an album and lovingly protected in a cardboard box.

Bill had shaken his head. 'Came home one day from work, and the bin men had just been. Joyce was crowing like an old cock, and pointed at the empty biscuit tin where I kept them.'

'What did you say?'

'Nothing. But it was another notch.'

Mark Jenkins made his way to the counter clutching one of the car boxes, and put it down, digging into his pocket and coming up with a handful of silver.

'That's it, Mrs Palmer,' he said. 'Mum said that was just right.'

Peggy counted the coins, and found that Mark was twenty pence short. She hesitated, then said, 'Quite right, Mark, well done. Which one did you choose?'

Mark read out the details of the car slowly and deliberately, then thanked Peggy politely and left the shop.

' 'E's a nice child,' said Ellen Biggs. 'All them Jenkinses is nice children, all credit to their mother. Jean's a good gel, always was.'

'You coming to me this afternoon, then, Ellen?' said Ivy. 'Don't know if I'll have time to bake, but I dare say I can find a biscuit or two.'

She only says it to annoy, thought Ellen. I shan't rise, shan't give 'er the satisfaction.

Peggy took Ivy Beasley's wire basket and added up the

small number of purchases quickly. The sooner she goes the better I like it, she said to herself. I could do without her custom, but then she'd not pick up the gossip in here and that would limit her ammunition considerably.

'That will be exactly three pounds fifty,' she said, not smiling.

Ivy put down the money on the counter and turned to leave, scarcely acknowledging Peggy, and certainly not thanking her as she put the few items in her string bag.

'See you this afternoon, Ellen,' she said, and added tartly, 'and see if you can be on time for once.'

Ellen stuck her tongue out at the retreating back, and smiled at Peggy.

'God forbid I ever get as crabby as old Ivy,' she said. 'I 'ope you'll 'ave me put down at once, my dear.'

Peggy glanced out of the shop window as Ivy Beasley crossed the road in front of Greg Jones's car, which drew up outside the school. Greg got out, waving and shouting to Robert Bates, who was carefully negotiating his way through the village on a tractor with a lethal hedge-cutter attachment. Ivy stood at the bus stop, watching.

'Greg looks worried,' said Peggy, turning back to old Ellen. 'Wonder why he's not at school?'

'More trouble with that daughter of 'is, I shouldn't wonder,' said Ellen. 'What she needs is a good talking to.'

Peggy shrugged. 'There's some would say it's too late,' she said, 'and anyway. I thought she'd been out with Tim Bright a couple of times and given up her pursuit of poor Robert.'

'That sort never gives up,' said Ellen knowingly. 'Not till it suits them . . .'

Greg Jones stood on the pavement waving vigorously at Robert Bates, until the tractor stopped and Robert leaned out.

'Morning, Mr Jones,' he said, 'you waving at me?'

Greg nodded and crossed the road. He looked up at the tractor cab, feeling immediately at a foolish disadvantage.

'Just wondered if we could have a private word some time, Robert?' he said, shouting above the engine noise. Jean

Jenkins, passing by on her way to the shop, heard what Greg said, and the word 'private' made her prick up her ears.

'What do he want a private word with Robert Bates for, Eddie my duck?' she said to her chubby son, already wriggling around in his pushchair ready to get out at the shop.

The rest of Greg's conversation with Robert was lost to Jean, as she could find no reason to hang about, and after a minute or two Robert drove off and turned down past the pub and into Bates's End.

'Morning, Jean,' said Peggy, as Eddie and his mother came slowly into the shop. Eddie's walking was still a little unsteady, and his rolling gait not quite up to climbing the shop steps without the aid of his mother. The large frame of Jean Jenkins beside her small son filled the narrow doorway and they eased themselves into the shop with much laughter and encouragement from old Ellen.

'That's it, Eddie Jenkins,' she said, 'what a clever boy!'

'Your Mark's been in already,' said Peggy. 'What can I get you, Jean?'

Jean Jenkins opened her purse and took out a twenty-pence piece. 'He was short, Peggy, and you never said. I saw the price ticket when he got home, and I come straight down. I must have seen it wrong when I was in yesterday.' She handed over the coin, and Peggy humbly took it, feeling somehow in the wrong.

'What's that Jones man want with our Robert?' said Ellen, hobbling towards the door. 'You hear anythin', Jean?'

'Just that he wanted a private word,' said Jean.

Ellen turned to Peggy. 'There, what did I say? It's that brat of 'is causin' trouble again.'

'I don't think you should jump to . . .' Peggy was interrupted by Jean Jenkins snatching Eddie from a wire basket full of cans of cola. Several had already rolled round the shop floor, and Peggy rushed round from the other side of the counter to help.

'Let me hold him for a bit,' she said, taking Eddie from his mother's scolding grasp. Eddie put his little arms round

Peggy's neck and buried his face in her shoulder. She laughed and cuddled him, loving his warm little body.

What a shame, thought Jean Jenkins for the umpteenth time, what a pity she's got no family, no one to love. Except Bill, she corrected herself, and that's a bit of non-starter.

'Here, wait a minute,' she said, when peace had been restored. 'I was comin' back from the phone box last night, and that Octavia Jones was comin' along by the pub, in the dark, all by herself. I reckon she saw me, and turned round and went back the way she come.'

'What could that 'ave to do with Robert?' said Ellen, looking interested.

Jean shook her head. 'Don't know,' she said, 'but Foxy said he saw him drivin' by slowly when he come out of the pub later on.'

The shop door opened again, and Pat Osman came in, bright and fresh, and with smiles for all.

Peggy reluctantly handed Eddie back to his mother, and returned to her post behind the counter.

'We should be careful,' she said, 'about putting two and two together and making five. Hello Mrs Osman,' she continued, greeting her new customer, 'what can I get for you this morning?'

'I might be a bit late for tea today, Mum,' said Robert Bates, getting up from the table and brushing crumbs of pastry to the grateful spaniel at his feet. 'Mr Jones asked me to call in and have a private word, so I'll go in before seeing Auntie Ivy.'

The farm kitchen was very warm, full of good cooking smells, and the big wooden table covered with a checked oil cloth bore the remains of a stout meal. Behind Olive's chair, a little light filtered in from the garden, through tiny panes steamed up from the constantly simmering kettle. Robert began to feel the need of fresh air.

'What kind of private word?' said Olive sharply.

Robert shrugged. 'Don't ask me,' he said, 'probably something to do with Parish Council business.' Robert was the youngest and keenest member of the Parish Council, and was often approached to sort out a problem when villagers would hesitate to tackle Tom Price. 'See you later, then,' and he gave his mother a peck on her cheek. 'Cheer up, it may never happen!' he said, and, pulling on his boots, prepared to get back to work.

'Don't you think we should have got the police or something?' said Gabriella, staring out of her sitting room window and twisting her hands together nervously. 'How are we going to put it to Robert Bates?'

Greg put down the paper he was trying to read. 'I shall just ask him outright if he molested Octavia last night . . . no, of course I shan't, Gabriella . . . we shall have to be very tactful indeed. And it would have been entirely the wrong thing to get in the police at this stage. We'll give the lad a chance to tell us his side of it, and then think again.'

Gabriella frowned and turned to look at Greg. 'You don't believe her, do you?' she blurted out. 'You think she's lying, made it all up, don't you?'

Greg was silent for a moment, and then sighed. 'I don't know, Gabbie, I really don't know. It's just that I clearly remember hearing a car door slam and then the sound of it moving off seconds before Octavia came in last night. And that doesn't tie up with her story of running home on her own in a panic.'

Robert Bates's tractor drew up outside the gate, and he clambered down from the cab.

'Here he is,' said Gabriella. 'You let him in.'

Greg went to the door, and the two men returned to the room in silence.

Robert sat on the edge of the Joneses' sofa, his feet in their grey socks placed squarely on the cream shaggy rug. He had insisted on removing his boots, and Greg was nonplussed at the sight of Robert's familiar, pleasant face smiling at him across the room. How the hell was he going to begin?

Gabriella had disappeared into the kitchen to make a cup of

tea, and Robert exchanged with Greg a few pleasantries about the weather.

'Was it something to do with Council matters you wanted to ask me?' Robert said finally, thinking he'd be here all afternoon if they didn't get on with it.

'No, not really,' said Greg, clearing his throat. 'It's about Octavia.'

'Ah,' said Robert. 'That one.'

'Well,' said Greg, 'I don't know how to say this, but she came in very upset last night and said you'd given her a lift along the road.'

'Quite right,' said Robert. 'I was very surprised to see her out on her own.'

Greg sat up straighter. 'What happened, Robert?' he said in the confiding tone he used to encourage schoolchildren to talk to him. 'You can tell us, you know, I'm sure we'll be able to sort it all out.'

Robert looked at him in amazement. Gabriella had come back with a tea tray and was staring at him anxiously.

'Happened?' said Robert. 'Bloody nothing happened!' He stood up. 'I come across your daughter wandering along the road in the dark, all by herself, and stopped to bring her back home. Which is what I did, making sure she came up the path and into your house before I drove off again. And nothing bloody happened!' he repeated, his face bright red with indignation.

They stood glaring at each other for a few seconds, then Gabriella put down the tea tray and said nervously, 'Would you like a cup of tea, Robert?'

'No thanks,' said Robert, marching towards the door. 'I've got work to do, no time to waste here. You'll have big trouble with that Octavia if you're not careful, Mr Jones. Best you do something to stop it straight away.'

The front door slammed, and Greg and Gabriella looked at one another in silence. Gabriella poured two cups of tea, and handed one to Greg.

'What is the truth, Greg?' she said wearily. Greg sat down beside her and put his arm round her shoulders.

'I'm afraid I'm inclined to believe Robert,' he said gently. 'There was something about the way 'Tavie looked at us when she came in, something not quite right.'

'I can't believe it,' said Gabriella pathetically. 'Not my baby girl. What on earth shall we do now?'

'Talk to her again,' said Greg. 'When she comes home from school, I'll talk to her alone. You are naturally upset, and there's far too much emotion flying around. Leave it to me, and I'll see if I can straighten it out.'

'What's eating you, Robert?' said Ivy Beasley, setting down a cup of good strong tea and a large wedge of chocolate fudge cake.

'Nothing, Auntie, at least, nothing very much,' said Robert, taking a grateful gulp of the tea.

' "Always something in nothing," as my mother used to say,' said Ivy, relying on her favourite saying to help things along.

'Well, yes,' said Robert. 'It's that Octavia Jones up to her tricks again. It's her mum and dad I feel sorry for. She twists them round her little finger.'

'Where do you come into it, then?' said Ivy, gently prodding.

'Oh, it was nothing at all – just that little tramp making up some story about me when I gave her a lift last night.'

Ivy bristled. 'She'd better not start causing trouble for you, Robert, else I shall have something more to say. And I'm not one to mince my words.'

Robert hastily assured her that it was nothing important and would all blow over, but he regretted mentioning it to Auntie Ivy, knowing her reputation for malicious gossip, and also her abiding love for himself.

'Enjoying the concert rehearsals, Auntie?' he said, changing the subject.

'Not so far,' Ivy replied. 'Mind you, Reverend Brooks is

doing his best with an unruly bunch. But there's too much laughing and joking for my liking. That Gabriella Jones is always making sheep's eyes at Reverend Brooks, and she has no idea about discipline. It wasn't like that in my schooldays. We all had to behave ourselves, and not be continually interrupting and making suggestions.'

'But it's not school, Auntie,' said Robert. 'It's supposed to be a bit of fun and something nice for the village at Christmas.'

Ivy sniffed, and took Robert's cup to refill. 'I shall carry on with it, anyway,' she said, 'for old Ellen's sake. She can't sing for toffee, but it's an outing for her and she won't go without me.'

'That's kind of you, Auntie,' said Robert, not really listening, but thinking he should be on his way.

'You're hedge-cutting early this year, aren't you, Robert?' said Ivy. 'There'll be no blackberries left to pick at this rate. They're scarcely ripe yet.'

'Try the bottom of Fenny Moor,' said Robert. 'You know that little old field? Well, Dad never cuts the hedge there by the stream. It's got loads of blackberries and crabs and hips and haws and all sorts. You go down there, Auntie, you'll find more than enough.'

He got up and kissed her on the cheek. 'Thanks very much, Auntie Ivy, see you next week. Mind how you go . . .'

Ivy watched him disappear up the street and, when he was out of sight, returned to the kitchen.

Looks like another job for me, Mother, she said to the quiet room.

Oh, speaking to me again, are you, said the voice in her head. Thought you'd sulk for ever. You always were one for sulking, Ivy.

Give it a rest, do, said Ivy. I'm just thinking how I can make those Joneses see they can't come to this village and stir up trouble for my Robert without so much as a by your leave. I blame that Gabriella, she's always been a flibbertigibbet with her long hair and her short shorts. She's never out of Nigel

Brooks's sight these days, with her 'Is this right, Nigel?' and 'What do you think, Nigel?'

You're very steamed up, Ivy. Not jealous, are we?

Mother, I'm only thinking of that poor wife of his, that Sophie Brooks. She's a poor thing, but that doesn't mean she deserves to be treated like dirt by a brassy bit like Gabriella Jones.

Ivy wiped her hands on her apron, then took it off and went out into the garden to pick a few last beans for her supper.

Octavia sensed trouble as soon as she opened the front door. Her father was standing in a patriarchal position with his back to the fireplace, and her mother was nowhere to be seen.

'Where's Mum?' said Octavia.

'In the garden,' said Greg. 'I'd like a word or two with you, young lady, before you do anything else.'

Oh shit, thought Octavia, they've been talking to Robert.

'Sit down,' said Greg, 'and tell me again exactly what happened last night.'

Octavia sat down with unusual obedience, and began to suck a strand of her ash-blonde hair.

'Well?' said Greg.

'I told you,' said Octavia.

'Tell me again,' said Greg.

Octavia went once more through her story, repeating the exact details and managing a few tears when she came to the part where Robert ripped open her blouse. Then she made a mistake.

'He stopped the car outside here and practically shoved me out,' she concluded, reaching for her father's hand, and sniffing loudly.

Greg shook her off, and stared at her.

'But you said you got out of the car way back up the road and ran home in a panic,' he said accusingly.

'No, I didn't,' said Octavia, her voice breaking in alarm.

'Tell me the truth, Octavia,' said Greg, grimly stern.

Octavia stood up and faced him. 'You wouldn't know the

truth if you heard it!' she screamed at him. 'And that's just it –
you can't hear it, you stupid . . . !'

She turned and ran from the room, yelling, 'Mum! Mum!
Where are you?' at the top of her voice.

Greg felt as if someone had hit him hard across the face. His
own daughter mocking him for being deaf. It was too cruel to
take in. He wiped his hand across his eyes and coughed. Well,
he thought, at least I think I have the truth now. I must ring up
Robert and apologise. He looked down at his hand and saw
that it was wet, and then sat down heavily on the sofa.

'Octavia Jones,' he said. 'Daddy's little 'Tavie . . .'

CHAPTER TWENTY-SIX

Ellen Biggs looked into her damp, narrow clothes cupboard and wondered what to wear for tea with Ivy Beasley. Every year, at the jumble sale in the Village Hall, Ellen handed in a small pile of worn clothes, and bought herself a new selection of outfits for the four seasons, to last until the sale came round again. In this way, for a pound or two, she could indulge her passion for dressing to please herself, delighting in bright colours and rich folds of material, not caring in the least what impression she made on other people, and certainly not fearing Ivy's scathing comments. Indeed, the more she could provoke her friend's disapproval, the happier Ellen was.

She glanced out of the small, dusty window at her sunlit garden, bright with late chrysanthemums and dark purple Michaelmas daisies. Looks warm out there, she thought, but you can't trust this time of the year. Better put on something warmish, don't want a chill on top of me rheumatism.

A tough old woman, Ellen put a brave face on days when her legs ached and she could hardly turn her head. Living alone, with nobody to sympathise or nurse her, she had a grim determination not to give up her comfortless, dingy cottage until carried out in her coffin, and so she told no one about waking in panic in the small hours, unable to get out of bed and terrified of wetting herself. She joked about old age, and watched her contemporaries disappear into Bagley

House, which she preferred to call the workhouse, with a secret terror that one day it would be her turn.

'This'll do well,' she said, taking out a royal-blue woollen dress with a dropped waist and shawl neckline. It had been Mrs Ross's best for several years, and was still in good condition, except for a few spots down the side, where the little dog had disgraced himself.

Ellen had struggled into the dress, and was sitting on the edge of her bed pulling on comfortable black plimsolls over beige ribbed cotton stockings, when she heard a light tap and her back door opening.

'Ellen? Are you there, Ellen? It's only me . . . Mrs Standing . . . Ellen?'

Well, thought Ellen, if it's only you, you can wait a minute or two 'til I've got me shoes on.

'Comin', madam,' she called, and stood up, pulling down the dress and admiring the effect in an old cracked cheval mirror which had once graced the nanny's bedroom in the Hall.

'Good morning, Ellen, how nice you look,' said Susan Standing. She had been frustrated and irritated by the old woman in her last years as cook at the Hall, but now she had a sneaking fondness for the independent Ellen, and called in frequently to check on her.

'Do sit down, madam,' said Ellen, always on her dignity with her former employer. 'Lovely day now, ain't it?'

Susan agreed, and sat gingerly on the edge of a rickety cane chair. 'Ellen,' she said, 'I need your advice.'

Oh yes, thought Ellen, I've heard that one before. Usually means she wants me to feed them 'orrible dogs while they're away.

'It's the concert,' said Susan, 'the Christmas concert. I believe you are singing in the choir, is that right?'

Ellen nodded and waited. So it wasn't the dogs. What's comin', I wonder.

'I would really like to contribute something, but my voice is certainly not up to choir standard,' Susan said modestly. 'I was wondering if Mr Brooks would want any kind of dramatic interlude. Perhaps a recitation or a reading from Dickens, or something like that . . . what do you think, Ellen? You always know what fits in . . .' Her voice trailed away into a vague, questioning silence.

'What, you mean like "The Boy stood on the Burning Deck"?' said Ellen blandly.

Susan shook her head. 'Well, no, not exactly that. More an extract from *A Christmas Carol*, or *Pickwick Papers*. Or perhaps that wonderful Hardy poem about Christmas Eve?'

Ellen reached for her long gaberdine mac that had been Mr Richard's, and began to fold it up and squash it into an old egg basket.

'I don't 'ave much idea about them,' she said. 'Best you ask Reverend Brooks. But I'm sure 'e'll be delighted, and that Gabriella Jones will be glad of a little break 'alfway through.' And anyway, thought Ellen, it could be good for a laugh, if nothing else.

'She's talkin' of recitin' at the concert,' said Ellen, setting down her basket in Ivy Beasley's hall.

There was an unmistakable, heavenly smell of baking in Ivy's house, and Ellen sighed with relief that the threat of a couple of biscuits had been forgotten.

'Lovely smell of cookin', Ivy,' she said, and made her way into the neat front room, sitting down in the best chair under the old wall clock.

'Who's talking of reciting?' said Doris Ashbourne, already seated on the overstuffed sofa, her handbag tucked down by her side.

'Madam,' said Ellen. 'Mrs Standing 'erself. She wants to contribute, she says, and asked me first, knowing as I'm in touch with what goes on.'

'Rubbish!' said Ivy, bringing in the teapot shrouded by a crinoline lady with satin skirts and haughty demeanour. 'She knows you're a regular old gossip, that's for sure . . .'

Tea poured, Ivy lifted a knife to the perfect coffee sponge

sitting without a lean in any direction on a fresh white paper doily.

'You'll take a piece of cake, Ellen?' she said. 'Don't feel you have to, I shan't be offended, knowing you're not over fond of coffee.'

One of these days, thought Ellen, I shall swipe her one with my 'andbag.

'Think you must be confusin' me with Doris,' she said, causing the innocent, coffee-loving Doris to look anxiously at the mouth-watering airy sponge yielding to Ivy's knife.

'My favourite,' said Doris firmly. 'Never could get it right myself, but that looks a perfect sponge, Ivy, nothing less.'

Ivy smiled in triumph. 'So we'll all have a piece, then, shall we?' she said, offering the plate round and making sure the smallest slice made its way into Ellen's hand.

'Now then,' Ivy continued, settling back into her chair by the window, 'what's all this about Mrs Standing and the concert?'

Ellen explained, and Doris said that she had always loved that poem by Thomas Hardy, 'Christmas Eve', and she thought Mrs Standing would read it beautifully.

'She went to dramatic school, you know,' Doris said, 'before she married Mr Richard.'

'Well,' said Ellen, squashing the remaining cake crumbs on her plate into a little ball and popping it into her mouth, 'I've certainly seen a drama or two up at the 'all in my time.'

'Could be a very good idea,' said Ivy. 'If Mrs Standing came to rehearsals, it would give a bit of order to proceedings, not so much larking about. Perhaps that Gabriella Jones would get on with it a bit better if Mrs Standing was there, perhaps she'd not waste so much time making eyes at Reverend Brooks.'

Doris and Ellen exchanged glances, and then Ellen began to laugh. 'So that's it, Ivy, is it?' she said. 'You're suspicious of Mrs Jones, as well as Peggy Palmer. What makes you think they're all after your precious Nigel?'

Ivy glared at Ellen, and move the coffee sponge further away from her. 'Peggy Palmer's disgracefully busy elsewhere,' she said, 'but if you'd been doing your duty with the brasses like I was, and seen Reverend Brooks and Gabriella Jones with their heads together over the organ, laughing and whispering over bits of old music, you'd be suspicious.'

Doris Ashbourne sat up straight, and opened and shut her handbag with a snap.

'Ivy,' she said, 'I can smell one of your campaigns coming on. For goodness sake, can't you just mind your own business for once? Reverend Brooks is a very nice, kind man, and Mrs Brooks is a nice, kind woman, and they're obviously very fond of each other. They can do without tittle-tattle such as this, and I for one intend to talk about something else.'

In the silence that followed this, Ivy stood up and turned her back on the others, staring angrily out of her window and across the Green.

'Go on,' then,' said Ellen, finally.

'Go on, what?' said Doris.

'Talk about somethin' else,' said Ellen. 'Otherwise we might just as well go 'ome.'

Doris shifted about in her sent, and said, 'Well, are you going to the Harvest Supper, Ellen?'

'You know I am, we got it all sorted last week,' said Ellen unhelpfully.

Doris was silent and discouraged. Then Ivy leaned forward and peered carefully through the lace curtain, turning her head to watch something happening in the street.

'What did I say?' she said gleefully.

'Well,' said Doris, 'tell us.'

'There he is again,' Ivy said, 'our handsome vicar going down the lovely Gabriella's path and knocking at her door. There . . . she's let him in . . . and Mr Jones not yet home from school. No wonder,' she added, turning in righteous indignation to the other women, 'her daughter's such a wicked miss. She's got no example to follow, none whatsoever.'

CHAPTER TWENTY-SEVEN

'It is much better here,' said Sophie Brooks, 'than it was in Wales, but there's still that invisible barrier between me and the rest.'

'What rest?' said Nigel, busy with notes for his sermon.

'The rest of the women in the village,' said Sophie. 'Even Peggy treats me with just a fraction more respect.'

'You imagine it, Soph,' said Nigel, looking up at her with a smile. 'You do have a kind of reserve, you know, always have. Took me all my courage to ask you out that first time.'

'Honestly?' said Sophie, putting down her paintbrush in surprise. She was touching up the white-painted wooden overmantel in Nigel's study, and though she knew he hated to be interrupted, she couldn't help remarks bursting out now and then.

'It's that nose of yours,' said Nigel. 'Makes you look as if you've just smelt something really disgusting. Come here, you silly girl, and give us a kiss.'

Sophie obediently crossed over the carpet and kissed Nigel on top of his head, leaving a couple of drops of white paint on his page of notes.

'Oh no, Soph,' he groaned, 'couldn't you paint some other time?'

'There you are, you see,' she said, 'even you don't want me around.'

Nigel sighed and put his pen neatly in the wooden

penholder on his desk.

'Go on, then,' he said, 'tell me everything.'

'Well, you're probably right, I expect I do imagine it. But I don't imagine the fact that no one ever comes to sit next to me in church. Or that at coffee mornings they all go into laughing huddles and then stop self-consciously when I go and join them. I just wish they wouldn't . . . oh, I don't know . . . you must notice it, Nigel, surely . . .'

'Of course, Sophie, it's one of the hazards of the job.'

'That's fine for you, then, it's your job. But it's not mine, and I just don't want to be treated like some plaster saint who must stay her side of the line and not cross into the real world.'

Nigel got up and stood looking out of the window into the orchard, where one or two shrivelled apples still clung to branches fast losing their leaves into the thick grass beneath. Suppose I ought to cut that before winter comes, he thought, then brought himself back to his wife's dilemma.

'Can be quite useful, sometimes,' he said. 'You used to think so yourself in Wales. At least you could distance yourself from the endless gossiping and scheming. And how many times did you say no to invitations to join this and that and every other organisation? I thought you were really happy here, Sophie? You can't have it all ways, nobody can.'

'Gabriella Jones can,' Sophie said sulkily. 'She's young, beautiful, talented, comfortably off, free and energetic, and popular with everybody.' Especially you, Nigel, you old smoothie, she said to herself.

Nigel frowned at her. 'You are not being fair, Sophie,' he said. 'Poor Gabriella and Greg have their hands more than full with that wayward daughter of theirs. Have you heard the latest?'

Sophie had heard nothing, but she had met Ivy Beasley in the street, and wondered why she asked if Reverend Brooks had any experience with delinquent children. And then again in the church, when Ivy was sorting hymn books into neat piles, Sophie has listened to half-hints of misbehaviour and lack of parental guidance in the Jones household.

'Poison Ivy has been hinting darkly once or twice,' she said.

'I don't think you should call her that, Sophie dear,' said Nigel. 'I'm sure she's not as bad as that.'

'Are you?' said Sophie. 'Well, what is the latest on the wicked Octavia?'

Nigel told her the edited version he had received from Gabriella when they met to discuss lighting and amplification in the church. Gabriella had been very upset, and it had taken several minutes comforting her in the vestry before she pulled herself together and concentrated on spotlights and microphones. Even Ivy Beasley, crouching with brush and dustpan at the back of the pews, had expressed her sympathy and offered to get a glass of water for Mrs Jones.

CHAPTER TWENTY-EIGHT

Colin Osman sat in his comfortable armchair watching the regional news on television. From where he sat he could see across the park to the Hall beyond, and thought once more how lucky they had been that Peggy Palmer had not wanted to sell the shop after all. At the time, of course, they had both been really keen, but his Pat was a great one for bees in her bonnet, and her enthusiasm for running a village shop had soon waned. Now she was involved in cooking for the Harvest Supper, having long discussions with Doreen Price on the best way of serving eighty-odd people, and offering Colin's services in carving and serving giant roasts.

He had taken on the rejuvenation of Ringford cricket team, and a possible junior football team as well. The pavilion on the playing fields had been vandalised so many times that the Committee had lost heart. Nobody ever saw the damage being done, and it was always blamed on either the Robertses or marauding teenagers from Tresham out for a cruise round the villages.

What we need, thought Colin, is to give Ringford more of a sense of community. The old people keep to themselves, and the women have the Women's Institute, where they had certainly welcomed Pat with open arms. But if you were not a five pints a night man at the Arms, there was little for a chap like himself to do. He fully intended to stand for the Parish Council when the elections came round again, but meantime he had thrown himself wholeheartedly into the cricket revival.

Some success had come to their revitalised team, and with volunteer help the pavilion had once more been set to rights. But Colin could the see the winter coming on and only the ragged beginnings of a young football team to keep him busy.

He turned off the television, and walked over to the window, staring across the park with its great trees still burning with autumn colours and sheltering flocks of chattering birds, all congregating in their miraculous way in preparation for their epic flights of migration. They must have some magical way of communicating with each other, drawing them all together at the right time, thought Colin.

'I know!' he said aloud, struck by a sudden idea. 'What we need is some kind of newsletter, something to report village goings on, so everybody reads it and feels part of the whole.'

He turned round and nearly ran out of the room in his excitement.

'Pat! Pat, where are you?' he shouted.

'Washing my hair,' came the muffled reply.

'I've got something really exciting to tell you,' he said.

'I know,' she said, emerging from the bathroom with a towel wound into a turban round her head. 'I know what it is, you're having a baby.'

'Oh, very funny,' said Colin, this being a matter of some controversy between them. 'No, Pat, seriously, I have just had this fabulous idea for the village.' He smiled at her pleadingly.

'Another one?' said Pat, who had supported Colin through the cricket and football projects, but was now quite looking forward to a peaceful autumn and winter, when she could get on with her dressmaking and watch some good programmes on television.

Pat Osman had an agency for make-up and accessories, and earned a good annual sum from her efforts. She was an attractive woman, vigorous and healthy-looking, eyes always bright and her hair thick and shining. With her cheerful personality she could sell most things to most people, and was on the whole happy with her lot. She would have liked a baby, but Colin said they must wait until the time was right. She was beginning to wonder when that would be, but for the moment held her peace.

'Go on, then, don't keep me in suspense,' she said, taking off the towel and shaking her wet hair like a dog.

'Careful, Pat!' said Colin. 'It's going everywhere . . .'

Pat went into the kitchen and turned on the oven, ready to start preparing their supper.

'What do you think about a village newsletter?' Colin said, following behind and taking a glass out of the immaculate kitchen cupboard.

Pat opened the refrigerator and pulled out a chicken, tightly enclosed in its vacuum polythene. The slithery packed slipped from her hand and fell to the floor, taking a small jug of milk with it. The jug broke and the milk spilled into a quickly spreading pool.

'Pat! What a mess! Here, let me mop it up and you go and fix your hair. Comes of trying to do several things at once.'

'Oh, shut up, Colin,' said Pat, 'and go away and I'll clear it up. It's you talking at me when I'm trying to concentrate on something else. Just go away and I'll come in and have a drink in a minute and we can talk about newsletters and any other improving ideas you may have for Round Ringford.'

Colin left the room feeling huffy, and sat down again in his armchair, picking up the paper and trying to bury himself in the sports pages.

Half an hour later they were talking amiably about his new idea.

'It could work well, Pat, with one or two of us acting as editors, and some encouragement to others to contribute all kinds of news and ideas.' Colin was getting into his stride.

'You'd be editor-in-chief, I suppose,' said Pat. 'After all, it is your idea.'

'No doubt the Rev Nigel would think it his right to claim the job, but I suspect he's one of those wanting to be in charge of everything, so he'll have to be satisfied with assistant editor.'

'He may not want to do it at all,' said Pat. 'He's got enough on his plate at the moment with the concert and his many consultations with the lovely Gabriella.'

Colin looked at her sharply. 'Pat? What are saying?'

Colin had one or two irritating little faults, like his obsession with tidiness and order, but one of his good points was his honest refusal to gossip. Pat had to acknowledge that this was a good point, but often she longed to chew over some interesting speculation about, say, Peggy Palmer and Bill Turner, and that loopy wife of his, but Colin would just shut down completely.

'Oh, *I'm* not saying anything, Colin,' Pat said, 'it's just all over the village at the moment that the vicar's handsome grey head and Gabriella's smooth blonde one are often seen in close conversation.'

'That seems very stupid to me,' said Colin, a touch pompously. 'Naturally they have a lot to discuss, with the concert hotting up and people adding new items and making all kinds of weird suggestions. Did you hear that the eldest Roberts boy had offered a couple of numbers from his pop group?'

Pat nodded. At the WI meeting the other night there had been a lot of talk over the coffee cups of unsuitable music for a village church, and of things getting out of hand.

'The latest,' she said, 'is Susan Standing's offer of a recitation. Old Ellen was saying she's going to do "Albert and the Lion", but you never know when that old devil's pulling your leg.'

'Do you think,' said Colin, getting back to his exciting idea, 'we should have an editorial committee, or just a couple of people doing the job?'

'Committees are a disaster, mostly,' said Pat, 'but you should perhaps get a few folks together to discuss the whole thing. You'll need to decide on format and how often it comes out, all that sort of thing.'

Now Colin was on firm ground. His work at a large printers in Tresham gave him all the technical knowledge he was likely to need in producing a village newsletter, and he immediately fetched a stack of paper from his desk and began to make notes.

'We'd better have one more meeting on the Harvest Supper,' said Doreen to Peggy in the shop.

The morning was dull and overcast, but it was not cold. A heavy dew had covered the Green in the early morning, and an intriguing pattern of footprints on the damp grass showed where the children had crossed to wait at the bus stop, and where old Fred Mills had taken a short cut on his morning stroll. A tangle of sodden grass marked where Gemma, Amy and Mark had scuffled over sweets on the way to school.

'Can you make tomorrow, about eight o'clock?' Doreen continued, and Peggy nodded.

'I'd no idea so much preparation went into the Supper,' she said. 'I bet most people don't realise.'

'We like a good do in Ringford,' Doreen said, 'though I sometimes wonder what it has to do with the harvest these days. Most of the folk who come have nothing to do with farming, and even the farmers talk about their favourite telly programmes or the beginning of the hunting season.'

'Don't matter,' said Ellen Biggs, joining Doreen at the shop counter. 'You got to keep up the village traditions, else we might as well all go and live in Bagley. You heard old Ivy on about it? You'd think she kept Ringford goin' single-handed, to listen to 'er.'

'It doesn't do to listen to Ivy Beasley too closely,' said Doreen with a frown. 'She's stirring things up again, I hear. Seems to have taken on a new lease lately, what with her smart hair-do and that bright green coat. Have you seen it, Peggy?'

'The less I see of my charming neighbour, the better I like it,' said Peggy, totalling up Doreen's purchases.

She and Bill had been very circumspect ever since Joyce's dreadful exhibition on Gardens Open Day. There were days

– and nights – when Peggy longed for Bill to hold her tight and share his warmth and strength with her for longer than a few clandestine short half-hours. But there was never a time when Ivy Beasley might not be on the look-out, and Peggy felt her presence even when she went into Tresham and knew that Ivy was extremely unlikely to be anywhere near.

'Spread the word, then, Peggy, would you?' said Doreen, and, lifting her heavy basket as if it were full of feathers instead of pounds of flour and sugar, she walked swiftly out to her muddy estate car and drove off.

Peggy's next customer was Pat Osman, and the message about the meeting was duly given. 'I could pick you up on my way to the farm, if you like?' said Peggy kindly.

'Thanks, Mrs Palmer,' said Pat, pulling a sheet of paper out of her document case.

'I'm all right for make-up at the moment,' said Peggy quickly, not wanting to hurt her feelings. She never bought any of Pat's wares, not liking the heavy scent which pervaded all the products.

'No, it's from Colin,' said Pat, spreading out a carefully written poster, advertising a preliminary meeting for all those interested in producing a village newsletter.

'Another idea from your Colin?' said Peggy, smiling.

'Ain't 'e got no work to do?' said Ellen, leaning over and squinting at the poster. 'We got on all right all these years without a newsletter, or whatever you call it. Everything gets round the village sooner or later, anyroad. Don't need to 'ave it all writ down.'

The door opened with a burst of energy, and Richard Standing marched in.

'In a frightful hurry, Mrs Palmer. Could you oblige me with a couple of stamps? So sorry, ladies, I really do have to catch a train.'

The peaceful atmosphere of the shop was transformed into immediate action. Old Ellen gathered together her few packages and left the shop, muttering about people who should know better with their upbringing. Peggy moved quickly to the Post Office cubicle and found a page of first-class stamps for the impatient squire.

'What's this?' said Mr Richard, picking up Colin Osman's notice.

'Something to do with a newsletter,' said Peggy. 'Pat asked me to put it up.'

Richard Standing read it in silence, and then chuckled. 'Could be a very jolly idea,' he said. 'Might give him a ring and offer my services. I used to like writing the odd poem or two once upon a time. Thank you, Mrs Palmer, I must rush . . .'

Peggy watched him duck his head to avoid the low doorway, and then nearly collide with old Fred, who had stopped at the foot of the steps to relight his smouldering pipe.

Should be interesting, she thought, rather wishing she was going to the newsletter meeting instead of a session on feeding the five thousand.

CHAPTER TWENTY-NINE

'Are we agreed, then, that Peggy and Doris and me will do the roasts, and Pat will organise puddings from all them as has offered to help?'

Doreen looked round her sitting room at the assembled women. Peggy and Doris Ashbourne sat on the sofa, and Ivy Beasley on an upright chair by the window. Pat Osman, Mrs Ross and Sophie Brooks occupied assorted chairs brought in from the rest of the house, and Doreen herself sat at a card-table with her notepad in front of her, making notes as decisions were taken.

Peggy looked at the massive stone fireplace, and saw Roundhead soldiers leaning on the mantleshelf, spitting into the flames and cursing the weather. Small leaded panes in the stone-mullioned windows rattled in the wind, and Peggy thought of all the Price farmers who had struggled through storms to rescue isolated animals, returning to this room to dry their soaking clothes and warm their chilled bones. The grating, matter-of-fact voice of Ivy Beasley brought her sharply back to the present.

'I'm to be in charge of laying up the tables as usual, then?' said Ivy. So far, no specific job had been handed out to her.

'Thank you, Ivy,' said Doreen diplomatically, 'that is one of the most difficult jobs. Have you got the posies for the tables organised?'

'Should be enough flowers, if we all chip in,' said Peggy, and Ivy frowned.

'I shan't need any chipping in,' she said, 'everything's arranged.'

Miserable old bag, thought Peggy, and turned to Sophie.

'Are you happy to make an apple pie, Sophie?' she said.

There was a tradition that apple pies were always part of the menu, but in latter years other, more sophisticated puddings had been added. Mrs Ross had offered a couple of large Pavlovas and now Pat Osman suggested a nice chocolate roulade would go down well with everyone.

'And biscuits and cheese, of course,' said Doreen. 'They're meant to be an alternative to pudding, but most people – especially old Roberts – take both. Old Roberts always calls for biscuits and cheese.'

'Don't forget soup,' said Ivy Beasley sharply, 'the men have to have their soup. Wouldn't be right without soup.'

'Would you like to organise that, then, Ivy?' said Doreen smoothly. 'Whatever flavour you think would be best. Your soup is always so good.'

How could you, Doreen, thought Peggy. But she had to acknowledge that Doreen was an excellent chairman, especially in a gathering of women. She always said exactly the right thing, and knew how to juggle the various warring personalities.

'I shall be providing the sherry, of course,' continued Doreen, 'that being my prerogative as churchwarden.'

'Should have thought it was Mr Richard's turn for once,' said Ivy.

'I'm only too pleased,' said Doreen, smiling sweetly. 'And now shall we get on to the entertainment?'

'Nigel said he'd like to say grace,' said Sophie, 'just to show it is a church occasion, but nothing further, no prayers or anything. We save that for the Harvest Festival service, don't we?'

She looked anxiously round the room, and saw relief in

their faces. Perhaps they thought Nigel was going to give them a sermon on loaves and fishes, she speculated. They forget he has two other parishes with harvest suppers and harvest festivals, and all wanting it differently.

'That's fine,' said Doreen. 'We have to decide between Robert Bates and his guitar, and an offer from Colin Osman.'

She smiled encouragingly at Pat, who shuffled her feet and looked embarrassed.

'Well, actually, Colin would like to withdraw his offer if that's all right, now that he's got involved in this newsletter idea.'

Once more relief flooded the room. Robert Bates always did a turn, singing folk songs and some ditties with words he made up, lampooning village personalities in the nicest possible way. It was a popular act, anticipated eagerly by the village, and it had become almost an insult not to be included in Robert's list of those he gently mocked. The problem raised by Colin Osman's offer now evaporated, and Doreen relaxed.

'We'll just leave it to Robert, as usual, then,' she said, ticking off the last item on her list. 'Now, is there anything else anyone wants to discuss?'

The women started to collect themselves together, ready to leave, but were stopped by Ivy Beasley clearing her throat purposefully.

'There was one thing we've forgotten, I think, Mrs Price,' she said.

Now what, thought Doreen. There's always one last little bombshell from old Ivy.

'It would be fitting,' said Ivy, 'if one of us regular churchgoers made a short vote of thanks to our new vicar for all his hard work and enthusiasm since he arrived.'

Wow, thought Sophie.

In the amazed silence that followed Ivy's uncharacteristic contribution, Doreen closed her note pad and fastened it with a rubber band. For once she was at a loss.

'Um, yes, Ivy, quite right,' she said, looking round at the others for help. 'Now, who would be the right person to do it?'

In unspoken agreement, they all turned and looked at Ivy Beasley.

She nodded, and said in her flat voice, 'Right, that's it then. I shall be happy to oblige.'

The lights burned late in the Village Hall as the newsletter meeting progressed. Colin Osman had been gratified to see so many people drifting through the door and sitting in groups round the hall. He had been even more pleased when, ten minutes after the meeting had begun, Richard Standing came bursting through the door and motioned to Colin to continue the meeting.

So many ideas were put forward it was difficult to keep up with them. A gardening column, said old Fred, with topical tips and hints on growing in the local soil. How about a monthly competition, said Mr Ross, perhaps a crossword using local knowledge: he would be quite happy to set one or two. Nigel Brooks sat quietly at first, tactfully allowing other, more experienced village people to have their say.

After Colin had summed up the ideas put forward, and added his own suggestions for layout and editorial control, Nigel spoke.

'In my last parish,' he said, 'the newsletter was used in a forum for discussion on topics of the day, broader issues perhaps than mere village concerns. Famine and civil war, for example, were subjects we put forward, and it was a most useful exercise. Many people had strong views, and it was a very cathartic experience to give them an airing.'

"Ere,' said Fred Mills to his neighbour, 'what's 'e talkin' about?'

'Don't we get enough of that in the daily papers?' said Bill Turner, who had been dragooned into attending by Greg Jones. 'I think a village newsletter should be just that: a monthly bulletin of news about the village, and a way of letting people know what's going on.'

'Absolutely,' said Richard Standing. 'Well said, Bill, them's me sentiments entirely. And maybe we could have the odd verse or two, perhaps a country couplet, just to break up the prose, you know. I'd be glad to have a stab at that.'

Jean Jenkins, sturdy and cheerful, stood up. 'I'd like to second Bill's opinions,' she said. 'We get enough doom and gloom in the papers and on the telly. I propose our village newsletter should cheer people up, get them going, helpin' with village events and such like.'

Nigel Brooks settled back in his chair. It wouldn't work, he knew that, but he saw it as his duty to try and broaden the village outlook. Well, he'd done his best.

'May I put in a first paragraph or two on the coming concert, then, Colin?' he said. 'Most people know about it, but just a reminder of the date and where to get tickets and so on. Gabriella will be getting a programme together soon, isn't that right, Greg?' Nigel looked across at Greg Jones with a smile. It was not returned.

'No doubt,' said Greg flatly.

It was cold and damp when they emerged into the night air from the Village Hall, but Colin glowed with success and walked home smartly, impatient to get on with the first issue.

'There was a good deal of support,' he said to Pat, 'and the Rev Nigel was not at all pushy, apart from a short-lived attempt to bring the outside world inside Ringford's cosy boundaries.'

'Who else was there?' said Pat.

'Oh, Mr Richard – he came in late – and good old Fred, and Bill Turner and Greg Jones . . .'

'And Gabriella?' said Pat, looking closely at him.

He shook his head, 'No, I expect she was at home with Octavia. They've been sticking to that child like glue lately. Not sure it's the right thing, but you can't blame them.'

'So did Nigel Brooks talk to Greg Jones at all?' said Pat casually.

'Goodness, I didn't notice, Pat,' said Colin. 'Except that Greg was a bit terse with the vicar when he mentioned the concert. I expect he's getting fed up with the demands on Gabriella's time.'

'Ah,' said Pat. 'Yes, you could say that, he must be . . . quite fed up.'

'And how did your evening go?' said Colin, perfectly aware of what Pat was up to, and determined to change the subject.

'Very smoothly,' said Pat. 'Doreen Price is a wonder. So calm and efficient, and apart from Ivy Beasley wanting to thank her precious Nigel for being so wonderful, it all went much as every other year, I should imagine.'

'Nice thought, though,' said Colin. 'Old Ivy's probably got a heart of gold lurking there somewhere.'

'Not a chance,' said Pat. 'No chance at all.'

Peggy lingered outside the shop, looking across the Green at the moon. It was on the wane, and veiled with a thin layer of cloud passing slowly across. The black woods on Bagley Hill were forbidding and impenetrable. How far away and cold that moon looks, she thought, how completely unaware of me and Round Ringford and this country and this planet.

'Makes you feel small, doesn't it, gel,' said Bill at her side.

'You made me jump,' she said. 'Where have you been?'

'Newsletter meeting,' he said, taking her hand and putting it with his own into his warm jacket pocket.

'Bill!' she said warningly. It was quite dark, but the hazy moon gave enough light for accustomed eyes to pick out shapes in the night, and certainly to identify two people standing too close outside the Post Office Stores.

'There's nobody about,' he said. 'I was last one out of the hall, and then checked on a few things before I locked up. The others are all gone home.'

He drew her quietly from the pavement into the little alley

going up beside the shop, and when they reached Peggy's back door he put his arms round her and pulled her close, kissing her cold face until the blood rushed into her cheeks and she tightened her clasp round his neck, twining her fingers in his thick, wiry hair.

'Dear, dear Bill,' she said. 'Mmm . . . it's just like being sixteen again, standing outside Mum's door and hoping she wouldn't come and open it too soon.'

Bill groaned. 'Peggy, come on, please . . . let's go in, for God's sake. We're not sixteen, we're nearer sixty, and grown-up people responsible for our own . . . oh God, Peggy, please . . .'

A window opened with a sharp clatter above their heads. It was next door, in Victoria Villa, and as they froze a voice yelled raucously out into the night.

'Get off, get off! Randy old tom cat! Get off, get out of it!'

The window banged shut, and silence reigned.

Bill backed away from Peggy and stood leaning his head against the wall. Peggy looked at him anxiously, then saw his shoulders begin to shake. He straightened up and looked across at the now blank window of Ivy Beasley's bedroom.

'Mee . . . ee . . . ee . . . ow!' he whined, in a very passable imitation of a tom cat on the prowl. Peggy began to laugh and stuffed her handkerchief in her mouth. Bill continued to call, walking over to the fence and following up the yowl with some spine-chilling fighting, spitting sounds.

'Bill, stop it!' whispered Peggy. 'She'll know it's you.'

'She knows anyway,' said Bill. 'Might as well give her her money's worth.'

Ivy Beasley, rigid and quiet in her white cotton nightdress, lay listening to the noise outside her bedroom window.

It's not right, Mother, she said. They'll both go straight to Damnation.

There was no reply from the voice in her head, and Ivy sighed and turned over between the cool cotton sheets. She's asleep, wherever she is, she thought, and began to think about

Nigel Brooks, and his lovely straight nose, and those warm grey eyes . . .

CHAPTER THIRTY

One day to go, and and the preparations for the Harvest Supper were going smoothly. Ivy Beasley had got up early, and, with the Village Hall key collected from Doreen the previous evening, had let herself into the dim, dusty interior long before the village street had come alive with children and cars disappearing off to Tresham and Bagley.

She had a flask of tea with her, and sat on the steps leading to the stage to have a break. She had already been round with the broom and duster, and now planned to clean the windows and give the curtains a good shake before old Fred and Robert turned up to help her set up the trestle tables.

Cupping a mug of good strong tea in her hands, she looked round the old hall, with its wooden floor and yellow-painted walls. The windows were certainly smudgy, and cobwebs looped across high corners. Ivy dipped a plain biscuit in her tea and ate it slowly. Dad helped build this hall, she thought, and remembered how particular her mother had been about keeping it clean and tidy, with all the crockery neatly stacked in the kitchen cupboard, and the spoons polished after every use.

Nobody bothers much now, she thought. The WI paid Jean Jenkins to come and have one of her quick turn-outs every so often, otherwise it was neglected. Cups and saucers, milk jugs and old lidless teapots were jumbled together in the cupboard, and most of the cups had tea-stain rings round the insides.

Pity you can't do more to keep it in order, said her mother's voice. People don't appreciate what they've got these days, not like when we built this place. And you're just as bad, Ivy. We were so excited and proud, all of us, when we had the opening dance. Your dad was a good dancer, Ivy.

She remembered Dad dancing, upright as a ram-rod, her mother held a good eighteen inches away from him, his feet twinkling and accurate.

She'd learned to dance herself, briefly, as a young girl, attending classes in this same Village Hall. Now she thought of it, it was her father who had persuaded Mother to let her go. Dancing? said the voice. What did you want with dancing? Dancing won't make the beds and cook the dinner.

But Ivy had stopped listening. She stood up and screwed the plastic mug back on her thermos flask, putting it down on the stage. She walked a few steps into the middle of the hall, and slowly put up her arms, one on an imaginary shoulder, the other resting lightly on a strong brown arm with its dark grey clerical shirt sleeve rolled up beyond the elbow in a manly fashion.

Slowly Ivy began to gyrate round the room. One, two, three – one, two, three. Dum dum dum de-dum, dum-dum, dum-dum, she hummed. And the handsome grey head bent down to whisper something in her ear, warm breath stroking her cheek.

'You all right, Auntie Ivy?' said Robert, coming in and finding to his amazement that the stern spinster was standing in the middle of the floor, her arms raised like a bird about to take off, and her face with a moony smile turned up to the ceiling above.

'Just wondering if that needs a bit of paint, up there where it's peeling round the light fitting,' improvised Ivy, collecting herself together rapidly.

Robert nodded and said he'd have a go at it some time. He was impatient to get the tables up, having decided to take the morning off and go with Mandy to buy the bridesmaids' presents. There were still months to go to the wedding, but

Mandy wanted everything organised, every item on her list ticked off, so she could enjoy the excitement of looking forward, discussing all the details with her ladies as they relaxed under her snipping scissors.

'There's always something left to do, something at the last minute that you've forgotten,' she had said wisely to Olive Bates.

The door opened again behind Robert, and old Fred stumped in, his pipe belching clouds of smoke like a bonfire of old motor tyres.

'You can put that thing out, for a start,' said Ivy, 'then we must get to work. I've a great deal to do here, and I doubt whether there'll be any help forthcoming after you two've gone.'

Robert and Fred manhandled the old trestle tables out from under the stage, where they had been since the last Roberts wedding reception, when daughter Sandra, carrying all before her, had married her Sam, and had a rowdy party to celebrate, just as if her parents had approved all along, and her father's attempt to knock all that bloody rubbish out of her had never happened.

'Still got bits of cake sticking to this one,' said Ivy, straightening the stained wooden top on its primitive trestles.

'It don't go there, Ivy,' said Fred Mills. 'It always goes up by the stage, that one.'

'No, it doesn't,' said Robert. 'That one goes by the wall there, and this one here goes by the stage. It's longer, and gives room for the vicar and his missus and Mr and Mrs Richard, and other nobs who think they should be on the top table.'

'No, no,' said Ivy, 'we have two tables shoved together for that, these two here, with the initials cut in them. Young Mr Richard did that with that Josie girl he was sweet on. His dad was not at all pleased, if I recall correctly.'

'Never mind about recalling the past, Auntie Ivy,' said Robert. 'I must be in Tresham by ten thirty, so we'd better get a move on. Come on Fred, heave ho!'

I could do it twice as quick on my own, thought Robert, but

that'd hurt old Fred's feelings. Doesn't do to make him feel unwanted, he'll sulk for weeks.

'I remember when each farm used to 'ave its own harvest supper,' said Fred, 'when there were dozens of farm workers livin' in the village. It were a kind of competition to see which farm give the best supper. Old Mrs Price, Tom's mum, were generally the best. 'Course, now it's all machinery and one man and his boy. Do you remember, Ivy,' he continued, resting his elbow on the edge of a vertical table top, much to Robert's irritation, 'do you remember 'ow we used to keep the last sheaf of the harvest for the next year? It were a kind o' good luck charm for the followin' harvest.'

'Fred!' said Robert, out of patience. 'Are you going to get these tables up or not? If you want to sit down and chat to Auntie Ivy, that's fine by me, but I got to get going.'

After more disagreement on placing, the tables were finally set up, and chairs arranged neatly down each side. Robert disappeared with a good-humoured wave, and Fred Mills relit his pipe and wandered off with his stick towards the shop, where with any luck he would find somebody else to listen to him.

Ivy set to work briskly, with armfuls of red and white checked cloths, stacks of red table napkins, and handfuls of knives and forks and spoons. After a break for dinner, when she met old Ellen along the road and told her what a lazy old devil she was, Ivy returned with a basket full of posies of small flowers, which she arranged at regular intervals along the tables.

'We having candles again?' she asked Doreen Price, who dropped in halfway through the afternoon to see how she was getting on.

'Yep,' said Doreen. 'At least, we've asked everybody to bring a red candle and candlestick with them. It looked so pretty last year, with just candlelight. Tom said it was really romantic.'

Ivy sniffed. 'Very dangerous, if you ask me,' she said. 'Whole place could go up in flames. Foolhardy, in a wooden building like this.'

There was a lot of sense in what she said, and Doreen felt momentarily discomfited. Why did old Ivy always look on the black side? Now the thought of fire would worry her all evening. But Tom, sitting at the kitchen table for his first cup of tea, told her not to give it another thought. 'We're all grown up, aren't we, Doreen?' he said. 'We know how to behave sensibly. Don't take any notice of old Ivy, she loves putting her spoke in.'

'For what we are about to receive, may the Lord make us truly thankful.' The simple grace was said clearly by a smiling Nigel Brooks, and the packed hall dutifully chorused, 'Amen.'

Welcomed at the door by Tom and Doreen, villagers of all ages had made their way to the festive tables, sipping their nutty-tasting sweet sherry, and watching anxiously to make sure all members of their party were comfortably seated. Miraculously, they all sorted themselves out, and families sat next to others they liked, and newcomers occupied a whole table, bunching together to give themselves confidence, overcoming their slight unease at being present at such an ancient rural tradition.

'All right, then, Greg?' shouted Colin Osman to the Joneses, seated with a sullen-looking Octavia at the end of his table. He glanced with pride at Pat by his side, and thought how right she looked, colourful in her woollen print, but not too dressy.

With efficient speed the food was served, and the bottles of wine, sold illegally from a bench by the door, disappeared rapidly. Conversation became loud and liberally interspersed with roars of laughter.

Nigel Brooks was in his element, flattering Susan Standing at the top table, and getting up to chat to his parishioners one by one as he moved like a shining star round the warm hall.

'You'd think 'e'd bin 'ere all 'is life,' said Ellen Biggs grumpily. 'Just look at that Gabriella Jones, gazin' up at him as if 'e was Ronald Colman.'

'Ronald who?' said Jean Jenkins, leaning over with a dish of roast potatoes and spooning a couple on to Ellen's plate.

'You tryin' to sink me, Jean Jenkins?' said Ellen. 'That's my third helpin'.'

At the next table, Peggy sat quietly next to Mr and Mrs Ross, and tried not to smile too much at Bill Turner opposite her. Every so often, she felt his foot touch hers, and then his hand gently caressed her knee under the table.

At least, she thought, I hope to God it is Bill's hand. Supposing it's Mr Ross? She looked sideways at the neat, moustached face, and heard the clipped voice talking about slugs and manure, and dismissed the thought.

All courses demolished, it was time for the entertainment, and Robert Bates climbed on to the stage, slinging his guitar over his shoulder and twanging a few trial chords. Silence fell on the hall, after much shifting of chairs to get a good view of the stage.

'Good lad!' shouted Fred Mills, and was shushed by Ellen Biggs. 'Save yourself 'til 'e's done something to shout about, you ol' fool,' she said in a very audible stage whisper.

Robert began with a few songs, rural in flavour, and humorous, sending ripples of laughter round the hall. Mandy, sitting with Mr and Mrs Bates, looked at him with pride, and blew him an encouraging kiss.

'Now,' said Robert, 'one of our old favourites: "I never seen a farmer on a bike!"' This was greeted by whoops and cheers, and when Robert began altering the usual words and took good-humoured swipes at Tom Price and Michael Roberts, and gently mocked Colin Osman and his marauding cricketers, the laughter grew and Jean Jenkins mopped her eyes, saying, 'Oh dear, oh my dear Foxy, stop him, do!'

There were still gales of laughter round the hall when Robert started on his last verse.

'And on his way the vicar goes, on a bike what rattles 'is bones,
He saves our souls, and the soles of 'is shoes,
And he cheers up them what's got the blues,

169

And it's only 'is collar what stops him proposing
A tandem with nice Mrs Jones.'

The laughter slowly died away, and a spatter of claps fizzled
out. Sophie Brooks stared at her lap, and Nigel nodded his
head in a puzzled but tolerant way. But Greg Jones pushed his
chair back with a loud scraping sound, waving his arm across
the table and saying in a fuddled voice, 'That's enough, Robert
Bates, quite enough.'

His sweeping arm knocked over a glass and wine spread
over the cloth in a vivid pool. A spindly candlestick teetered,
the flame on the red candle guttering, and then it fell, the
candle rolled out, and the flame licked at a paper table napkin,
blazing quickly as it caught fire.

Suddenly there was pandemonium. Everyone stood up at
once, and one or two children screamed. Tom Price, emerging from the gents at the back of the hall, took one look and
then tore off his jacket and threw it violently over the leaping
flames. He leaned his whole weight over the table and the
noise of the panic ebbed. Gingerly he lifted up his jacket,
revealing a charred mess of tablecloth, wine and smouldering
jacket lining, which he quickly doused with a jug of water.

'All done, then,' he said, looking round the room, 'no
damage to speak of. Take your seats, ladies and gentlemen,
and let's hear Robert sing our own special song.' And Tom
began to sing, 'When you come to the end of a perfect day,'
jollying along a few tentative voices joining in, and waving to
Robert to continue.

'Of course,' said Doreen to Peggy next morning, as they
walked up the church path together to morning service. 'Tom
didn't hear what Robert said, him being in the gents at the
time. When I told him, he said it explained a lot, and looked
grim. Said he'd have a word with young Robert, but I told
him it was only a joke, them Joneses always being about the
village on their bikes.'

'I felt sorry for Sophie,' said Peggy. 'She looked as if she was about to burst into tears.'

'Ah well,' said Doreen, as they took their hymn books from Mr Ross at the door, 'it'll soon blow over, best forgotten.'

Peggy had reservations about this. In her short experience of Round Ringford, she had learned that, although things like this appeared to be forgotten, no longer mentioned, giving way to the next bit of gossip, the village was like a murky pond, where larvae rise to the surface, ugly and alarming, and old mischief would emerge again, just when you thought it was gone for good.

CHAPTER THIRTY-ONE

The date of the concert was fixed for the second week in December, and Gabriella Jones doubled up the number of rehearsals each week as the performance came closer.

Sophie Brooks, walking along the path from the vicarage to the church for the second choir session this week, looked up at the dark yews outlined against the sky, and shivered. Winter had come to Round Ringford slowly, autumn reluctantly relinquishing its hold on the bright trees and the sparkling mornings. But now the branches were bare, except for the yews which bore their nasty little spiky leaves all the year round, dense and funereal, thought Sophie, as she pushed her way past laurels and brambles lining the path.

The black, moonless night matched her mood. Ever since the fiasco on Harvest Supper night, she and Nigel had been edgy with one another. She knew she was being ridiculous, but every time she went in the shop she was convinced the conversation stopped abruptly, that they had been talking about Nigel and Gabriella, and she collected her groceries and left as quickly as possible. Every friendly word that Nigel exchanged with Gabriella at concert rehearsals was marked down by Sophie, and, she was sure, by every other member of the choir.

It was a ridiculous situation, and she dare not mention any of it to Nigel. He had had a rare explosion of anger and contempt when she had countered him with a jealous accusation after the Supper. He had made her feel so small, so petty and immature, that she didn't mention it again, although her sleep was disturbed by lurid dreams of an avenging Ivy Beasley swooping with an axe on an entwined Nigel and Gabriella.

Ivy Beasley had been extremely charming to Sophie ever since Robert's terrible gaffe. Sophie could not understand this change of heart, and, not liking the sharp-tongued woman, did not reciprocate, and refused offers of tea and elderflower wine, preferring to maintain her friendship with Peggy, although with her too she felt some holding back, an embarrassment never explained.

An owl hooted from the churchyard, and the lamp by the gate snapped on with a welcome yellow light. Nigel must have put it on, thought Sophie, and, making up her mind to put all pettiness behind her and start afresh, she greeted Gabriella with enthusiasm as they met at the church door. Gabriella's cheeks were pink from her bike ride, and her blonde hair, twisted into a knot over a soft black woolly scarf wound warmly round her neck, shone in the lamplight.

'Let me open the door,' said Sophie, 'you've got such a lot to carry.'

To everyone's surprise, and to Nigel's delight, the music was coming along very nicely. Once the choir had mastered four-part singing, and learned that there are pleasant alternatives to belting it out at full pitch, the seasonal pieces chosen by Gabriella and Nigel were sounding tuneful and, on occasion, quite professional.

'Right, everyone,' said Gabriella, clapping her hands for silence. 'Let's begin with "Adam Lay Y-Bounden", and then we'll go through as we shall sing it on the night. Colin has kindly agreed to time us with his stopwatch, and we'll include the readings just as they will slot into the programme.'

They were halfway through 'Adam' when Susan Standing slid into the front pew and sat quietly, waiting for her turn to read. She had settled on the Christmas pudding passage from Dickens's *A Christmas Carol*, and had rehearsed it many times in front of a patient Richard. He could almost recite the whole thing by heart. She found the account so moving that by the time she came to Tiny Tim's 'God bless us every one!' she had difficulty keeping back her own tears.

She looked up at the choir, singing earnestly, and watching Gabriella intently with the fearful concentration of amateurs. The medieval carol was a difficult one, and when the tenors wandered off key Gabriella frowned at them and they looked at each other, each one sure that it was his neighbour and not himself who had transgressed.

It's all a great credit to Nigel Brooks, Susan Standing thought, knowing that he had with difficulty smoothed down Ivy's ruffled feathers when she was relegated to an end-of-the-row position in the altos. He had also comforted old Fred Mills after Gabriella had turned down his offer of 'The Fireman's Wedding' monologue, done many times to great acclaim in the past. Perhaps for Harvest Supper next year, Nigel had said.

We are very lucky that he has turned out so well, thought Susan, getting up and stepping to the front of the choir to say her piece.

Ivy Beasley would have agreed wholeheartedly, but she was deeply worried. Something seemed to have gone very wrong that night in the Village Hall. After the drama over the fire – and they wouldn't listen to me about those candles, she thought – there hadn't been a suitable moment for her to make her thank-you speech to the vicar. And everyone had turned away from her as they left the hall, a more subdued crowd than usual after the annual feast.

Robert had not visited her for two weeks now, sending a message via his mother that he was too busy on the farm at the moment. Too busy with that Mandy of his, more likely, she thought.

She had tried to be nice to poor Sophie Brooks, who could not have failed to get the drift of Robert's timely warning. But Sophie had shrugged off Ivy's advances, which consequently reverted from spurious sympathy to the usual acid reproach.

174

'We will rock you, rock you, ro-ock you,' she grated in as quiet a voice as she could manage. Gabriella had her finger to her lips, shushing the exuberant and unrepentant Colin Osman, who as usual was singing at double forte.

The programme was fifteen minutes over its intended time, and Nigel and Gabriella went into a huddle, discussing which of the pieces could be tightened up, whether they could persuade Susan Standing to cut down on the dramatic pauses.

Sophie turned her head away, desperately trying to think of something to say to Peggy, anything to take her mind off the awful gnawing suspicion that seemed to be with her night and day, and to grow with every small remark, however, inoffensive.

'Thought of everything, haven't they,' Ivy Beasley had said to her the previous day, when several women had been in the shop discussing the coming concert, 'your husband and Gabriella Jones. They should be very proud of what they have got together, the pair of them.'

. . . the pair of them, thought Sophie. Now what did she mean by that?

'That will do for tonight, thank you everyone,' said Gabriella, smiling at the anxious faces in front of her. 'You did very well, and if we can cut just five or ten minutes – speed up our introductions and so on – we shall be spot on.'

'Dress rehearsal, don't forget,' said Nigel, 'everyone in church by seven o'clock sharp. That includes the readers,' he added. 'We want everything exactly as it will be on performance.'

Groups of people stood about, gossiping and laughing, and Peggy came up to Sophie as she tidied up the chairs.

'Everything all right?' Peggy said, looking closely at Sophie Brooks's downcast face.

'Of course,' said Sophie, forcing a smile, 'I'm just a bit tired, that's all. It's a busy time for us, you know, with the three parishes and all the various Christmas activities.'

Peggy nodded. 'Come back and have coffee with me,' she said. 'It's not too late, and I'd be glad of the company.'

Sophie looked round the church, empty now, except for Nigel and Gabriella, still deep in conversation by the old piano.

'Do you mind if I go in for a coffee with Peggy?' she called across the pews, and Nigel looked round absently, almost as if he'd forgotten who she was.

'Fine,' he said, 'fine . . . see you later . . .' And he turned back to where Gabriella had got out notebook and pen, and was jotting down notes for the dress rehearsal.

'No, Peggy, there's nothing wrong, really,' protested Sophie, sitting in Peggy's kitchen sipping coffee, with her cold hands round the mug for warmth.

'It's not this ridiculous Gabriella Jones business, is it?' said Peggy bluntly. She had heard so much gossip and innuendo in the shop that she had become worried and stamped hard on any conversation which looked to be going that way.

Sophie shook her head, but her eyes filled with tears. 'No, of course not,' she said, 'that was just a bit of Robert's nonsense. He rang Nigel the next day and apologised, said he meant to say "Miss Jones", because of Octavia's reputation, but it came out "Mrs" by mistake.'

'Do you believe him?' said Peggy.

'No, I think he meant what he said, and I think it was partly revenge on Greg Jones for that wicked accusation Octavia made about being molested.'

'I wouldn't have thought Robert was that petty,' said Peggy, opening a tin of shortbread biscuits and offering them to Sophie.

'No thanks, Peggy, I'm not very hungry these days,' she said. 'But if it wasn't revenge, then Robert really meant to make trouble. And he seems to have succeeded,' added Sophie quietly.

'Cheer up, Sophie!' said Peggy. 'I thought you were so happy in Ringford? It will soon be Christmas, and all the lovely things to come . . .' Peggy's voice tailed away, as memories of last year's Christmas overcame her. They sat without speaking for a few minutes, and then Sophie saw Peggy take out a handkerchief and wipe her cheeks, sniffing and getting up to refill the Rayburn.

'Peggy?' said Sophie.

'Yes?' said Peggy, shovelling fuel noisily.

'You're crying,' said Sophie.

'Not really,' said Peggy, sitting down again at the table and taking a deep breath.

'Oh, Peggy,' said Sophie, mortified, 'here am I going on about something totally unimportant, and forgetting completely that it will soon be the anniversary of Frank's death. Please forgive me, my dear.'

Sophie looked anxiously at Peggy, and she put out a hand across the table.

Peggy began to sniff again, and then the tears rolled faster down her cheeks.

'Oh sod it,' she said, her voice muffled by her handkerchief.

Sophie frowned, and then she too began to cry. Gilbert looked in alarm from her basket by the Rayburn, her ears pricked and her eyes wild. She stood up and miaowed loudly, jumping on to Peggy's lap and pummelling her skirt frantically.

'Oh Gilbert,' said Peggy, beginning to laugh, 'this won't do, will it?'

Sophie pulled herself together, and although she agreed and began to smile at the ridiculousness of it all, she returned home through the darkness slowly, her mind still revolving all the small scenes and conversations of the concert rehearsal. And she could not rid herself of that final dismissive phrase of Nigel's: 'Fine, see you later . . .'

How much later? Would he be home now, or would the house be dark and empty? And what would she do if it was?

Dear God, she prayed to the distant sky, please make it go away, please . . .

CHAPTER THIRTY-TWO

'Thank God it's not snowing,' said Peggy, as she got reluctantly out of bed and gave Frank's photograph the ritual good-morning kiss.

Exactly a year ago, it had been snowing heavily, the village transformed and coldly beautiful. But it had been the ice and snow that caused Frank's accident, and Peggy dreaded the reminder, watching the sky for the tell-tale yellow luminosity that heralds a snowstorm.

She had a quick bath and dressed warmly for a routine day in the shop. Her Christmas corner was going well, and she would have to ask Bill if he would fetch more supplies from the wholesaler. By the time she had served in the shop all day, her feet were either frozen solid or achingly hot, and she accepted with relief his offers of help. She made a list of things she needed, but there were always one or two extras tentatively included by Bill.

'Should go well, gel,' he would say, and then watch the shelves anxiously to make sure he hadn't lumbered her with slow movers.

She pulled back the curtains in the kitchen, and unlocked the back door, opening it and calling, 'Gilbert! Gilbertiney!' She looked down at something bright and colourful.

On the back doorstep was a large bunch of chrysanthemums, bronze shaggy heads and dark green leaves, vibrating with life in the cold air.

Peggy looked at them for several seconds before picking them up. Then she buried her nose in the chilly, special scent, and took them back into the kitchen. She knew who had left them there, and why, but she looked nevertheless for a card.

She found it tucked into the leaves. 'Thinking of Frank, and of my love for you, Peggy. Bill.'

A good ten minutes passed before Peggy was able to get up from the kitchen chair and look for a vase. She arranged the flowers and took them through to the sitting room, putting them in the window where Bill would see them if he passed.

The hours went slowly. It was one of those winter days which never get much beyond the cold grey light of dawn. The incessant humming of the cool cabinet in the shop, and a flickering neon tube which needed replacing, combined to get on Peggy's nerves, and she snapped, 'Please shut the door!' when William Roberts drifted in, leaving it open behind him.

Peggy watched him making for the Christmas corner, where he stood in silent contemplation. How he's grown, she thought, looking at his long, thin legs in their rubbed jeans, and the back of his neck, spindly and somehow vulnerable, with the shock of short hair sticking up in angry spikes above. His anorak was a couple of sizes too small, and she wondered whether the Roberts children had to wait for outgrown clothes from the one above.

'How's Sandra and the baby?' she asked.

'All right,' said William.

'Are they coming for Christmas?' said Peggy, wondering why she was bothering with William, who clearly did not want to talk.

'Dunno.'

Peggy began to stack new packs of butter in the refrigerated display, and left William to it. After a minute or two, he came to the counter, carrying a pen and pencil set in a plastic bubble pack.

'D'you think our Andrew would like this?' he said. Andrew was the next one down, and Peggy confirmed that he would love it.

William handed over the money, and then fumbled in his anorak pocket, bringing out a tiny metal screwdriver, with an elaborate criss-cross machine-tooled pattern on the brass handle.

Peggy picked it up, and said, 'It's lovely, William, where did you get it?' She had an uncharitable thought about the Robertses' light-fingered reputation.

'Made it,' said William, 'at school, in metalwork. It's for you.'

Peggy stared at him. 'For me, William? But it's not my birthday, or anything . . .'

'No, but . . . you know,' said William, shifting from one foot to the other in embarrassment.

'Oh, William,' said Peggy, rescuing him, 'yes, of course, I do know. And it's very, very kind of you. Thank you.'

'Should be useful for doin' electric plugs, and that,' said William, sighing with relief, and making for the door. 'Bye, then, Mrs P.'

Peggy sat over a ham sandwich at lunchtime and wondered how to get through to the end of the day. Jean Jenkins had come in and given her a hug, and little Eddie had been bidden to give one of his warm, chocolatey kisses. Doreen Price had rung up, ostensibly about eggs for the shop, but really to make sure Peggy was all right.

The shop bell jangled, and Peggy got up wearily. It was Ivy Beasley, and her face was grim.

'Half of lard,' she said, banging the money down on to the counter.

Peggy fetched a packet from the fridge and put it in a white paper bag.

'Anything else?' she said.

'Yes,' said Ivy, 'yes, I've something to say, and you'll do well to listen, especially on this particular day.'

Peggy felt her heart begin to thud. She wouldn't, surely, not even Poison Ivy, not today.

'Just as well there's nobody else in the shop,' continued Ivy, 'because what I have to say is for your ears only. No doubt you will convey the meaning to Bill Turner yourself.'

Peggy gripped the edge of the counter, and waited.

'The pair of you,' said Ivy Beasley, her eyes glinting, 'should be ashamed of yourselves. The whole village knows what you're up to, but even worse, poor Joyce Turner knows and it's driving her mad.'

What shall I do? thought Peggy. I'm trapped here in the shop. Why doesn't somebody come in?

The hard voice droned on, piling recrimination on exhortations to examine her conscience, until Peggy thought she would never stop. And then the door opened, and Ellen Biggs came in.

'Mornin', my dear,' she said to Peggy, and then, seeing her white, horrified face, she turned to Ivy Beasley.

''Ere, Ivy, what you bin sayin'?' she said, ''Ave you bin 'avin' a go at Mrs Palmer?'

Ivy Beasley was breathing hard, and began to push her way past Ellen to leave the shop.

'Oh no,' said Ellen, immovable as a rock, 'just you stay 'ere a minute, Ivy.'

The cold silence in the shop told Ellen all she needed to know, and she leaned her face close to Ivy's.

'I wouldn't be you, Ivy Dorothy Beasley,' she hissed, 'for all the tea in China. You will reap what you 'ave sowed, mark my words. You'd better go 'ome and pray as 'ard as you know how, because you're surely goin' to need some 'elp from the Almighty.'

Ivy backed away from her, pushing at her with grey-gloved hands, and then turned and ran out of the shop.

Ellen hobbled up to the counter, where Peggy stood without moving, her face bleak and withdrawn.

'It's no good my sayin' to take no notice, dear,' said Ellen, 'I can see that. But don't forget that 'er wickedness will be punished, nothin' surer than that.'

Peggy shook herself, and stared across at Ellen.

'And what about my wickedness, Ellen?' she said. She

looked away, all colour and life drained from her face, looked out of the window and over the Green towards the church-yard. 'It's a year ago today, Ellen,' she said. 'Frank died a year ago today.'

CHAPTER THIRTY-THREE

It was very quiet in Victoria Villa. Ivy Beasley had not taken off her coat, or her grey woollen gloves, and was walking rapidly round the house, from room to room, not looking for anything, just walking.

She stopped eventually, and found herself in her mother's bedroom. The quiet was so thick in here that she crossed to the window and opened it a fraction, replacing the heavy net curtains quickly.

The Green was empty, except for the distant figure of Mr Ross, muffled and disguised, taking his little dog for a walk by the river. As Ivy looked, old Ellen came out of the shop and headed for home. She did not once glance in the direction of Victoria Villa.

Ivy took off her gloves and coat, and let them fall in a heap on the floor. Then she sat down on the dressing-table stool and looked at herself in the mirror. That can't be me, she thought, that's not me. She got up again quickly, and began to walk towards the door.

Stand still! Stand still at once! said the voice in her head. Ivy halted, for once relieved that her mother was still there.

What exactly do you think you are doing? said the voice.

Ivy tried to speak, but words would not come.

You've really messed it up now, haven't you, you stupid girl. Ellen Biggs will tell everyone and the few friends you have got will turn against you. Why did you have to choose today of all days?

Ivy sat down on the edge of the bed, her hand repeatedly smoothing the cold white cover.

I thought you'd given up on Pushy Peg? said the relentless voice. Thought it was Gabriella Jones you were after? Well, answer me, girl!

But Ivy could find nothing to say. She slowly slid off the edge of the bed, down on to the rag rug made by her mother in winter evenings long ago, and curled up like a child, closing her eyes tight against a hostile world.

CHAPTER THIRTY-FOUR

Gabriella gathered her music together and put it into her old brown music case, the one she had had at school, and had promised to give to Octavia if she wanted to follow her mother's career in teaching music.

'That old thing?' Octavia had said. 'No thanks. I'm going to be a model, anyway, marry some rich old man who'll die quickly and leave me lots of money to enjoy myself.'

It was a bitterly cold evening, and Gabriella looked at her cosy sitting room with some regret. Greg had built up a big log fire, and sat buried behind the newspaper in his deep armchair.

'Hope not to be too late back,' she said, wrapping her scarf several times round her neck. Greg did not answer, and she walked over to him.

'Greg, you might say good luck, or something,' she said.

He put down the paper with deliberation and looked up at her.

'It's only the dress rehearsal, isn't it?' he said. 'I'll save the good wishes for tomorrow night.'

Gabriella frowned. 'Is something wrong, Greg?' she said. He shook his head and began to read.

'It's not that ridiculous thing Robert said that night, is it? You're not still brooding about that?'

'Don't be silly, Gabriella,' he said. 'You'd better be going, you don't want to be late.'

'Is it Octavia, then, is there something you're not telling me?'

'Gabriella, there is nothing wrong . . . and I have never kept anything important from you, you know that. I hope you can say the same thing. And now leave me in peace, there's a good girl.'

It *is* what Robert said, thought Gabriella. Sophie Brooks has been very off with me ever since, and Doreen and Peggy have been giving me funny looks. And then there's old Ivy, dripping her poison all over the village. She's probably been spreading untruths, as usual. Perhaps I shouldn't have moved her to the back row, mortally offended her, no doubt.

Most of the company, including Susan Standing, were already in the church, and from the excited level of conversation Gabriella knew that tension was mounting. It was all very well to sing just for themselves, and have a lot of fun doing it, but now the prospect of an audience was sending shivers through many of them.

'Here she comes,' said Nigel Brooks, dignified in his full cassock, his face shining with benevolence and encouragement.

'Hello, everyone,' said Gabriella, forcing her mind back to the concert, and the importance of conveying confidence to her nervous choir.

'Take your places, and we'll make a start,' she said. 'Remember the stopwatch, Colin?'

'Yes, Miss!' said Colin, full of good cheer.

The Reverend Nigel Brooks had stepped forward to welcome the invisible audience and announce the first item, when the door opened and Ellen Biggs hobbled in. She looked cold and furious, and Nigel halted mid-sentence.

'Ellen,' he said, 'come along in, we're just about to start.'

'Where is she?' said Ellen, her voice cracked and gruff with the cold.

'Where is who?'

'Ivy,' said Ellen. 'Ivy Beasley – where is she?'

Nobody had noticed Ivy's absence, but now they all began

to talk at once, and Gabriella moved into her conductor's position.

'Quiet, please, everybody, quiet.' She took Ellen's arm and helped her up the chancel steps into the altos, telling her to keep on her scarf and gloves until she had warmed up.

'Anybody seen Miss Beasley?' said Nigel. He turned and looked at the choir, his face genuinely concerned.

Nobody had, and various suggestions of indisposition and unexpected visitors were put forward.

'Well, it's most unlike her to be late.' said Gabriella, 'but we must begin.' She looked at Nigel. 'Will you do the welcome again?' she said, and nodded to Colin Osman, who restarted his stopwatch with a flourish.

It was a ragged, unsatisfactory dress rehearsal, and, despite her best efforts, Gabriella felt the choir's exuberance draining away. By the end of he programme, everyone looked miserable and low. Small groups formed as usual, but the conversation was quiet, desultory.

Sophie Brooks found herself at odds with the rest. She had a nasty, mean feeling of pleasure that things had not gone well. I don't care, she thought, if it is a disaster. In fact, I rather hope it is a disaster, then Nigel and his beloved Gabriella will stop preening themselves like a couple of love birds and get back to their proper work and families.

'Now, everyone,' said Nigel, standing on the chancel steps, 'you know what they say, a bad dress rehearsal means a good performance, and vice versa, of course. So I, for one, am not downhearted, and with the good Lord's help we shall have a triumph tomorrow night. So let's cheer up, and away to our beds.'

Bill Turner offered to run Ellen home in his van, and the rest walked away from the church in twos and threes, chattering in a more lively way, their spirits somewhat restored by Nigel's little pep-talk.

''As Peggy told you about Ivy?' said Ellen, as she settled back in Bill's sagging front seat.

Bill wiped condensation off the windscreen with an old rag

187

and grunted. 'She did say something, but didn't want to talk about it when I asked.'

'It was wicked, on this particular day,' said Ellen, pulling up her coat collar against the draughts. 'Shouldn't be surprised if old Nick hadn't come for 'er. That's where she's gone, I shouldn't wonder, straight to Purgat'ry.'

'Who? Peggy?' said Bill, only half listening.

'No, old Ivy,' said Ellen. 'What you and Peggy Palmer mean to each other is your own business. And don't let that Ivy tell you it's driving Joyce mad. You and me and most of the village know that Joyce has been unhinged for years. You done your best by 'er, Bill, and no man could 'ave done more.'

'Thanks, Ellen,' said Bill. 'You're not such a bad old devil yourself.'

Ellen chuckled, and scrambled out of Bill's van outside the Lodge.

'Ta, Bill,' she said. 'You'd best go and check on old Ivy. Wouldn't want even that old misery lying cold on 'er kitchen floor and nobody to find her.'

Sophie lingered in the church, putting away chairs and helping to move the piano back against the wall. Nigel seemed in good spirits, but Gabriella would not be cheered up.

'It was terrible, Nigel, wasn't it. Sophie, wasn't it terrible?' she said. 'The tenors were flatter than usual, and Ellen went wrong several times. Her mind seemed to be elsewhere, and with her strong voice the mistakes are really noticeable. Then Susan Standing was stammering with nerves – she's never done that before – and the Gloria at the end sounded more like a Requiem . . .'

'It wasn't nearly as bad as that!' said Nigel, patting her on the shoulder. 'You'll see, they'll all come up trumps tomorrow. It's a sense of occasion does the trick, always works.'

But Gabriella shook her head, her blonde hair swinging, and walked disconsolately to the door.

'Come back with us and have a cup of tea,' said Nigel, an

impulsive offer made on the spur of the moment. 'I hate to see you disappearing into the night with such a long face. We always have a cuppa last thing, don't we, Soph?'

I don't believe it, thought Sophie, how can he be so insensitive? Does he think I am some dutiful handmaiden, who will jump to the kettle and the teapot when he feels like indulging his fancy woman?

'Of course,' she said. 'Do come over, Gabriella. I am sure you and Nigel still have final details to discuss.'

'Are you sure?' said Gabriella, unwilling to go back to the unresponsive Greg. 'Well, then, thank you very much, Sophie.'

In the big kitchen at the vicarage, the three of them sat drinking tea round the table, and, as they talked sensibly about the rehearsal, Gabriella seemed more optimistic.

'I suppose it wasn't all that bad,' she said. 'It was just that I was so anxious for it all to be perfect.'

She stood up. 'I must be going, Greg will be wondering where I am,' she said, and Sophie and Nigel also got to their feet.

'I'll walk back with you,' said Nigel. 'It's a very dark night.'

Sophie felt sick. He can't do that, she thought. If he walks her home, I shall leave. Straight away. I shall just get in the car and go, anywhere, anywhere to get away. I can't take any more.

'Shan't be many minutes, Soph,' said Nigel, pulling on his coat and following Gabriella across the black and white tiled floor and out of the heavy front door. It shut with a thud behind them, and Sophie rushed to the cupboard, pulling out her own coat. She took her car keys from the board over the hatch, and walked quickly out of the kitchen. At the foot of the stairs in the hall, she stopped.

Ricky, the old black dog, stretched out on the door mat where everyone fell over him, lifted his head and looked at her with his bluey-black eyes. It wasn't an invitation to a walk, he knew that. He also knew that his favourite person was in trouble. He walked in his meandering way over to Sophie and pushed his nose into her hand, tentatively wagging his ratty old tail.

She looked down at him, and patted his bony head. Then she took off her coat, put the keys back on the board, and went wearily upstairs to bed.

CHAPTER THIRTY-FIVE

Ivy Beasley stared out of her mother's bedroom window at the falling snow. Her face was closed, and the thin skin under her eyes bruised and black from crying and restless sleep. She had heard Bill Turner banging at the door the night before, and finally, to get rid of him, she'd gone down and yelled, 'Go away!' through the locked door.

She turned and went out on to the landing, where she hesitated, then continued on downstairs and into the kitchen. The range fire was out, and the house cold and damp-smelling. She put on the electric kettle, given to her by Robert last Christmas, spooned tea into the pot, and went to sit down by the dead grate. The kettle boiled and switched itself off, and Ivy did not stir.

Two hours later, with the village transformed into a picture postcard by the snow, thick and soft, Robert Bates found her still sitting in the same chair, staring into space, her hands idle in her lap.

'Auntie?' he had called through the letterbox. Receiving no reply, he fished out the key which she had given him on his insistence, and let himself in.

'Auntie?' he repeated, seeing her sitting there, not even looking up as he came in the kitchen. He took her hands, and felt that they were ice cold. He rushed up to her bedroom and took a rug off the bed, running down again and wrapping it round her shoulders. The fire was quickly lit, and Robert piled on dry logs to give off as much heat as possible.

Handing her a steaming cup of sweet tea, he said, 'Come on, Auntie, drink this, it'll warm you up.' She shook her head, dazed, and looked up at him. Like a child, she allowed him to hold the cup to her lips, and slowly tip the hot liquid into her mouth.

At last she took the cup from him, and finished the tea down to the last dregs. Without speaking, she pulled the rug closer round her and closed her eyes. Robert sat and watched her until her breathing became light and regular, and then he went quickly into the shop and asked Peggy to ring for the doctor.

'Could've died, Doris,' said Ellen, as they sat having a cup of coffee in Doris's sitting room. The white morning light, reflected from the snow, filled the room, and old Ellen shivered.

'Doctor said it were 'yperthermia, or some such. She were ice cold, I 'eard Robert Bates telling Peggy in the shop.' Ellen shifted her chair closer to Doris's glowing gas fire.

'What brought it on?' said Doris. 'Our Ivy's always been one for a good fire. I don't understand it.'

'She weren't at choir last night. Nobody seemed to care much, but I thought it were very unlike Ivy to miss out on anythin'. I asked Bill to look in on 'er, but 'e couldn't get 'er to open up.'

They sat silently for a minute or two, appalled at the thought of Ivy, strong and invincible in the order of things in Round Ringford, brought low by some strange force which they could only guess at.

'Perhaps it were a brainstorm,' said Ellen, not yet ready to tell Doris about her set-to with Ivy in the shop. ''Er mother were a funny one, used to have these turns where she'd go all peculiar. Or it could be a judgement . . .' she added darkly.

Doris shrugged. 'There's been such a lot of bad feeling in the village, ever since the Harvest Supper,' she said, getting up and collecting the cups. 'I for one shall be glad when this concert's over and we can get back to normal. We all thought the Brookses were such a good thing, but now I'm not so sure.'

Sophie Brooks was standing in the high-ceilinged drawing room of the vicarage, a small address book in her hand, her face pale and oddly set.

She leafed through until she found what she wanted: Jones G., Barnstones, High Street – Ringford 956474.

She had woken early in the morning, and said sleepily, 'Nigel? What time is it?'

When there was no reply, she awoke properly and sat up. She was alone in the big bed, and there was no sign of Nigel or his clothes.

She shot out of bed and on to the landing. The small guest-room door was closed, and standing uncertainly outside she could hear snoring. What is he doing in there, she thought. And then the old evil thoughts began, and before she had reached the foot of the stairs she had constructed a terrifying scenario. He had stayed out with Gabriella, somewhere secret, and had come in too late to sleep in the marital bed.

'Didn't want to wake you, Soph,' Nigel said at breakfast. 'I peeped in and you were fast asleep, with your thumb in your mouth – dear little thing.' He reached out to give her an affectionate squeeze, but she dodged, taking the dishes to the sink.

Now she stood with the little yellow book in her hand, willing herself to make the call that would put it all straight.

The snow had drifted during the morning, forming little mounds at the corners of Gabriella's garden. Young trees, fragile in the strong wind, shed powdery showers, and a robin perched on the edge of the bird bath like an animated Christmas card.

I remember a time when Octavia would have been out there in her little red boots, joyfully making a snowman with Greg, thought Gabriella. The telephone rang, and she turned away from the window.

'Hello?' said Gabriella. 'Hello, who's there?'

A strained voice said, 'It's me, Sophie Brooks. I have something to say to you.'

Gabriella frowned. 'Is it a message from Nigel?' she said.

The slow-burning fuse finally reached its destination, and Sophie began to talk, softly at first, and then shouting, blaspheming, accusing.

Gabriella said nothing. Her hand holding the telephone receiver began to tremble, and after a while, but not soon enough, she put it quietly back into its cradle.

CHAPTER THIRTY-SIX

The Reverend Nigel Brooks strode through the snow, pleased with the crisp air and fresh wind, happily contemplating the prospect of a successful concert. After Christmas, he thought, I can start on the regular church choir. Several of the men, chaps like Colin Osman, could surely be persuaded to join, and then he would visit the parents of some of the likely children and see if he could enlist their support.

As he approached Barnstones, he saw Gabriella at the gate, without a coat, her arms wrapped around herself in a protective gesture, and as he came up he was startled by her greeting.

'You'd better not come in, Nigel,' she said, unsmiling. 'I'll just tell you here and now. The concert's off, unless you can do it without me. I shall never set foot in your lousy church again, and if you want to know why, ask your loyal little wife!'

She turned and ran back into the house, slamming the door shut with a wood-splitting crash.

Nigel stared at the house for a moment, then began to open the gate.

'Reverend Brooks!' It was Michael Roberts, a shovel over his shoulder, coming along on the opposite side of the road.

'Mornin', Vicar,' he said, 'just off to see if you want the snow cleared from your drive?'

They set off together, Nigel reflecting that perhaps he had

better not tackle Gabriella, and anxious to see what exactly Sophie had been up to. She had certainly been acting rather strangely these last few days.

He left Michael Roberts shovelling mounds of snow and gravel, and approached the front door. To his surprise, he saw it stood wide open, and no Ricky bounded to greet him. There was nobody in the kitchen, and he went around the rest of the house, calling loudly for Sophie.

Finally he gave up, took off his cloak and hung it in the echoing hall, and went to sit in his study. I need to think, he said to himself. There's something very wrong here.

The study was quiet and warm. It was a dark room, and Nigel put on his desk lamp, throwing a pool of yellow light on to the polished leather top. He bowed his head and said a small prayer for help and guidance. A few clues would be useful, he muttered.

Almost at once the ridiculous verse of Robert's harvest song came into his mind. Sophie had made a little scene about that, he remembered. But he'd soon set her straight, thought she'd put it out of her mind.

> 'And it's only 'is collar what stops him proposing
> A tandem with nice Mrs Jones.'

Round and round it went in his head, until he put his hand over his ears and stood up. That was it. Sophie was jealous, jealous of Gabriella Jones. And now all the words and occasions which could have fuelled her jealousy came flooding back to Nigel. Oh, my dear God, he groaned, what have I done?

Bill Turner was heaving boxes of supplies on to shelves in the store room at the back of the shop, with Peggy directing operations. It was nearly lunchtime, and a quiet time for custom.

'This should last you well into the New Year,' said Bill.

'There's always a last-minute rush before Christmas,' said Peggy. 'Doris said it was the same every year. Then I expect January and February will be the usual dreary months, when I shall be lucky to take enough to keep the shop going.'

'Don't worry, gel,' said Bill, 'we'll think of . . .' He broke off, listening to the sounds from the shop.

'You've got a customer, I think,' he said.

Peggy walked through, and saw Sophie Brooks standing by the counter, wearing an old jacket, buttoned crookedly, her hair covered with snow. Her face was pale with her mouth drawn into a narrow line. She held a leather lead tightly in her hand, and the old black dog stood obediently at her side.

'Sophie!' said Peggy. 'What on earth's the matter?' She was so shocked by her friend's appearance that she forgot to remind her that no dogs were allowed in the shop.

'Can I speak to you, Peggy?' she whispered. And then, seeing Bill in the kitchen, she added, 'It's very urgent and very private.'

'I'm off, Peg,' said Bill, knowing a crisis when he saw one. 'Let me know if you need any help.'

For the first time since Frank died, Peggy locked the shop door in the middle of the day and put up a little note saying, 'Re-open at two o'clock.' She led Sophie, still clutching Ricky's lead, through to the sitting room, and sat her down in a comfortable armchair.

'Don't move,' Peggy said. 'I shall be back in one minute.'

She returned with a glass and a bottle of brandy. 'Drink this,' she said, 'but not too quickly.'

Sophie sipped the brandy with shaking hands, and after a minute or two said, 'Peggy, I've done a very stupid thing. It is so stupid that I hardly dare think about it . . .'

Peggy walked to the window and looked out. Maybe it will be easier for her if she doesn't have to see me, she thought. I think I know what's coming, anyway.

She waited for Sophie to begin, and watched old Fred, slipping and sliding, heading home from the pub. Jean Jenkins was helping Eddie to make snowballs on the Green, throwing them ineffectually at Mark. The children were in the school playground after lunch, making more noise than usual in the excitement of snowfall.

'And the worst of it, Peggy,' said Sophie, more fluent now after a hesitant start, and gulping down the last of the brandy, 'was that the more I ranted and raved, the more convinced I became that there was absolutely nothing in it. It was all for nothing, and I couldn't stop. I seemed to be listening to someone else . . .'

'Oh Sophie,' said Peggy, 'but are you sure you said really bad things? Maybe you just thought them, and in the heat of the moment thought you'd said them.'

She saw old Ellen looking crossly at the notice on the shop door. She turned away, walking off towards Bates's End and keeping to the middle of the road where it had been gritted and was comparatively safe. I shall have to send somebody down to ask if she wanted anything urgently, thought Peggy, can't have her coming up again today in this weather.

'I said them,' said Sophie. 'Oh yes, I certainly said them.'

Peggy returned to sit opposite the hunched figure, and tried desperately to think of something helpful to say.

'Look, Sophie,' she said, 'if Gabriella didn't say anything, just put down the phone, ten to one she won't do anything either. It will have to be sorted out, of course, but after the concert, when everybody's calmed down, you can see her and explain.'

She wondered whether to say anything about the rumours which had been rife in the village for weeks, but decided against it.

'I haven't told you the very worst,' said Sophie.

Peggy waited. The clock ticked away, and she saw there were only a couple of minutes left to opening time. Bang goes my lunch, she thought. I shall have to grab a sandwich between customers.

'I threatened to tell Greg,' said Sophie, 'said that maybe then he'd be able to keep her in order. Then I said . . .' She stopped, and Peggy nodded encouragingly. 'I said,' whispered Sophie, 'that maybe Greg should keep his women under lock and key, for the peace of mind of the village.'

There was a small silence, and then Peggy began to splutter. 'You said that?' she said. 'Oh, Sophie, how absolutely . . .' But she couldn't continue, as mirth welled up and threatened to burst out. She swallowed hard, and realised with shame that there would be no laughing Sophie out of it this time.

There was certainly no laughter in Barnstones. Gabriella had paced about the house, snapping at Octavia and watching the clock move at a snail's pace until it was time for Greg to be home from a school football match.

'Thank God,' she said, as his car appeared at last. 'Here, Octavia, take my purse and run down to the shop. Bring a tin of that new soup, you can choose – off you go, now.'

Octavia, seeing her mother's desperate face, for once did as she was told, did it at once, without arguing.

'I might call in at the Brights – see if Tanya's there,' she said.

It was a pity that Gabriella did not register her daughter's unselfish thought, but she was already rehearsing her first words of explanation and appeal to Greg.

They sat by the leaping fire in their quiet, neutral sitting room. Greg had taken one look at Gabriella, and retired to the kitchen to open a Christmas bottle. She had begun at the beginning, with rumours spread by Ivy Beasley, and her own unthinking close association with Nigel over the concert. She blamed herself for blindness in not seeing Sophie's distress and ill-concealed jealousy.

'And it was all for nothing!' she said vehemently. 'I never even thought of him as a man, he's just a vicar in a long dress to me . . .'

Greg looked at his wife, beaten and angry at the same time, her shining hair scraped back into an elastic band, and her face bare and sallow, with no make-up, stained with tears, and he felt a real stab of hate for the Brookses – for both of them. What a fool the man must be, how unsuited to his job. And that sniffy, carrot-haired Sophie, so superior and sure of herself. What a complete mess they'd made of something that could have been a great contribution to the village Christmas.

He reached out and took Gabriella's hand.

'Don't worry, Gabbie,' he said, his voice odder than usual, charged with emotion, 'you can leave it to me now, I'll sort it out. It is a very serious matter, and will need a great deal of thought.'

'I've told him the concert's off, anyway,' said Gabriella, Squeezing Greg's hand gratefully.

Greg frowned. 'Are you sure that's a good idea?' he said. 'It could look like an admission of guilt. I think you should carry on, keep your head high and make the concert a real triumph. Then the village will see you have nothing to be ashamed of, and the Brookses will look the complete fools they undoubtedly are.'

'But I've told him –'

'Leave it to me,' repeated Greg. He crossed to the telephone and dialled the vicarage. His face was set into stern, classroom-quelling lines.

'Mr Brooks?' he said. 'This is Jones here. I am ringing to tell you that Gabriella will be conducting the concert as planned. As to the other matter, you will be hearing from me in due course.'

A log of applewood spat, sending a glowing spark on to the shaggy cream-coloured rug, and Gabriella rushed to brush it back into the hearth. Greg put down the telephone and walked over to her as she straightened up. He put his arms round her and hugged her tight.

'I'll be there,' he said, 'and so will Octavia. Trust me, Gabbie, I could slay dragons for you when you look at me like that.'

They were still standing there when Octavia returned.

'Brights were out,' she said, 'and the shop was shut. But have you heard the latest on old Beasley? Robert's had to take her up to the farm, she went and collapsed in his arms. Why didn't I think of that?' She looked at her parents' faces, and

added, 'What's up with you two anyway? Did the world come
to an end while I was out?'

CHAPTER THIRTY-SEVEN

The choir had gathered early, as instructed. It was warm in the church, Mr Ross having put on the heaters two hours before, and the altos and sopranos took off their coats, revealing colourful outfits, some quite sparkly and festive, others more conservative, but newly bought for the occasion, and worn a little self-consciously.

Old Ellen had surpassed herself. Free of Ivy's restraining influence, she had selected a long black velvet skirt, a size or two too small, but well anchored with safety pins, and a dazzling blouse covered with gold sequins and once worn by Pat Osman during her ballroom-dancing phase. For warmth, Ellen had added a scarlet mohair stole, only a little moth-eaten, and almost matching her carefully applied lipstick.

The men had had serious discussions about whether or not to wear dinner jackets, but in the end settled on dark suits and white shirts, in the interests of equality. It had been Nigel who had gently pointed out to Colin Osman that not all the chaps would necessarily have dinner jackets.

Gabriella had been first to arrive. She had brought Octavia with her, and the two of them arranged music and pushed chairs into the right places, until the side door of the church had opened, and Nigel had come in. His face shocked Gabriella. The usual pink, healthy complexion was grey, and his expression haunted.

'Good evening, Gabriella,' he said quietly, 'are we all ready?'

Octavia turned her back on him, but Gabriella nodded and managed an 'Uh-huh,' before sitting down at the piano and running through a series of conversation-stopping arpeggios.

It was easier as the others began to arrive, and now she clapped her hands and called for a few la-las to warm up their voices before they retired to the vestry to line up in twos for the procession. The church was full, the atmosphere expectant.

Sophie slipped into the church through the side door, and crept into her place next to Pat Osman. The choir was ready, all bunched up and silent, waiting for the signal from Gabriella.

The lights in the church were dimmed, and a hush fell on the audience. The tall Christmas tree, cut from the plantation and safely anchored by Tom Price in half a beer barrel, twinkled and shed a glow on the swags of holly and ivy along the high windowsills.

Gabriella, waiting at the piano, played a soft chord, and from the vestry came a high, heavenly voice, echoing round the still, quiet church.

'Once in Royal David's city, stood a lowly cattle shed,' sang Octavia, a reluctant soloist, her naturally clear, true voice coached for the occasion by her mother.

Octavia's blonde hair, drawn neatly back with a black velvet hairband, shone in the flickering lights of candles carried by the choir, and her face was bland and innocent. The singers slowly processed round the aisles of the church, serious and concentrating hard, nervously acknowledging their friends and relations as they passed the ends of packed pews.

Once the concert got going, all Gabriella thought about was the music and the choir. She prompted readers to step forward smartly, and even smiled at Colin Osman as he launched into his solo spot, quavering on his high notes and losing the beat in his anxiety.

Every seat in the church was taken. The audience, chilly in their responses at first, soon warmed up, and, encouraged by Nigel to applaud, clapped loudly. The readings were popular, even when words were forgotten and stumbled over. Susan Standing's passage from Dickens was especially well received, not only because she read it very movingly, but because she was there, the squire's lady, doing her bit.

As Gabriella turned to announce the interval, the church door creaked open slowly. Puzzled, she waited before speaking, looking anxiously at the front pew. But Greg was still there, solid and reassuring, smiling at her and making thumbs up, going well, signs.

In the silence, several of the audience looked round at the slowly opening door. The lights had come up after the last item, and the doorway was spotlit, emphasizing its graceful Norman arch and ancient oak door.

Into the light, blinking but standing straight as a ramrod, stepped Ivy Beasley. She was pale as a ghost, but neat and smart in her best black coat and grey silk scarf, her hair smooth and curled under in the new style. She handed her ticket to a stunned Mr Ross, and muttered, 'Not too late for the second half, I hope.' Then she walked slowly and quietly to a seat in the back pew, waiting for a startled-looking Doris Ashbourne to make room for her.

As the audience slowly got to their feet and began milling about, mingling with the choir and offering comment and opinion on the show so far, old Ellen struggled down the chancel steps and made her way to the back of the church.

She found Ivy sitting in her pew, looking around with an apparently mild eye.

'Glad you made it, Ivy,' said Ellen generously. ''Ow you feelin' now? Shall I get yer a cup of coffee?'

'Our Doris is gone for one already,' said Ivy, looking squarely at the old woman. Her voice grew stronger as she continued.

'I don't know what you think you look like, Ellen Biggs,'

she said, 'but if you ask me, a cross between Guy Fawkes and
the fairy on the top of the Christmas tree wouldn't be far off.'

CHAPTER THIRTY-EIGHT

Well, come on, Ivy, how did it go? The voice had a taunting edge.

Ivy Beasley took off her coat and carefully folded her new silk scarf into a neat square. She glanced at herself in the mirror of the hall-stand, and patted her hair.

Not quite in the pink, are we, Ivy? said her mother's voice inside her exhausted head.

At least, said Ivy, being pale makes me look less like a boiled lobster.

Iron tablets, that's what you need, get yourself some iron tablets from the chemist.

Ivy put on the kettle, and sat down heavily in her chair by the range. I'm glad I made the effort, she said. It was worth going just to see Ellen Biggs. You've never seen anything like it, Mother, she was a real sight.

That's nothing new, said the voice. Tell me about the concert, and that Gabriella Jones and her fancy man.

If you mean Reverend Brooks, said Ivy coolly, he never looked at her once. And his thank-you speech was much shorter than I expected. Mark my words, something's been said there. And about time too. Mrs Brooks looked like death warmed up.

Bit like you, Ivy, said the voice, unsweetened by concern.

I must say it was all very well done, what I heard of it. It was halfway through by the time I got away from Olive Bates.

Them Bateses were always ones for fussing, said the voice.

Ivy leaned forward, warming her hands by the fire. She slipped off her best shoes, and, easing her painful toes, put on her comfortable, worn carpet slippers.

Go on, then, Ivy, said the voice impatiently.

Well, the music was good, Mother, and you'd have liked the readings, especially one about a farmer's wife and all the goodies she'd got in her larder for Christmas. Jean Jenkins read that. Pity she can't read a bit better, but still, you don't expect much from a Jenkins.

Ivy got up and made tea in the brown earthenware pot, putting a folded teacloth over it while it brewed to the right strength.

We have got a tea cosy, Ivy Beasley, said the voice.

Give it a rest, Mother, do, said Ivy. It's all I can do to keep on my feet.

Better go and see Dr Russell again, then, get a tonic.

Maybe, said Ivy. I'll give it another few days.

She drank the hot tea, and closed her eyes, falling almost immediately asleep, the empty cup tipping sideways in her lap. She was woken half an hour later by a coal falling noisily in the grate, and stood up awkwardly, taking the cup and saucer to the sink. She rinsed it under the tap, and riddled the grate, making it safe for the night. Then she checked the locks on both doors, put out the kitchen light, and, hugging a hot-water bottle to her flat chest, climbed the stairs slowly and went to bed.

You didn't clean your teeth, Ivy Dorothy Beasley! said her mother's voice.

Nor I did, said Ivy, and, turning on her side, went instantly to sleep.

The champagne cork came out of the bottle with a dull thud, but Gabriella flung her arms round Greg nevertheless, causing Octavia to sniff in embarrassment and disgust. The fire in the sitting room had gone out, and they sat in a threesome round the kitchen table.

'You two,' she said. 'What's brought on all this luvvy-duvvy stuff?'

'Just a treat for your mother, 'Tavie,' said Greg, pouring out a fizzing glass and handing it to Gabriella. 'She did extremely well tonight – better than you could possibly know. The concert went without a hitch, and honour was saved.'

'What d'you mean, Dad, "honour was saved"?' said Octavia.

'Nothing,' said Gabriella quickly, 'nothing at all. Are you sure you'll be all right with that champagne, 'Tavie, it won't make you too excited to sleep?'

Octavia smiled at her, humouring her fussy mother. 'It'll take me at least a week to calm down after the excitement of Peggy Palmer reading "How far is it to Bethlehem?",' she said. 'How can the school trip to Stratford and *Lady Macbeth* possibly come up to that?'

'That's quite enough of your schoolgirl wit, Octavia,' said Greg. 'Drink up and off to bed with you. See you in the morning.'

'Night, my pet,' said Gabriella.

'Night, Mum,' said Octavia, and hesitated. Then, rather awkwardly, she leaned over the back of her mother's chair and kissed her on the top of her head. 'It was quite good, actually, Mum,' she said. 'I have to admit I was even a bit proud. 'Night both.'

Greg looked at Gabriella, and he could see she was near to tears.

'Drink up, Gabbie my love,' he said, 'then it's up the wooden hill to Bedfordshire. Tomorrow's another day.'

It was cold in the big vicarage kitchen, and Sophie opened the Aga door to find the fire had gone out.

'Damn,' she said, 'must have forgotten to fill it up at lunchtime. Ah well, end of a perfect day.'

She slammed the firebox door shut, and walked out of the kitchen, making for Nigel's study, where he had gone the moment they arrived home. She looked apprehensively across the hall, shadowy and chilly, and saw with relief that he had left his door open. At least he's not shut me out altogether, she thought.

Nigel was sitting in his big leather swivel chair, still wrapped closely in a black cloak, staring out of the window at the silvery night. The temperature had dropped at dusk, and now the snow was frosted with fiery sparks. The moon was frighteningly bright, as if its turn had finally come to outshine the sun and take possession of the earth.

Sophie shivered, and pulled her black cardigan closer round her small body.

'Nigel?' she said.

He turned and looked at her, and his eyes were as cold as the moon.

'Would you like a cup of tea?' Sophie said meekly. 'I think I'll have one to warm up. The Aga's out.'

She knew the showdown had to come, but also knew it was no good trying to force Nigel into it. He would take his time, while she suffered agonies of self-recrimination and shame, and then he would justly and charitably put it all straight. At least, that is what Sophie hoped. Or thought she hoped.

'Thank you,' he said flatly, 'that is a good idea. I will light the Aga in the morning.'

Sophie did not say the whole water system in the house would probably be frozen up in the morning if he left the relighting till then. She returned to the kitchen and switched on the electric kettle. She arranged mugs and a plate of biscuits on a tray, and carried it all into the study, setting it down on Nigel's desk.

'It all went well,' she said, giving him an opening to talk.

He looked across at her, screwing up his eyes as if trying to get her into focus.

'Yes,' he said, 'very well.' And then he added, 'It was nice to see Miss Beasley up and about again.'

Something inside Sophie gave way.

'Don't speak to me about that woman!' she said. 'I wish Ivy Beasley could vanish off the face of the earth, never be seen again. I suppose I wish she was dead!'

'What do you mean, Sophie!' said Nigel, his voice rising. 'She is a poor old spinster, unloved by anybody except perhaps a very little by Robert Bates. How can you be so cruel?'

'Cruel?' screamed Sophie, rapidly losing control. 'Cruel? How dare you say that! Ivy bloody Beasley has nearly wrecked my life . . . maybe has wrecked it. Her wicked lies and serpent stories have poisoned our marriage, just about, and made me a pathetic laughing stock in this village that I so hoped to love and make my home . . . and . . .' She ran out of breath, and glared angrily at Nigel.

The cold moon cast shadows in the garden, like giant night people watching the unlovely scene in the study, and a couple of owls hooted to each other from the yew trees in the churchyard.

'It is not Ivy Beasley who has nearly wrecked our marriage,' said Nigel.

He stood up, knocked his cup over and sent steaming brown tea over his desk and on to the carpet. He did not appear to notice. 'It is nobody's fault, Sophie,' he said, and his voice had suddenly dropped to a quiet, calm level.

Here we go, thought Sophie, now for the sermon. She reached quietly for an old copy of *Church Times* and soaked up the spilt tea.

'I was so keen, you know that, Soph, to get things going well in the village.' He ran his fingers through his hair, an habitual gesture, without vanity. 'And then, when the Joneses had had such a rotten time with Octavia, it seemed an ideal thing for Gabriella, take her mind off things, make her feel optimistic again . . .'

Sophie felt the old pain rising in her stomach, and quelled it firmly by strength of will. No more of that, not ever again.

'It never once occurred to me,' Nigel continued, 'that tongues would wag. I suppose we are used to a different way of going on, a freedom to make friends with all kinds of people, opposite sex, different class, without comment. I am right about that, aren't I, Sophie?

Sophie nodded. Thin strips of cloud were crossing the moon, trails of vapour, making little impression on the bright, relentless shining light. I shall have to draw the curtains, thought Sophie, I can't take much more of that moon. But she stayed in her chair, scarcely moving except for the occasional nod or shake of the head, helping Nigel along.

'Well, now we know. Villages are different. And I can see that either we accept their rules, or . . .' He paused and looked at Sophie closely.

'Or go,' she said flatly.

They sat in silence for a few moments, and then Sophie spoke.

'So you think it was just the village, Nigel, no blame attached to either of us?'

He shook his head mournfully.

'Nigel,' said Sophie firmly, 'could you just for once forget that you are a priest, and tell me honestly, straight from your heart, what you think has happened to us?'

He sighed. 'All right, Sophie, let's pretend. Let's pretend I am still a solicitor in a flourishing practice, and you have been brewing up a fierce jealousy of my lovely blonde secretary.'

'Fine,' said Sophie, sitting forward. 'And you have been going to her house, often when her husband was at work, supposedly to plan the strategy on an important case. I have seen your heads close together, your hand on her shoulder, her eyes looking into yours. She has been to our house many times, closeted with you in your study, and you have walked her home late at night when it was dark and nobody about.'

Nigel was very still in his chair, his hands gripping the smooth wooden arms.

'And I've spoken to you on occasion when she was there too,' continued Sophie, her cheeks glowing, 'and you've looked through me, as if I wasn't there. All these things,' she continued, 'and many more, have led me to believe – fuelled by gossip in the neighbourhood and in your office – that you two are having an affair.'

It was very quiet in the study. Not a relaxed quiet or a

peaceful quiet, but the quiet of atmosphere charged with tension. Not even Ricky, asleep in his basket in the corner, moved a muscle.

Nigel got up slowly from his chair, and went to look out into the moonlit garden.

'It's Christmas, Soph,' he said. 'Do you remember how the children would open the doors on their Advent calendar, taking turns, and then do the last one, Christmas Day, together?' Sophie said nothing. Nigel continued, 'those old bashed plaster figures, the nativity, came out year after year, do you remember? They'd always give the baby Jesus a goodnight kiss before putting him in his cradle . . . Soph, do you remember?'

His voice was choking, and when he turned round to look at Sophie, the tears were running down his cheeks unchecked, and his hands hung defeated at his side.

Sophie stared at him without sympathy. She walked over to him reluctantly, and took hold of his hand.

'What a mess, Sophie,' he said. 'What a horrible mess.'

CHAPTER THIRTY-NINE

Greg Jones sat at the table in the tidy dining room of Barnstones with a blank sheet of paper in front of him. He looked up at the Christmas decorations and reflected that it was time they came down. Twelfth Night tomorrow, thank goodness. There was nothing more dead than left-overs from Christmas.

After the excitement of the successful concert, Greg had been unable to shake off a growing obsession, turning over in his mind the horrors of Sophie Brooks's telephone call, and the hurt suffered by Gabriella. Instead of going away, the whole episode festered in his mind, causing him to lose sleep and interrupting his concentration on planning for next term. Should he do something about it, or let it all calm down and forget the whole thing, hoping that stupid bugger, Nigel Brooks, had learned his lesson, and that they wouldn't have anything much to do with them in the future?

But Gabriella was talking about giving up playing the organ in church, and when Greg saw Nigel striding with apparent confidence past the window on his pastoral duties, his resentment and anger returned, and he finally decided that the vain twit needed a bit of a jolt to make him think.

To this end, Greg bought a paperback on church laws and procedures, and read it carefully. It seemed to him that a protest could be made, but that more than one parishioner was needed to make it. Who else would join him? He knew Mr

Ross had been horrified by the whole thing, had never much liked the Brookses, and might well agree to help. Then there was Colin Osman, always game for a bit of involvement. And old Don Cutt at the pub, he couldn't stand vicars at any price. Price, thought Greg, what about Tom Price? Tom had never thought the concert was a good idea. A carol service as usual was all the village needed. He'd said so, several times, in the pub. Well, that was four for a start. Shouldn't be too difficult to find a couple more.

Greg took up his pen and began to write. In formal, factual terms he described what had happened, and how in total it added up to the unsuitability of Nigel Brooks to be a priest in the village of Round Ringford. This, he knew from his researches, would have to be presented to the Bishop, who would then proceed on a carefully laid-down course.

'Greg?' It was Gabriella, back from a ride round the lanes on her bike. The snow had not lasted beyond Boxing Day, and now the roads were wet and gravelly where the gritting lorry had discharged its load. It was a dismal time of the year, but Gabriella always came back refreshed, full of sighting some small, strange bird or a premature sign of spring in the hedgerow.

Greg hastily turned his paper over and began to jot down a specimen plan for school. He wouldn't tell Gabriella until he'd really decided to go through with it.

Bill Turner had seen Gabriella cycling slowly down the lane through Bagley Woods, and the sight of her had interrupted his thoughts about Peggy and how much he loved her, never mind Joyce and her continual, undermining campaign to destroy him.

That's a good-looker, he thought, as she free-wheeled down the hill, her blonde hair streaming out behind her, no wonder old Nigel fancied her rotten. Peggy had given him an edited version of Sophie's end of the story, and he wondered if it had all been sorted. Dramas in Ringford had a habit of boiling up and then going off the boil when something turned down the heat. Now the concert was finished and done with, perhaps everything would get back to normal.

He came out of the wood, and on to the road. His boots were thick with mud, and the old canvas bag on his shoulder was heavy with a couple of rabbits, one for Joyce and himself, one for Peggy. I'll have to skin and draw it for Peg, he thought, she isn't that much of a countrywoman yet.

A strong gust of wind caught him and nearly blew off his old cap, so oily and shiny with use that it was difficult to see the original tweed pattern underneath. He saw the tiny figure of Gabriella at the bottom of the hill, blown from one side of the road to the other. A flurry of dead leaves whirled about his feet, and as he looked at the sky, over the village and to the hills beyond, the clouds scudded across, rain-filled and threatening.

He and Peggy had met infrequently, their weekend walks in the woods curtailed by the weather. She would still not allow him to visit her in the evenings, sure that Ivy Beasley was back on duty, monitoring their movements, and ready and waiting to convey any suspicious circumstances to Joyce. Joyce had been relatively quiet lately, but Bill had learned over the years that this kind of behaviour from her usually presaged a storm.

Peggy had been upset by Sophie's distress, after her first reaction to the funny side of it. She had seen a happy woman, a very cheerful, optimistic woman, slowly collapse into depression before her eyes. And all because of a possible love affair, the speculation mounting in the village, and the dangerous, one-sided nature of gossip surrounding it. She had not been blind to the parallels. She and Bill had taken second place in the agenda of conversation at the bus stop. But that did not mean that they were forgotten. Joyce was still the vulnerable, deserted wife in some people's eyes, and Peggy the wicked woman. The whole concert saga had made her think very seriously, and Bill had sensed a cooling-off in her, felt himself being pushed away and held at a distance.

He looked into the bluey grey landscape before him, and had a hard job to think of something cheerful. Must be something to look forward to, he thought, if it's only a pint with Tom in the pub.

A car pulled up behind him, and he looked round. It was Robert Bates, in his new, smart little run-around. Beside him sat Ivy Beasley, prim and straight, her basket on her lap and her gloved hands neatly folded over its handle.

'Morning, Bill,' said Robert. 'Got yourself something for the pot?'

Bill answered pleasantly, leaning over, resting his elbow on Robert's car.

'Morning, Ivy,' he said, looking at the tightly pursed lips, the face still pale and closed. She did not reply, and remained staring straight ahead through the windscreen.

'Auntie's still not quite a hundred per cent,' said Robert, embarrassed by Ivy's silence. 'We've just been into Bagley to do a bit of shopping.'

'How's the wedding preparations going, then, boy?' said Bill with a smile. Everyone liked Robert Bates, and since his childhood he had had the village people eating out of his hand, with his ready smile and willingness to help.

'Pretty well, thanks, Bill,' he said. 'Mind you, Mandy's getting in a state. Only hope she hasn't got cold feet by the time the big day comes!'

'Knows when she's on to a good thing, don't you worry,' said Ivy in a sharp voice.

'I think it's me that's on to a good thing, Auntie,' said Robert gently, taking off the handbrake and slowly moving off down the hill.

'Cheerio, Robert,' said Bill. 'That'll all come right on the day, you'll see!'

Bill walked on, thinking of his own wedding day, with Joyce a picture in her wedding dress. She'd been such a pretty girl, brown curly hair and lively hazel eyes – always a bit thin, but a good figure and enough flesh in the right places. He'd known her since school, watched her flirting with all the most popular boys, and teasing him for his dogged faithfulness.

216

When she'd finally settled on him, he couldn't believe his luck, though he knew his mum and dad had been a bit uneasy.

'Once a flirt, always a flirt,' Mum had said.

But she was wrong. Joyce had never once looked at another man, not even when things were bad between them.

Bill moved the heavy canvas bag from one shoulder to the other, and stood in the middle of the road without moving.

She'd been so excited when, a year or so after they were married, old Dr Russell had told her she was pregnant. Doc Russell wasn't so old then, of course; and there was no doubt he'd done his best.

Five months she'd lived in the womb, their little girl. They knew it was a girl, the hospital had told them. Joyce had been near to death, losing far too much blood, and then that dreadful hunt for the right blood group. And Joyce's mum and dad standing at the bottom of her hospital bed, looking like ghosts, but not as white as Joyce.

She'd said afterwards, Joyce had, that she felt herself leaving, floating up a long corridor of light, with specks in it, like motes in a shaft of sunlight.

But she hadn't left. They'd nursed her back to health. Well, health of a sort.

Bill walked on, his head down, unable to shake off the memories, willing himself to think of something else. As he approached the playing fields, he looked up to see Warren Jenkins and William Roberts rushing about the muddy football pitch, dribbling the ball, passing to each other, and shooting goals between the leaning goalposts. Forty years ago, it was me and Tom Price out there, he thought. What have I got to look back on since then?

It hadn't been all bad, he scolded himself. Joyce had seemed to rally for a while, but then no more babies had come along, and she wouldn't go near a hospital for tests. Said she'd had more than enough of hospitals, couldn't face it. Her mother hadn't been much help, either, putting Joyce off the tests with those terrible stories of women she'd known. Put herself like a wedge between them in the end, and by the time she died it was too late. Joyce was a stranger to him, had made herself his sworn enemy. They lived in the same house, but that was about it.

He had arrived at the shop, and automatically climbed the steps. He needed to see Peggy, and hoped the shop would be empty.

'Mornin' Bill,' said old Ellen, as he opened the door. 'What you got in that bag, then?' she continued. 'You look like a jolly swagman. Least, you would if you smiled.'

Bill smiled broadly at the old woman. Trust old Ellen to sort him out.

' 'Ad yer invitation, then?' she said.

Peggy was looking at him warmly from behind the counter, and he felt his spirits rising steadily.

'You mean Robert's wedding?' he asked, dumping his bag on the floor and stretching his shoulders.

'I've had mine,' said Peggy. 'It was very nice of them to ask me, I wasn't really expecting it.'

'No,' said Bill, 'I haven't seen an invitation. Maybe it'll come tomorrow. I saw Robert on the hill, but he didn't say anything.'

'Sure to ask you, Bill,' said Ellen, fishing into her old rexine bag, and bringing out a crumped envelope. 'Here,' she said, 'I got mine yesterday. Took me answer up the farm this mornin'. It says to reply to Mandy's folks, but I thought I'd save a bit of postage.'

She began to gather her packages together, and turned to the door.

'Just a word,' she said, looking quite seriously at Bill. 'Old Ivy's done 'er worst with them poor Brookses. She'll be on the warpath again shortly, so just watch it, both of yer. She may look poorly, but looks deceive. Don't want to see yer in trouble, neither of yer. Cheerio then, Bill, Peggy . . .'

Bill helped her down the steps, then came back into the shop, closing the door behind him.

Peggy was grinning.

'What's so funny?' Bill said. 'Old Ellen's always right, and she knows Ivy Beasley better than most.'

'It was just the thought of the pair of us in trouble . . . what sort of trouble does she have in mind? Ducking in the village pond? A day or two in the stocks?'

Bill leaned over the counter, and took Peggy's hand.

'You're cold,' he said.

'It is cold,' she replied.

'Let me warm you up,' he said.

'No,' said Peggy.

'All right, then,' said Bill, 'give us half a pound of Cheddar instead.'

Nobody else came into the shop for the next quarter of an hour, and Peggy made Bill a cup of coffee. They sat in the kitchen, with the connecting door giving them a view of the shop, and chatted idly.

Mandy Butler was the next customer, coming in for a bar of chocolate before going down to Bates's Farm for yet another conference with her future mother-in-law.

Bill got up, shouldered the canvas bag, and, giving Peggy a surreptitious peck on the cheek, walked through to the shop door. 'How's it going, Mandy?' he said.

Mandy sighed heavily, and turned an exaggeratedly tragic face to Bill.

'If only you knew,' she said. 'If I'd known what I know now, I'd have settled for elopement, or even living in sin with my Robert. You lose sight of what it's all about, don't you.'

Bill smiled at her very kindly. 'Don't worry, Mandy,' he said, 'you'll be the most beautiful bride Ringford's seen for many a year. Just imagine yourself, gliding down the aisle on your dad's arm, and then you see dear Robert's face, smiling at you as you join him . . . it'll all be worth it, take it from me.'

It had been worth it for Joyce, he thought sadly, for a while.

CHAPTER FORTY

Bill let himself into his back door, pushing aside the heavy curtain shrouding the panes of dusty glass. There was something different about the kitchen, and it did not take him long to see that Joyce had cleared up.

This was a very rare occurrence. It usually meant that she had done something bad, smashed something precious to Bill, and wanted to get one up on him before the inevitable scene.

She was upstairs. He could hear her moving about the bedroom, and he called up the stairs, 'Joycey! I'm home.' He got no reply, but this did not surprise him. Better go and see what's missing, lying in pieces in the dustbin, he thought. But everything seemed to be in order, the sitting room tidy and the dusting done.

Bill went outside and poked about in the bags of food waste and old newspapers. Underneath a pile of magazines, brought to Joyce weekly by Ivy Beasley, he saw some torn-up scraps of paper. He pulled them out and saw pieces of an envelope with handwriting on it. There were more bits of card, and he saw printed words. He could read some of it: '. . . pleasure of . . . at the marriage of their daugh . . .'. He knew then what Joyce had done.

She came downstairs with her head down. She had dressed carelessly, and was carrying her old teddy bear, moth-eaten and no longer growling. She held him carefully, her hand supporting his back, in case he should fall.

'Joyce,' said Bill. 'Did we get any letters this morning?'

She shook her head, and went into the sitting room, shutting the door behind her.

Bill shrugged, and went back into the kitchen. What's the use, he thought. She won't own up, and anyway, what if she does? Just one more row, getting nowhere. Best ignore it.

But Joyce had other ideas. She appeared at the kitchen door, still holding her teddy bear, now with his face into her shoulder, while she patted his back gently.

'Not been asked to the wedding, then?' she said mockingly. Bill did not answer, but filled the kettle and put it on the gas ring.

'Still,' continued Joyce, 'it's not surprising, is it? Snubbed by the whole village, I shouldn't wonder. You and your fancy woman, canoodling in front of anybody who happens to look out of the window. Not that I care, but it's disgusting!' Her voice had risen to a shout, and Bill turned round to face her.

'Ivy been round, has she?' he said coldly. Joyce flushed, and avoided his eyes. 'Not content with stirring up real trouble with the vicar and the Joneses, she's on to us again, is she?'

He picked up a women's magazine from the kitchen table and waved it under Joyce's nose. She backed away.

'Been charity visiting, has she?' he said, louder now in mounting anger. 'I should have thought you could think for yourself for once. First your mother, and now old Ivy – always ready for a bit of juicy gossip, aren't you, Joyce?' He raised his arm, as if to strike her, but quickly turned away, letting it fall.

What can I say? he thought. Ivy's right. I'd be in there with Peggy every moment of the day and night if I could. Guilty as charged.

He took the boiling kettle off the stove, and poured the scalding water into the teapot.

'Go back in the room, Joyce,' he said flatly. 'I'll bring you a nice cup of tea.'

Looking disappointed, her colour retreating and leaving her face its customary greyish white, Joyce hugged her bear tightly and went to sit down.

Doris Ashbourne's sitting room was warm, the gas fire popping reassuringly and her bits of brass twinkling in the light.

'Nearly dark already, Doris,' said Ellen, 'and only half past three.'

She sat in Doris's most comfortable chair, close to the fire. Her usual bulk was increased by three layers of woollies, purple upon black upon scarlet. The effect was ecclesiastical, but watered down by the baggy brown tweed skirt and scuffed fur-lined boots, too big for their former owner and not much worn.

'Don't know if Ivy will make it today,' said Doris from the kitchen. 'I saw her yesterday, and she wouldn't say for definite. At least it's not raining now.'

''Ere she comes,' said Ellen, looking out of the big window with its commanding view of Macmillan Gardens. 'Goin' at her usual crackin' pace – she must be feelin' better.'

Doris brought in the tray of tea, and went back for a plate of yellow lemon-cake slices, crunchy on top where she had sprinkled granulated sugar and lemon juice on the hot sponge.

'Come on in, Ivy,' she said, 'I've just brewed up.'

Ivy Beasley took off her coat and hat and sat down. She leaned over and looked at the lemon cake.

'You didn't cut that when it was still hot, I hope, Doris,' she said, picking up a small knife and pressing with the flat blade on top of a piece of cake.

'Course not, Ivy,' said Doris, nettled. 'You're not the only one who knows how to bake.'

Tea was handed round, and the lemon cake began to disappear rapidly.

'Very nice indeed, Doris,' said Ellen. 'I'll 'ave the recipe off you later.'

Ivy laughed scornfully. 'You haven't baked a cake since you

stopped cooking at the Hall,' she said. 'Probably forgotten how. Mind you, you should have more idea than that Mandy Butler. I had a slice of fruit cake she'd made at the Bateses, and didn't know how to get it down.'

Doris and Ellen exchanged glances. 'All the fruit sunk to the bottom, Ivy?' said Doris.

'And dry as sawdust,' said Ivy, nodding. 'She hasn't the first idea.'

Doris tried to turn the conversation to the next WI meeting, but Ivy was not to be deflected.

'Beats me,' she said, 'why Robert couldn't marry a girl from his own village, or at least a farmer's daughter. What good is a slip of a hairdresser going to be to him on that farm?'

'She's very nice,' said Doris weakly.

' "Nice" is not what's wanted,' said Ivy firmly. 'Olive Bates has been a good half of that farm for years. Won't be long before she and Ted want to step down and let Robert take it on. Can't see that Mandy up at the crack of dawn doing the chickens, can you?'

'I 'eard as Robert don't necessarily want to take on the farm when 'is father goes,' said Ellen, hoping to be one up on Ivy Beasley.

'Never said anything about it to me,' said Ivy, glaring at her, 'and Robert tells me most things.'

'Won't for much longer,' said Ellen slyly. 'That Mandy'll soon put a stop to them Monday afternoon visits of 'is. Your little boy's grown up, Ivy, and you'll 'ave to let go.'

'Don't talk nonsense, Ellen Biggs,' said Ivy. 'You don't get any better as you get older.'

They settled down with a last slice of lemon cake, and Doris used all her skill to get the talk round to the next speaker at the WI, a cheery lady from Fletching who demonstrated Indian cooking for English palates.

'You won't catch me making any of that curry muck,' said Ivy, and then leaned forward in her chair, staring out of the window.

'There he goes,' she said with satisfaction. 'Back to his tea, and the arms of his loving wife.'

The others watched Bill Turner get off his bike and push it through the garden gate.

'You can be very cruel, Ivy,' said Doris. 'It's not all black and white there, not by any means.'

'What do it take to learn you a lesson, Ivy?' said Ellen, with force, and she struggled to her feet. 'I'm glad to see you better,' she continued, 'but you should beware the good Lord don't strike you dumb one o' these days.'

Doris Ashbourne took a white invitation card from her mantelshelf, and looked at it with a smile.

'What shall we get Mandy and Robert for a wedding present, then?' she said, fed up with Ellen and Ivy and their constant bickering.

'I got mine already,' said Ivy, standing up and straightening her skirt. 'A nice new book from Smith's in Tresham, reduced in the sale I'm glad to say: *Cookery for Beginners*. What do you think of that, Doris?'

CHAPTER FORTY-ONE

Tom Price stood at the top of his farmyard, his brown overall stained with pig muck, his big hands stuffed into ragged pockets. He watched as Greg Jones approached, leather shoes sliding on the wet concrete of the yard.

At first light, when Tom had gone out to check on early lambs, the village had been a uniform grey, hills misty and blurred, a landscape without dimensions. Clinging fog had imperceptibly turned to rain, and this had become torrential, filling rutted tracks and bursting through a hole in the guttering above the back door of the farmhouse, spouting a clear stream of water on to the yard and Doreen's tubs of straggly wallflower plants.

The wind, a wilful litter-lout, had blown waste paper out of bins and round the village, and a mangy old farm cat, its tail erect and fur staring, like a bottle brush, chased a torn paper bag across the yard, pouncing and then losing interest, embarrassed at its own foolishness.

The pavement outside the farm had been fouled by a wandering dog, and Tom watched Greg Jones wiping his shoe on a tuft of grass by the stable door.

'Morning,' said Tom. 'What can I do for you, Greg?'

'I wondered if I might have word,' said Greg, 'if you're not too busy, that is.'

Greg had chosen this Saturday morning to make his first approach, whilst Gabbie was out shopping in Tresham. No point in worrying her. He might find nobody willing to support him in his complaint against Nigel Brooks.

Tom stumped off down the yard, Greg in tow, and, taking his boots off at the door, he beckoned Greg into the kitchen.

'Got some coffee on the go?' he said to Doreen, who was deep in a flower arrangement, bits of wire and languishing flowers strewn all over the table.

Doreen frowned at him, saw Greg, and went to fill the kettle. Tom led Greg into the sitting room and indicated a seat.

After a few pleasantries about the weather and the farm, Greg seemed unable to come to the point of his visit, and Tom began to wonder what the little bugger wanted. Doreen brought in a tray of coffee and biscuits, and tactfully disappeared.

'Right, then,' said Tom, 'what was it you come about?' He looked at Greg trying to balance a cup and saucer on his bony knee, and wondered what that lovely girl Gabriella saw in him.

Greg put his cup down on the low table in front of him and cleared his throat.

'I expect you heard about the fracas at Christmas over the concert, Tom?'

'The what?' said Tom, speaking louder than usual, remembering Greg's deafness.

'Gabriella's difficulty with Sophie Brooks?'

Tom shook his head. 'Better begin at the beginning,' he said, 'but don't take too long. Time and tide and pigs wait for no man.' He smiled kindly at Greg.

Stumbling over his words at first, Greg gave Tom a well-organised account of what had happened, and outlined his plan for a complaint.

Tom looked dumbfounded. He shifted his bulky figure uneasily in the big armchair. 'We never done that before,' he said, 'though I've heard of it in other parishes. You sure it were that serious, Greg?'

Grey sat up straight. 'It was sufficiently serious to bring Gabriella and myself near to the first major dispute in our marriage,' he said stiffly. 'Anyway, I can't take it further unless I get five other people in the parish to join me in making the complaint.'

Tom knew from long experience on the Parish Council that it didn't do to make a decision on anything straight away. Bide your time, boy – that had been his father's most useful piece of advice.

'Well now, Greg,' he said, 'this'll take a lot of thinking about. You'd best give me a few days to consider what's the right thing to do. Villages are difficult, you know,' he added. 'It isn't just what you do today that matters. You have to look to how things'll be next week, next year. We've all got to get along together somehow, you know.'

Greg stood up. He thought he knew what Tom's considered answer would be, and wanted to be gone. He was not at all sure now that the plan was viable, seen in the light of Tom's reaction. Still, he would canvas one or two others. He needed to do some more thinking.

On his way back to Barnstones, he met Colin Osman, walking along with a new puppy. It was a very small brindled Cairn pup, and bounced all over the pavement, not yet sure what was required of it. It looked so incongruous at the end of its narrow lead, in turn attached to the tall figure of Colin Osman, that Greg laughed.

'What have you got there, Colin?' he said.

Colin Osman looked embarrassed, and laughed loudly. 'It's not mine, of course,' he said. 'It's Pat's new toy.' He pulled at the lead and said, 'Sit, Tiggy! Sit!' The little dog looked at him in surprise.

'Tiggy?' said Greg.

'Short for Mrs Tiggywinkle,' said Colin, looking even more embarrassed. 'It's a she.'

They stood for a few minutes, discussing the junior football team, and then Colin asked Greg if he had anything he'd like to contribute to the Newsletter, now coming along nicely, but in need of a few more general items.

'I'll give it some thought,' Greg said. 'What's the deadline?'

'Next Friday,' said Colin, and tried to ignore the little dog, now crouching in the gutter with a pained expression on its whiskery face.

'You should praise it,' said Greg. 'It's like training a child, so they tell me.'

'Yes, well, I think it's time we were getting on,' Colin said, tugging at the lead. 'Come on, Tiggy . . . Cheers, Greg, speak to you soon.'

Greg went on his way, aware that he had not sounded out Colin Osman, but with the germ of a new idea stirring in his mind.

By Monday, Greg had talked to Don Cutt, the Rosses, and the new chap, Bright, who lived opposite the school. He'd had varying responses, but in general there was an unwillingness to take a step as serious as a formal complaint to the Bishop. Don Cutt had advocated a good going over on Ladies' Path on a suitably dark night. 'Get him where it hurts,' he guffawed, 'that'll cool him down!'

Greg was horrified, and retreated from the pub without buying a drink, thereby forfeiting any support he might have got from the landlord.

Roger Bright, a straightforward man with a pleasant wife and easy-going children, was sympathetic but detached. 'Not a churchgoing man myself,' he said, 'but it would have to be pretty serious to do what you suggest, I would say.'

Mr and Mrs Ross both looked terrified at the suggestion that they should join him in a course of action which would mean drawing attention to themselves in the village. 'We agree that Reverend Brooks is not half the man Cyril Collins was, but he must be given time to settle.' Mr Ross spoke for them both, and his wife nodded meekly from behind the teapot.

Greg was forced to admit that his idea for a complaint had foundered, but on Monday evening he came home from school in a cheerful mood. The day had gone well, and he'd been congratulated by the headmaster on his new plan for fieldwork in the spring.

'There's a nice concert on the radio this evening,' said Gabriella after they'd had tea and stacked the dishes in the machine.

'Great,' said Greg. 'You switch on, and I'll join you later. I must just jot down a few words for Colin Osman – promised him something for the Newsletter.' The new idea had begun to take shape.

He took a pad of paper from his document case, settled down at the dining-room table, and began to write.

CHAPTER FORTY-TWO

The entrance hall in the vicarage was cold, a chill rising up from the black and white tiles, and Sophie thought for the hundredth time that they should have the telephone moved to another room, where she wouldn't have to put on a coat to make a call. She'd had one or two lengthy chats to Paris, usually when Nigel was out on his rounds. She knew they were expensive calls, but she needed to talk, especially to someone outside the village. And anyway, she rehearsed her excuse, since Milly had announced her pregnancy with such excitement, she had wanted to keep in touch, wishing they were nearer.

Nigel wouldn't have the telephone in his study. His sermons were difficult enough to write, he said, without his train of thought being interrupted by the telephone. He had found it particularly difficult lately, ever since that terrible business with Gabriella Jones. He wasn't guilty of anything but stupidity and thoughtlessness, he believed, but didn't feel quite so sure as before of his right to stand in the pulpit and preach.

'Hello?' said Sophie. 'Ringford Vicarage – who is it?'

'Hello, Sophie, it's Peggy here.'

Sophie moved from one foot to the other, in an effort to keep her circulation going. Old Ricky, stretched out on the draughty door mat, bony and arthritic, watched her hopefully.

230

'Peggy, how nice,' she said. 'How are you?'

'Fine,' said Peggy, 'And you?'

'So-so,' said Sophie. 'We are still a bit gloomy up here at the vicarage. Why don't you come and have a coffee and cheer me up?'

'That is just what I was going to suggest,' said Peggy. 'I'll be up soon after I've shut up shop.'

That's odd, thought Sophie. It sounded more than just a casual call.

Peggy put down the telephone and went to serve Jean Jenkins in the shop.

'Eddie Jenkins,' she said, 'you've grown several inches since yesterday!'

Eddie laughed at her, putting out his arms to be lifted up on to the counter. Peggy cuddled him close, then sat him on the edge in front of her, supporting him with one hand and reaching into her apron pocket with the other.

'What have we got here?' she said, and brought out a small fruit sweet wrapped in paper. 'Healthy ones, so it says on the packet,' she reassured Jean, who shrugged.

'It's a losing battle, Peggy,' she said. 'Once they start school you might as well forget it. All mine have got good teeth, thank goodness. Foxy says it's his fresh vegetables, and he could be right.'

'Well, this one's not starting school yet awhile,' said Peggy, lifting him down carefully, and leading him by the hand into the kitchen. 'There you are,' she said. 'There's Gilbert waiting to say hello.'

'If you ever give up the shop,' said Jean Jenkins, 'you should start a play group, you're a natural.'

Peggy smiled, and came back into the shop. 'What's new today in the village, Jean?' she said.

'Not a lot,' said Jean, retrieving Eddie from a shelf stacked with packets of biscuits. ''Cept they say Greg Jones is getting up a petition against the vicar.'

'Ah that,' said Peggy. 'I don't think there can be any truth in that one, Jean, do you?'

'Not so sure,' said Jean. 'Mrs Ross were telling Mary York, and her Graham told Fox, that Mr Jones had been to see Mr Ross, wantin' his support.'

Peggy shook her head. 'Well, I think the less we say about it the better,' she said. 'I think Sophie Brooks has probably had just about enough of it. And after all,' she added, looking directly at Jean and hoping she would take in what she was about to say, 'nothing at all happened. It was all rumour and gossip, spread mostly by you-know-who, and blown up out of all proportion.'

'Enough to cause a lot of trouble, though,' said Jean obstinately. 'They say Mr and Mrs Jones were at each other's throats, not to mention the Brookses . . . and anyway, Peggy, there's no smoke without fire, you know that as well as me . . .'

Peggy ignored the heavy hint, and took Jean's wire basket. 'What's important, though,' she said, 'is that we don't make it any worse than it is. It might be very serious for Reverend Brooks, could cost him his job. I'm not sure Greg Jones realises that.'

But Peggy's well-meant advice was too late. Almost every person who came into the shop during the day referred to Greg Jones's perambulations round the village. By the time Peggy shut up the Stores, had a quick wash and put on a warm coat, she was very worried.

'My goodness, it's cold!' she said, as Sophie opened the heavy front door of the vicarage. Peggy remembered the first time she came to see the Brookses, when Sophie had been waiting with Ricky at the open door, beaming with delight at her new home and the bright prospect of country life ahead of her.

They went into the big kitchen – 'The only warm room in the house,' said Sophie – and Peggy sat down at the table, taking off coat, scarf and gloves.

'How's Nigel?' she said.

Sophie made a face. 'Not really back to his old bounce,' she said. 'It's really knocked him for six, this one.'

'Have you ever had anything happen like this before?' Peggy said. Nothing was spelled out. It wasn't necessary.

Sophie shook her head firmly. 'Never,' she said. 'We've had our ups and downs with the children, but never anything like this before. But then, we've never lived in a small village before.'

'Have you heard about Greg Jones?' Peggy said, getting round to the purpose of her visit.

'What do you mean?' said Sophie. 'We haven't seen or heard anything of either of them. Gabriella beetles off after church, and anyway, Nigel is trying to keep out of their way for a bit.'

'Oh dear,' said Peggy. 'Then I think I should warn you that Greg is thinking of making some sort of complaint against Nigel.'

Sophie's colour changed. 'Complaint?' she said. 'Who to? What about, exactly?'

Peggy sighed. She explained that once more it was all rumour, but that Greg was said to be trying to drum up support for a statement of Nigel's unsuitability for the parish of Round Ringford. If he got the backing he needed, a formal document would be sent to the Bishop.

'Oh my God!' said Sophie. She sat down heavily opposite Peggy, and stared at her. 'It's my fault, isn't it, Peggy. If I hadn't lost my wits and telephoned Gabriella Jones, it would all have come to nothing. What can we do?'

She looked pleadingly at Peggy, as if there might be some way of stopping the gathering storm. But Peggy was silent.

'It could drive us out,' Sophie said, her voice rising. 'It could be the end for Nigel! Do they realise that?'

'Did I hear my name?' said Nigel, coming in with a smile for Peggy. 'How are you, my dear?' he said. 'Heavens,' he added, looking at them both. 'Is the end of the world nigh, and no one told me?'

Sophie took a deep breath, stood up and went over to Nigel, taking his hand and leading him to a chair by the table. 'Sit down, dear,' she said. 'We need to talk, all three of us.'

★

Colin Osman stood at the big picture windows overlooking the park, and studied a sheet of closely written paper. I can't print this, he said to himself. What can he be thinking of?

When he'd met Greg in the street, he'd been pleased to see his interest. At least Greg could be relied on to write reasonable English, unlike some of the contributors he'd had. Something jolly about school, or geography trips to Cheddar Gorge, anything of that nature would have been welcome. But this? Colin read it again, and wished Pat would come back. She had gone round to Jean Jenkins with the new pup, ostensibly to ask her to do a bit of extra cleaning, but really to show off Tiggy to anyone who happened to be around.

It was nearly dark, but Colin could see well enough across the park. The trees were still bare, black branches against a cold sky, and in the distance there were lights at the Hall windows. Standings must be back, he thought. They're always pleading poverty, but seem to manage a skiing holiday every year.

He heard Pat at the front door, and turned to greet her.

'Can she oblige?' he said with a smile. Then he saw small, muddy footprints on the cream carpet, and his smile faded. 'At this rate,' he said, fetching a floor cloth from the kitchen, 'we shall need Jean Jenkins as a permanent fixture.'

'Sorry I'm a bit later than intended,' said Pat, bending down to take off Tiggy's lead, her cheeks rosy with the cold, 'but you know Jean Jenkins. There's no such thing as a quick word with Jean.'

'What's the latest, then?' said Colin, sitting down in his chair and picking up Greg's piece of paper.

'Oh, it's still the Brooks–Jones saga,' said Pat, 'Same old thing.'

'Speaking of which,' said Colin, 'take a look at this.'

Pat read through to the end without comment. Then she echoed his own thoughts. 'You can't print this,' she said. 'We'll be sued for libel.'

'I don't think it's libellous,' Colin said. 'Greg's too clever for that. But it will put the cat among the pigeons in a big way. What the hell am I going to do about it?'

'Don't print it,' said Pat. 'Tell them you haven't got the space. Tell him that's not what the Newsletter is for. Tell him anything, but for God's sake, don't print it!'

Colin absentmindedly patted Tiggy's fuzzy head, and she wriggled with delight, sprinkling the carpet with a few excited droplets.

'Bloody hell!' said Colin, getting up for the cloth.

Pat smiled indulgently and took the puppy on to her lap. She read through the paper once more, and shook her head.

'It's quite clever really, isn't it,' she said. 'It's what he doesn't say that's really shocking. All this stuff about the problems of a modern-day parson, and the difficulty of selecting the right man for the right parish . . . and then this bit at the end, it's quite obvious what he means.'

She read aloud, causing Colin to shudder. ' "Those most at risk of forgetting their calling," ' read Pat, ' "are the late-comers to the cloth. Too used to a worldly life, to its pleasures and temptations of the flesh, they do not see the danger signals in time. Vanity and insensitivity are the chief enemies of the contemporary parson . . ." '

'No more, please,' groaned Colin. They sat in silence for while, and then Pat jumped up. 'I know,' she said, 'you can edit it. That's part of your job, remember.'

Colin grasped at the straw. 'Right!' he said. 'That's the solution. I should be able to water it down and make it relatively harmless.'

Ivy Beasley watched Peggy return from the vicarage in the twilight, and concluded she had had another secret assignation with Bill Turner.

Now the weather's on the turn, Mother, she said, they'll be off to the woods like rabbits again.

She drew the curtains against the falling darkness, and took up her knitting, a pullover for Robert, a Fair Isle pattern and needing concentration. She had had television for several years, but seldom turned it on. It was such rubbish, and even when she was enjoying a programme she had a faint feeling of guilt, of her mother looking over her shoulder, shocked and disapproving.

She looked up at the photograph of her mother and father on their wedding day. Ivy's mother's face had a faint, worried smile, and the tips of her fingers rested lightly in her new husband's palm.

You weren't exactly the radiant bride, were you, Mother? said Ivy.

There was no reply. There never was, when Ivy got personal.

Ivy looked at her father's face, straight and stern. His thick, wavy hair was cut brutally short, and his eyes had a startled, staring expression as if he were being slowly throttled by his stiff white collar.

But he was a handsome man, said Ivy. I can see why you married him, Mother.

Silence.

Reminds me of Reverend Brooks a bit, Ivy thought, this time to herself, when he's up in the pulpit, serious and thoughtful, preaching his sermon and trying to change the wicked ways of this village. Mind you, there's precious few of them there to listen. Poor man, I feel sorry for him. And now there's this petition, or whatever it is, from Mr Jones.

Satisfied, are you, Ivy? Her mother had found her voice again.

Don't know what you mean, said Ivy, twisting in her chair, and yanking more wool from her knitting bag.

Who was it spread the rumours about him and Mrs Jones? You had a big success there, Ivy Dorothy.

Somebody had to stop what that Jones woman was up to! Ivy gripped her knitting needles hard. Her hands were sweating, and the wool struck, making it difficult to slide off the stitches.

Backfired, though, didn't it, said her mother's voice, sharply knowing.

Shut up, do, Mother! I'm getting this all wrong.

Can't change the subject, Ivy.

Ivy threw her knitting, with all the colours tangled, into her knitting bag, and went through to the kitchen. As she filled her kettle, turning the tap on full to drown her mother's relentless voice, she thought she heard scratching at the back door.

'Tiddles!' she said, opening the door a crack. 'What you doing here at this time of night?' She opened the door wider, and the little cat rushed in, rubbing herself ingratiatingly round Ivy's stout legs.

'Forgotten to feed you, has she? Her thoughts elsewhere, no doubt,' she said, pouring a saucer of milk and setting it down on the tiled kitchen floor. Gilbert began to lap enthusiastically, purring at the same time.

Ivy made a pot of tea, put a large piece of fruit cake on a plate, and, with milk, sugar and a cup and saucer, took the loaded tray back into the sitting room. She turned on the wireless, and settled down to listen to the play.

Don't think you can forget I'm here, said the voice. You always were one for not facing up to things. If your beloved vicar loses his job, it will be thanks to you, Ivy Beasley.

Ivy put her teacup back on the saucer with a shaking hand, spilling hot tea over her mother's embroidered tray cloth, and stood up. She reached for the photograph in its heavy, dark wooden frame, and turned into the middle of the room, her eyes wild. She walked over to the oak drop-leaved table, and, lifting the wedding portrait high over her head, brought it down with a splintering crash, face down on the polished surface.

CHAPTER FORTY-THREE

Richard Standing stood at the long windows of his drawing room, a glass of red wine in one hand, and in the other the latest issue of the Ringford Newsletter. He had turned directly to his own poetic contribution, and smiled and nodded to himself as he read it again.

'Not bad, not bad,' he said. 'It really looks quite good in print. What do you think, Susie?' He turned to hand the Newsletter to Susan Standing, resting with her feet up on the long sofa, a glass of sparkling mineral water and a dish of cashew nuts on the table beside her.

'Let me see it, darling,' said Susan. 'Dear Jenkins brought it in this morning, but I only glanced at it.'

'Mind on other things?' said Richard, with a conspiratorial look.

Susan took the newsletter and began to read aloud:

> 'Now is the winter nearly spent,
> And merry spring is on the lea,
> Soon will the bullfinch be content
> With yellow crocus for its tea.'

She began to laugh, and hastily turned it into a choke.

'Are you all right, Susan?' Richard said anxiously, and rubbed her back gently.

She nodded. 'Fine,' she said. 'I'm perfectly all right,

Richard, just a piece of nut caught in my throat.' She adjusted the cushions behind her head and continued reading.

'Well?' said Richard.

'Oh, yes, well, it's really good, Richard. As you say, it looks better in print. Really moving, darling.'

Richard refilled his glass from a dusty bottle on the shaky-legged table by the great fireplace, easing George along with the toe of his shoe, and managing a very small dig in the terrier's ribs without Susan noticing.

'I'm getting supper tonight,' he said. 'You stay there with your feet up. Take it easy, and tell me all the village news later.' He left the room, and the little dog lowered its beribboned head on to its front paws with a sigh.

There were a dozen or so pages, reports of village events and dates for the coming month. Colin had written a cheerful editorial, and made Fred Mills's gardening tips comprehensible to the average amateur. Mr Ross had written a memoir of his boyhood in industrial Bradford, and Miss Layton at the school had compiled a page of puzzles for little ones.

Susan turned to the last page.

Headed 'Comment for Today – An Endpiece', Greg's contribution had been reduced by at least a third. But in spite of Colin's best efforts, the message came through loud and clear. The job of the parish priest was a difficult one, it needed a very special person to do it well. Most failed, and some failed dismally. Colin had cut out the bit about vanity and insensitivity, but the comment on latecomers to the job was still there. 'Greg does have a point,' Colin had said to Pat, 'and it is very relevant to the issue.'

Pat had been doubtful, but Colin had begun to see himself as a questing editor, righting a few wrongs in the village, and left it in.

Susan once more sat up, and put her feet to the floor. She went to the door and called. 'Richard! I say, Richard! Come here a minute.'

He came at the double, rushing into the room and saying, 'What is it? What's the matter?'

'Calm down,' said Susan. 'It's just something in the Newsletter – read it for yourself. I think we may have some trouble brewing here.'

Richard sat down, breathing fast, and read Greg's piece.

'That's awkward,' he said. 'I suppose it's all about that nonsense with Jones's wife?'

'Gorgeous Gabriella,' said Susan. 'Yes, I'm afraid so. But what a sneaky way of getting his revenge! I hate these slow-burning campaigns – give me a short, sharp shock any time. Why doesn't he just kick him in the balls and be done with it?'

Richard laughed. 'Poor old Nigel, he's a good fellow,' he said, 'but we're not done with it yet, I fear. Now, do you fancy a nice piece of salmon, lightly poached, with a delicate sauce and buttered potatoes?'

Susan's usual pallor took on a greenish tinge. She shook her head. 'I think a Marmite sandwich is what I really fancy,' she said.

Bill cycled down Macmillan Gardens and turned right, past Victoria Villa, the shop, the Brights' new house and the Village Hall. It was a beautiful afternoon, and as he turned up the Bagley Road he got off his bike to retie his shoelace. He leaned against his cross-bar and looked back across the Green.

The sun was still travelling on a low arc in the sky, but it shone with brilliance in the cold, clear air, turning humps of damp moss on the school extension roof to a vivid shade of lime green. Away over the park, Bill could see growing wheat, furrows still visible, a reminder of a new season's bounty to come.

Afternoon playtime had sent the children into the play-ground shrieking and pushing at each other. One or two hefty boys hadn't bothered to put on anoraks, but smaller, more timid ones had heeded their mother's warning to wrap up warm.

Bill looked away over the park and to the hills beyond, sharply outlined against the shining sky. Ted Bates's old barn stood out, black and solid on the horizon, and a couple of crows hung in the air, then wheeled on the wind and disappeared behind the trees. Bill pulled his scarf tighter, and set off again up Bagley Hill. As he propped up his bike against the rickety fence, his eyes were held by a patch of pure white snowdrops, sudden and unexpected, gleaming against dark ivy under the trees.

'Here you are, Peg,' he said, as they met at the clearing by the tree stump. He handed her a tiny bunch of exquisite white flowers, anthers and petal tips a delicate green, carefully arranged with a shiny ivy leaf and held by an elastic band from his pocket.

'How lovely, Bill,' she said, reaching up to kiss his cold cheek.

'Would have brought you orchids,' he said, 'but these were going free.'

'We'd better keep walking,' Peggy said. 'It's too cold to hang about.'

'Madam's hide is coming along nicely,' said Bill, taking her hand and squeezing it. 'Come the spring, we should be able to have a few bird-watching sessions . . .'

'We'll see,' said Peggy. 'I shouldn't really have come today, with all this going on in the village with Greg and the Brookses. Have you seen the Newsletter?'

Bill shook his head. 'Haven't looked at it yet,' he said, 'but if Joyce doesn't decide to tear it up first, I'll probably get round to it this evening. Anything exciting in it?'

Peggy told him about Greg's broadside at the vicar, and how it had been the sole topic of conversation in the shop all day.

'I tried to stop people speculating and making it worse,' she said, 'but it's gone too far. Still, Sophie and Nigel are now at least prepared for something like this.'

'Not serious enough to reach the Bishop's ears, then?' said Bill, pulling brambles aside on the overgrown path. 'That first idea of Greg Jones was a real killer, could have had the Brookses out on their ears.'

They walked on, through the mud and snagging briars,

holding hands and talking about Ringford affairs. Totally at ease with each other, they now had no need of passionate declarations, were content for the moment to be in each other's company.

Coming out of the wood, they were alarmed to see a figure approaching down the side of the wheatfield.

'No good trying to pretend we're not here,' said Bill. 'And anyway,' he added, 'we've nothing to be ashamed of. Well, not much,' he added, seeing Peggy's expression.

They waited until the figure was close enough to recognise. 'It's Mr Richard,' Peggy said. 'He's got his gun, been shooting.'

'Afternoon, Turner,' said Richard Standing, and lifted his hat to Peggy. 'Lovely afternoon, Mrs Palmer.' he added, 'wonderful weather for walking.' He smiled kindly at them both, and walked on.

'Whew!' said Bill. 'I was waiting for him to ask me about the fence I'm supposed to be putting up in the long field. He must be in a real good mood about something.'

'Couldn't stop smiling, could he,' said Peggy.

'Well,' said Bill, 'I've witnessed one or two of *his* secret assignations in the past. Village memories are long, as he well knows.'

'No, I don't think it was us,' said Peggy. 'There was something in his walk, very springy, it was. He's either in love or inherited a fortune.'

'Or both,' said Bill. 'Some buggers have all the luck.'

The lovely afternoon had caused Ivy and Doris Ashbourne to walk slowly on their way to the Lodge for tea with Ellen.

'Old Fred was out there digging when I came by,' said Doris, 'making it look terrible hard work. One of these days he'll have to give it up, take it a bit easy.'

'He's an old fool,' said Ivy. 'Never knows when to stop. I saw him at the bus stop yesterday, and he said the soil was lovely, just like Christmas puddin', he said. Going senile, if you ask me.'

'Well, we've all survived another winter,' said Doris. 'You can feel the turn of the year, I reckon, it's in the air.'

Ivy had no time for such metaphysical thoughts, and stepped carefully round a large puddle outside Ellen's front gate. She had for the first time been reluctant to turn out for the weekly tea party. Her sleep had been disturbed by nightmares, in which she rescued Nigel Brooks singlehanded from a number of fatal situations. She had woken exhausted and with a splitting headache. Now she shrank from the inevitable topic of teatime conversation, and wondered if she could plead illness and go back home.

But it was too late. Ellen was at her door, smiling a welcome, dressed as usual in an outlandish assortment of other people's cast-offs. She would have to go in with Doris and make the best of it.

The small log fire, spitting and cheerful, warmed a half-circle of the room to a radius of about four feet. The rest of it was cold and damp, and the chill seemed to rise from the floor. Under the odd pieces of worn carpet were bricks laid on earth, common enough in the village years ago, but now unique to Ellen's cottage. To give Mr Richard his due, he had offered her proper concrete flooring, but she couldn't face the upheaval, and got used to wearing several layers of clothes against the cold.

It smells in here, thought Ivy. She's not really fit to be on her own. Soon be time for her to go into Bagley House. The thought depressed her more than usual, and she looked at Ellen, busy with the tea things and wincing as she bent down to pick up a dropped spoon. Poor old devil, she thought, and went into the kitchen.

'Shall I carry that tray, Ellen?' she said, in her sharp voice. 'We don't want to see our almond slices all over the floor, do we, Doris?'

Ellen growled that she was quite capable of carrying a tray of tea things, thank you very much. She would have been really worried if she'd heard compassion in Ivy's offer.

For once, however, Ivy did not snipe at Ellen's hospitality, and the three women sat quite amiably drinking tea and chatting about the buses being late, and the kids breaking the medieval glass in the church porch windows.

'I blame the parents,' said Doris. 'They'd come into the shop with their offspring, and then they were all over the place, into everything, with never a sharp word from their mothers. Jean Jenkins was the only one who ever stopped her kids from picking things off the shelves and that.'

'Not like in my day,' said Ivy. 'We knew how to behave, and woe betide us if we didn't.'

'You mum went too far, Ivy,' said Ellen. 'Spoilt your chances, she did, without a doubt.'

Ivy didn't rise to this. For one thing, she knew Ellen was right.

'Look at them Joneses with their Octavia,' said Ellen, and Ivy's heart sank.

'What can you expect,' said Doris, 'when there's no example for her to live up to?'

'They could've given her a sensible name, for a start,' said Ellen. 'Only makes her think she's somethin' special, calling her that fancy name.'

'Some funny names about,' said Ivy, hoping to steer the conversation in another direction. 'Don't care much for "Mandy", come to that, sounds like a piccaninny to me.'

'Bein' called Gabriella is bad enough,' said Ellen, seeing Ivy's drift and successfully thwarting her. 'Did you see 'er Greg's been writin' in the Newsletter? Couldn't make 'ead nor tail of it myself.'

Ivy drew her knees up tightly together, and pulled down her skirt, pursing her lips and saying nothing.

'He was definitely having a go at Reverend Brooks, no doubt about that,' said Doris. 'But there was nothing in it, Peggy says, not from either side. It was made worse by gossip, making that Sophie mad with jealousy.'

Ellen's eyes sparkled. This was more like it.

'Makes you wonder,' she said, 'whether she'd had

somethin' o' this sort before? You never know what 'e got up to before they came to Ringford.'

Ivy stood up, her hands twisting and a deep frown on her plain, worried face.

'That's nonsense, Ellen Biggs,' she said. 'There were references from all kinds of important people, and he would never think of doing anything like that. It was just that Jones woman, throwing herself at him night and day. He didn't stand a chance.'

'Quite right, Ivy,' said Ellen, nodding slyly. 'Specially when some busybody, supposed to be doin' the brasses, dropped words of poison into 'is poor wife's ear.'

Ivy stared at her and said nothing. She reached for her coat and gloves, and put them on. Without a word, she pushed her chair back against the wall and left the room. The old front door creaked and banged behind her and Doris and Ellen, aghast, heard the gate latch click shut.

'You've done it now, Ellen,' said Doris.

'She were near to tears, Doris,' said Ellen, looking guilty. 'I swear our Ivy were near to tears.'

CHAPTER FORTY-FOUR

The sun had gone behind a bank of dark cloud over Bagley Woods as Ivy marched down Bates's End and across the Green, careless of the mud and wet grass dirtying her polished brown shoes. So much for Doris's ideas about the season turning and that rubbish, she thought, shivering and scraping her shoes on the mat outside her front door.

The kitchen at Victoria Villa was warm from the range, quietly glowing under the bank of coal dust Ivy had shovelled on before she went out. She gave it a poke, and flames licked round the black iron bars, brightening the room. Without taking off her hat and coat, she stood looking out of the kitchen window to where sparrows quarrelled and fought in the bare branches of the apple tree.

She stood waiting, but there was no disembodied voice. Just as well, thought Ivy. She never says anything nice, never a word of comfort. And if you're listening, Mother, you won't catch me twice. I know you'll be back.

She hung her coat and hat in the narrow hall, and returned to the kitchen window. As she watched, Gilbert squeezed through the hedge and stalked across the neatly dug earth. She crouched behind a thick viburnum shrub, her tail slowly thrashing from side to side. Then, with a releasing quiver, she sprang up the trunk of the apple tree and all the sparrows flew off crossly, scolding and chattering.

Ivy opened the back door and called, 'Tiddles! Come

on, Tiddles, come and have some milk with Ivy.'

The tabby climbed out of the tree and came at a trot towards the house. She lapped happily at the creamy milk, the top of the bottle saved especially for her, and then jumped on to Ivy's lap, arching her back to the stroking hand and purring loudly.

'What shall I do, Tiddles?' said Ivy, her voice cracking. She cleared her throat and leaned her head back on the hard wooden spokes of her father's old chair.

Too late to put it right now, Ivy. The unwelcome voice intruded without mercy on Ivy's thoughts.

Ah, said Ivy, you're back.

If you're not careful, you'll lose the few friends you have got. The nagging edge wormed its way into Ivy's already aching head. But it wasn't finished yet. That Ellen Biggs isn't much, granted, the voice continued, but she's better than nothing, and Doris Ashbourne has always had a soft spot for her. You'll turn the two of them against you, you'll see. Then Robert'll be off with Mandy, and who'll you have left?

Ivy's head felt swollen and hot. She closed her eyes. Maybe if she could have a nap it would be better, stop her brain churning. She was just beginning to doze when the heavy front door knocker jerked her awake. Gilbert jumped off her lap and ran towards the door, miaowing.

'Now what?' said Ivy, and let out the cat. Then she went down the hallway to the front door and opened it a crack.

'Ivy?' said Doris Ashbourne, standing solid and calm on the scrubbed stone step. 'You all right, Ivy? Can I come in for a minute?'

Ivy thought for a moment, then opened the door wider. 'Of course I'm all right,' she said. 'Why shouldn't I be? What do you want, anyway?'

'You don't make it easy, Ivy Beasley,' said Doris, pushing her way into the hall, and walking through to the kitchen. She sat down, her handbag on her lap, and looked up at Ivy, standing uncertainly in the doorway.

'Better put the kettle on,' she said. 'We might as well have a cup while we talk.'

Ivy frowned. 'There's been plenty enough talking, I would say,' she replied, but began to fill the kettle nevertheless.

'Yes, well,' said Doris, 'that's what it's all about really, isn't it. We haven't had anything like this in the village since that stupid feud between old Price and Joe Barnett all those years ago.'

Doris's reasonable tones soothed Ivy, and she made the tea, pouring two cups and handing one to Doris. 'It's warm in here, Doris,' she said. 'Give me your coat, else you'll not feel the benefit.'

CHAPTER FORTY-FIVE

Robert Bates's car had been parked in a layby on the Tresham road for fifteen minutes, and the row which had blown up between him and Mandy had run out of steam. The rain hurled itself against the windscreen, insulating them from the outside world. They sat rigidly upright, not touching, a wall of ice between them.

After a few minutes, Robert said, 'Mandy . . .' He choked, cleared his throat, and began again. 'Mandy, you don't really mean it, do you?'

She turned and looked at him, and her face was unforgiving.

'Yes, I bloody well mean it,' she said. 'I'm fed up with the whole thing, and I'm especially fed up with your mother and all the bloody Bateses, generations of 'em, wonderful bloody farmers every one.'

Robert's features contracted, as if someone had punched him. He looked away from Mandy and hunched his broad shoulders.

'It isn't Mum's fault,' he said. 'She's never been away from the farm, not much, anyway, and then always with Dad. She doesn't know about anything else. She just wants to help you get used to it all, I'm sure that's it.'

Mandy said nothing, and Robert soldiered on.

'It'll be different once we're wed, and settled into the cottage,' he said. 'It will be our home, and –'

' – and your mother will be on the doorstep every day,'

interrupted Mandy vehemently, 'telling me what you like to eat, how you like your shirts ironed. Christ!' she added, her temper rising, 'I shouldn't be surprised if she comes on the honeymoon with us!'

Robert flinched. He reached out and turned the key, pressed his foot on the accelerator and drove out on the dual carriageway. There was a squeal of brakes and fierce hooting from behind, and he realised he had pulled out without looking in his driving mirror.

'I'd better take you home, Mandy,' he said. 'There's no point in our going to the farm if you're in this mood.'

'It's not a mood!' said Mandy, bursting into tears. 'I just don't want to go through with it. I don't, Robert, I really don't.'

Robert drove stolidly on, back into Tresham, and drew up outside the Butlers' house.

'I'll phone you tomorrow, Mandy,' he said. 'Don't fret, my duck, we'll sort it out.'

The rain eased off as he drove back to Ringford, and as he came down the long hill a watery sun lit up the village. Over Bagley Woods, where heavy clouds still hung threateningly above the trees, a shimmering, miraculous rainbow appeared, and Robert stopped the car. It was just here, he thought, that I found Mr Palmer that day. It's a funny old world. He sat for several minutes looking at the rainbow, and then set off again, back to the farm to explain to his mother why Mandy had not come to tea after all.

In the morning, Mandy still felt miserable and confused. She had not told her parents anything about the big row, just saying she was tired and going up to have a good rest. She had not reappeared for supper, in spite of her mother calling up the stairs.

'I think she's gone to sleep, poor little thing,' Mrs Butler said. 'There's such a lot to think about with a wedding, she's quite worn out, don't you think?'

Mr Butler dared not say what he really thought. He had

watched Mandy lose weight over the past weeks, looking thin and pale. He had seen his own bank balance dwindle alarmingly, and was certain it was all a lot of unnecessary nonsense. When he'd led his wife to the altar, they'd had a knife and fork tea at the pub afterwards, and gone off on the train to Yarmouth for a week.

But Mrs Butler was revelling in the whole fantastic edifice of dresses and flowers, wedding presents, reception, speeches, limousines and confetti, horseshoes and photographers.

'Do we need all that?' he'd said mildly to his wife. 'We're only ordinary people, you know, my dear.'

'Our only daughter is not ordinary!' Mrs Butler had replied. 'Don't be such an old killjoy.' So he had held his peace.

Mandy rang the salon and said she thought she had a touch of flu, and would stay at home for the day, just to be on the safe side. With only four weeks to go, she didn't want to risk a major bout of illness, she said. She went back to bed, but could not sleep. She looked round her room, at all the souvenirs of her childhood. Her battered baby doll sat in the little chair that had been hers, and the pictures on the walls were of rabbits and squirrels having picnics, going to school, playing among autumn leaves in the woods. And then her teens: posters of pop concerts and pictures cut out of magazines, made into a collage and framed by her dad. Photographs of herself, camping, swimming, acting in the school play, laughed at her from the chest of drawers.

I wouldn't really care if I never saw it all again, she thought, burying her face in the pillow. It's Mum that's kept it all going, dusting it all and arranging it round the room. It isn't me any more. Oh, I don't know what to think. Why does it all have to be so complicated?

She considered going down to have a chat with her mother, but she could hear her parents talking in the kitchen. Dad's not gone to work, she thought. Probably having a worry session about me. The person I really want to talk to is Robert, but I've messed that up good and proper. Anyway, we argue all the time these days, and it's usually my fault.

Mandy got out of bed and looked down on the rows of back gardens. She knew every square of lawn and vegetable patch, who worked in them and what they grew from year to year. The cat climbing over the wattle fence belonged two doors down, and she remembered it as a kitten. She thought of Bridge Cottage in Ringford, with no neighbours except the lofty vicarage and the dark, damp churchyard. Ellen Biggs would be her nearest neighbour. Well, that would be a real ball of laughs.

Then Mandy remembered Ivy Beasley. Robert had taken her to Victoria Villa once or twice, and Ivy had been polite but not particularly friendly. But there was no mistaking how she felt about Robert. Her eyes warmed when she looked at him, and her voice changed. No doubt at all, she loves him like her own son, thought Mandy, and she's known all the Bateses for years. Mandy began to dress, pulling on an old sweater and jeans.

'Ah, here she is,' said Mr Butler, as Mandy came into the kitchen, pale but composed.

'Would you like some breakfast, duckie?' said her mother.

Mandy shook her head and reached for her jacket. 'I'm not hungry, thanks, Mum,' she said. 'I'm off out for a bit. May not be back for dinner, but soon after. Don't save me anything. See you later, then.'

At the bus station she had half an hour to wait, and bought herself a cup of coffee and a sandwich. Now she was out of the house, with people around her going about their lives and taking no notice of her, she felt hungry. On the bus, there were one or two people going to Waltonby, but only one person besides herself asked for Round Ringford.

Ringford main street was completely empty when the bus drew up opposite the Stores. Mandy stepped down, and waited to cross the road. As she lifted her hand to knock on the front door of Victoria Villa, Ivy Beasley drew the bolt and opened it.

'Mandy,' she said, 'this is a surprise. You'd better come in.'

★

Perhaps this wasn't such a good idea, thought Mandy, sitting on the edge of a hard chair in Ivy's immaculate front room. There was a strong smell of furniture polish, and although a small electric fire burned in one corner, the air was chilly.

Ivy came in, carrying a tray with cups and saucers, teapot and fruit cake. Mandy was too nervous to notice that Ivy's hands were shaking a little, making the teacups rattle.

'I won't ask why you've come to Ringford on the bus,' Ivy said. 'No doubt you'll tell me in your own good time.' Her voice was even, flat, but not unfriendly. She had looked at the girl's face as she stood on her doorstep, and knew something was up.

'What a lovely cake, Miss Beasley,' said Mandy. 'Looks like a picture in a cookery book! It's perfect. I'd never be able to . . .' Her voice tailed away, and Ivy said, 'You'd better call me Auntie, seeing as you'll be a Bates very shortly.'

Mandy choked on a mouthful of tea, and set her cup down carefully in the saucer. Ivy got up and took it from her. Then, hesitantly, she gently patted the girl's shoulder.

'What is it, then?' she said. 'You'd best tell me, if that's what you came about.'

There was a long silence, and Ivy settled herself in her chair, folded her hands and waited.

'I'm not sure,' said Mandy, 'not sure about anything. I'm not sure about being a farmer's wife, or living in Ringford when I've always lived in town. I know I'll never be good enough for Robert's mum, and I just can't see myself being the other Mrs Bates. I have nightmares about that Bridge Cottage, and the churchyard and old Ellen Biggs. I don't know who to talk to. Robert and me quarrelled yesterday and he turned round and took me back home. Mum's so excited about the wedding she can't talk of anything else, and if I told Dad he'd look at me as if I was barmy.'

'So you came over to me,' said Ivy.

Mandy nodded. 'You've known the Bateses a long time,' she said.

Ivy chewed her lip, and poured another cup of tea.

'I've got one thing to say, Mandy,' she said, 'and it's the only important thing. Do you love our Robert?' Ivy seemed to have difficulty getting out her words, but she repeated it, to make sure Mandy understood.

'Of course I do.' Mandy's voice was low, but she looked Ivy straight in the eye, and they understood one another.

'Right, then,' said Ivy. 'Now you listen to me, young Mandy.'

The children came out of school, squealing and shouting under Ivy's window, and then the bus from Tresham Comprehensive disgorged its Ringford contingent. They all made for the shop and emerged eating chocolate and drinking from cans, throwing down wrappers and banana skins on the grass verges.

Ivy Beasley and Mandy Butler still sat in the quiet front room, as Ivy talked slowly, in fits and starts, and Mandy listened without speaking. It was a sad story, of chances missed, misunderstandings of love forgone in the name of duty. Ivy told Mandy all she knew about the Bateses, and tried to be fair to Olive and Ted and their much-loved only son. She also said that if anyone asked her, she would give it as her opinion that Robert Bates was one of the best, if not *the* best, of the lads Ringford had produced.

From over towards Bates's End, the church clock struck a sonorous five o'clock, and Mandy jumped up. She helped Ivy carry the tea things into the kitchen, drying up the cups and saucers, and carefully putting the fruit cake back into its tin.

'What now, then, Mandy?' said Ivy, tipping out the washing-up water and squeezing the dishcloth.

'Well,' said Mandy, 'I think I might go up the farm, see if Robert's come in for his tea.'

'Good girl,' said Ivy, and helped her on with her jacket.

'Thanks, Auntie.' Mandy leaned forward and kissed Ivy Dorothy Beasley lightly on her cheek, then quietly left the house.

Ivy went upstairs and into her mother's bedroom. She

picked up a book, still in its Smith's bag, from the little table by the bed.

I think I'll take this back next week, Mother, she said. 'Change it for something more suitable.'

CHAPTER FORTY-SIX

Several days had gone by since the Ringford Newsletter had hit the streets, and Greg's article had fuelled village gossip. Reaction had been mixed, from Jean and Foxy Jenkins threatening to bang Brooks's and Jones's heads together, to Mr and Mrs Ross refusing to speak to anyone about it in case they should be thought to be taking sides.

'Why 'e can't come straight out with it, face to face, like a man, I don't know,' said Fred Mills, leaning on his gate and chatting to Michael Roberts. 'No need for all that fancy stuff in the Newsletter, takin' up all the space. My gardenin' tips were squashed into a bit of a corner.'

'I know what I'd do with 'er, that Gabriella Jones, I'd put 'er over my knee and –'

'Oh yeh,' said Fred. 'We all know what you'd do with 'er. It ain't Mrs Jones I worry about. Not that I lose much sleep over any of 'em, but it don't seem fair on that poor vicar chap. He ain't been here five minutes, but what he's under fire from several quarters.'

Michael Roberts nodded, and reached out to cuff William ritually round the ear as he went by on his bike. Bill Turner came out of his gate on the opposite side of Macmillan Gardens, and the three men nodded a greeting.

'And as far as I can see, Reverend Brooks ain't done nothing wrong,' continued Fred. ' 'E's bin a bit of a silly bugger, but that ain't no crime. Forget the whole thing, and give him another chance, that's what I say.' He heaved his fork over his bent shoulder, and left Michael Roberts standing at the gate, with no chance to reply.

Up at the vicarage, Nigel and Sophie worked hard and spoke little. Sophie was busy with domesticity and long walks with Ricky. In the evenings she knitted small garments and watched television, occasionally switching it off in disgust, but always turning on the radio or playing a music tape, not wanting a silence between them.

'The best thing we can do,' Nigel had said that evening when Peggy came to warn them, 'is ignore it. The more you prolong these things with accusations and denials, the longer it takes for the whole thing to be forgotten.'

He went about the parishes, comforting the sick and dying, rejoicing with proud parents at the arrival of new babies, planning his confirmation classes and a revived church choir. His confidence seemed totally restored. Surely, thought Sophie, the sight of Nigel flying round the village in his black cape, Superman of the Church of England, will quell the rumours and restore his position in the village. She felt herself slowly recovering, getting back to normal.

But alone in his study, Nigel brooded on the cold, monosyllabic conversations with Gabriella, and the sight of Greg crossing the road to avoid him was like a wound that would not heal. He prayed for guidance, and knew that the answer was patience. It was not one of his strong suits, patience, and he spent far too much time plotting ways of healing the rift instead of thinking out his sermons.

'Not quite back to the old Nigel,' said Richard Standing to Susan after morning service on Sunday. 'The sermon was a bit simple-minded, I thought. Not much to think about there.' He handed Susan carefully into the passenger seat of the car, and they drove off for lunch with Richard's brother over at Fletching.

'Did you notice anything different about Susan Standing?' Doreen Price walked down the little path from the church with Peggy. It was a grey morning, heavy layers of fog hanging over the wooded hills, and a thick claustrophobic mist enveloping the Green. The air was quite still, not a breath of wind to stir the trees.

'No,' said Peggy, 'but I did think Mr Richard was fussing over her more than usual. Not the usual marching out of church with his little wife following meekly behind.'

'Yes, well,' said Doreen, 'there was something about the way she got into the car. Don't laugh, but I think she's pregnant.'

'What!' said Peggy. 'But she must be past it, surely?'

'Need not be,' said Doreen. 'Their son's only nineteen, and she was very young when she came to Ringford. Had her twenty-first after they were married. She's not more than forty, forty-one.'

'Oh, Doreen, do you really think so?' said Peggy, feeling excited. It was just what was needed in the village, after all the doom and gloom of the Brooks affair. And even the Bates wedding was rumoured to be having problems.

'I'm not taking bets,' said Doreen, 'but you can treat me to a box of chocolates if I'm right. Come on, now, Peggy, step out, the beef will be overdone and Tom hates that. You sure you won't eat with us?'

Peggy shook her head and thanked Doreen, but said that she had a lot of work to do in the stock room and this afternoon was her only chance. This was partly true, but she had also told Bill that he could come round and fix a broken window catch in the sitting room.

As she opened the side gate and bent down to greet Gilbert, Peggy heard a shout from the road.

'Peggy! Can you spare a moment?'

It was Greg Jones, standing with one foot on the ground, the other on his bicycle pedal. He had been for a ride in the fog, and droplets of moisture clung to his hair and beard.

Peggy stood leaning on the gate, not making any move towards opening it, and waited as he crossed to her side of the road.

'What is it, Greg?' she said. Ever since the article in the

Newsletter she had avoided the Joneses. Maybe right was on Greg's side, but it was on Nigel's too. It was a conflict without a guilty party, unless you looked at the real root of it, and that lurked, if anywhere, in Victoria Villa.

Old Ivy was on a better wicket with me and Bill, thought Peggy. At least we are obviously guilty.

'We were wondering if you would like to come to supper some time?' said Greg, nervously clicking his gears. 'Gabriella's been a bit low lately, and we've decided to do more socialising in the village.'

Peggy was taken aback. She had lived in the village for nearly two years, and the Joneses had never asked her to supper before, not even after Frank died. She thought quickly, and thanked him kindly, saying she was rather busy at the moment, but perhaps in a few weeks' time it would be very nice.

He nodded, complimented her on the creamy white magnolia in her garden – 'Amazing, isn't it, how those great waxy blossoms come out so early!' – and rode off on his bike towards Barnstones.

Peggy made herself a quick omelette with three cracked eggs from the shop, and sat at the kitchen table, eating and reading the Sunday newspaper at the same time. Solitary meals were not much fun, not like when she and Frank lingered over the roast and chatted about the shop and the village, relishing Sunday's peace and quiet. It had been her favourite time of the week, and now she got it out of the way as soon as possible.

Stacking and sorting in the stock room absorbed her attention, and it was only when she heard Ivy chopping wood next door that she looked at her watch. Half past three, and Bill had said he'd be round soon after two. Peggy finished unpacking a large, slithery polythene pack of toilet rolls, and went back into the kitchen. She washed her hands and looked again at the old clock over the Rayburn. A quarter to four, and no Bill.

She stared out of the window, up and down the street. A

breeze had sprung up, and the mist had cleared. Small patches of blue sky allowed momentary shafts of sunlight to warm up the village. Gemma and Amy Jenkins were walking hand in hand along the side of the Green, prim and neat in their new dark blue raincoats. Behind them came Warren, obviously deputed to keep an eye on them, but unable to resist occasional running passes with his football up and down the pavement, and round the empty seat under the chestnut tree.

But no Bill.

Well, I'm not going to worry, thought Peggy. he must have been held up. He wouldn't forget, and there's no way for me to find out what's happened. She reflected on the impossibility of ringing up the Turners and asking to speak to Bill.

Better just get on with something, and put it out of my mind, she thought. I shall see him tomorrow, sure to.

Bill sat in the reception office of St Lucien's, waiting to see the doctor. He was used to crises and dramas with Joyce, but this afternoon had been a nightmare. He'd cooked a nice lunch, and she had thrown it at him. After he'd cleared up the mess, he'd said he had to go out for an hour or so, and she had exploded.

It had been a real explosion, thought Bill, a horrible, frightening explosion with poor Joyce at the centre of it all. In the Sunday quiet of the hospital reception office, he went over and over the past couple of hours and felt again the terror of seeing Joyce in the grip of a fierce convulsion.

He had been in the kitchen, clearing up, when he heard her scream. It was a different scream from usual, high and full of fear. He had rushed into the sitting room to see her fall, hitting her head on the fireplace's tiled surround. Then the convulsions had begun, racking her poor body. Not realising what was happening, he had put his arms round her, trying to contain the awful jerking. It finally quietened, and he looked at her face, calling her name. Joyce! Joycey! Her eyes were shut, and she was blue. Then she stopped breathing, and he had panicked, trying to remember from long-distant first-aid classes what was the right thing to do.

After an interminable time of stillness and silence, she suddenly gulped in a choking mouthful of air and began to breath again. He had held her close, stroking her face and saying her name over and over again. When she opened her eyes and looked about her in a dazed, blinded way, he had laid her gently down on the sofa and gone to ring for an ambulance.

'Mr Turner?' Bill looked up and saw a young doctor in a white coat, holding a blue file and smiling kindly at him.

'Mrs Turner is sleeping quite peacefully now,' he said. 'You can go in and sit with her for a while.'

Bill stood up. 'When can I take her home?' he said.

'Not today,' said the doctor. 'We need to keep her in overnight, do a few tests, that sort of thing. You can telephone tomorrow, and then we shall have something more definite for you.'

Bill handed over the battered canvas bag containing Joyce's pitifully few, scruffy belongings, and made his way into the ward, where he almost walked past Joyce's bed, not recognising her exhausted face on the pillow.

CHAPTER FORTY-SEVEN

The day was one of those deceiving February miracles, when the sun shines warmly and pigeons swoop in pairs, crooning and keening, pretending that it's spring and seeing off marauding suitors.

It isn't really spring, thought Peggy, brushing down the yard and trying to avoid Gilbert, who followed the broom in a ridiculous, kitten-like game. We could still get snow, she thought with a shiver. And in the yard, hidden from the sun, it was cold and damp.

She took her broom through the shop and out to the pavement, where she brushed up the previous day's litter and muttered about children who couldn't be bothered to use the wire basket provided.

'Lovely morning, Mrs Palmer.' She looked up quickly, but it wasn't Bill. He wouldn't call her Mrs Palmer, anyway. It was Mr Ross, walking his little dog and tapping the ground smartly with his stick as he disappeared swiftly into the Bagley Road.

Peggy stood in the sun, looking across the Green to the willows glowing orange where their long, whippy shoots moved in the light wind. The roofs of the Hall showed clearly today, not a trace of mist. Smoke rose vigorously from one of the chimneys, and Peggy wondered if Susan Standing was feeling sick this morning.

The hunt is meeting at Fletching today, Peggy's thoughts

wandered on inconsequentially. I expect we shall have them all riding through later on, horse dollops all over the road and the hounds rooting in people's gardens. I must make sure the side gate is shut.

She heard the telephone ringing in the shop, and ran up the steps to answer it. It stopped as she picked up the receiver, and she frowned. Didn't give me much time, whoever it was, she thought. Probably Susan Standing wondering *if* I happened to be going that way, *maybe* I could possibly take half a pound of butter as they have run out.

She unlocked the till, and made the Post Office cubicle ready for the day. Nearly nine o'clock, might as well open up. Peggy drew the blinds on the shop door and the big window, and sunshine streamed in, taking off the overnight chill and glinting on the plate-glass window of the cubicle.

The telephone began to ring again, and Peggy walked quickly across the shop to answer it.

'Peggy?' It was Bill, and Peggy knew instantly that something was wrong. He was not in a telephone box, and he would never normally ring her from home. She perched on the edge of the stool behind the counter, listening without interruption.

'. . . so I'm just off to see her at St Lucien's,' Bill said. 'They're doing tests, and I should get some news. Must go, Peggy, I know she's going to be terrified in there, a strange hospital and all those people . . .'

Peggy said all the right things, and put the telephone down feeling cold and dismal. Bill's voice had been distant, his mind on the still, pathetic figure in a hospital bed. Joyce has won, Peggy thought, and then was horrified at her reaction to a terrible experience for the poor woman.

It was, of course, the chief topic of conversation in the shop all morning, and those who hadn't heard were swiftly informed by those who had. Peggy had the difficult task of appearing objectively sympathetic, while her concern for Bill and herself mounted to near panic by lunchtime.

She gave Gilbert a saucer of milk, and walked down to the

bottom of the garden, where a patch of golden crocuses shone in the weak sunlight. The fields around Walnut Farm in the distance were empty. It was too early in the season for the beasts to be out, and the sun lit up bare branches and leafless hedges.

Peggy unbuttoned her cardigan and turned to go back into the house. She saw Ivy Beasley hanging out washing, pillowcases and sheets, sensible knickers and an icy white nightdress. Peggy walked along the garden path, ignoring her neighbour, not expecting any conversation.

But Ivy Beasley had seen her, and, smartly elevating the washing line with an old wooden prop, she called, 'I expect you've heard the news, Mrs Palmer?'

Peggy hesitated. She was tempted to carry on as if she hadn't heard, but that would be childish and silly. She turned and looked over the hedge to where Ivy stood, hands on hips, feet squarely placed on the concrete yard.

'Yes,' said Peggy, not bothering to pretend. 'Very worrying, poor Mrs Turner.' She took a step towards the safety of the house, but Ivy Beasley hadn't finished.

'You'll remember what I said on Gardens Open Day, Mrs Palmer,' she continued. 'You can drive a person too far.'

Then she turned her back on Peggy, picked up the empty washing basket and disappeared into Victoria Villa.

Could've been worse, thought Peggy, nibbling at a piece of cheese in her kitchen, and waiting for the kettle to boil. At least she spared me the worst of her poisonous tongue.

She sat down at the table, and sipped hot tea, rejecting the biscuits and cheese she had put out for herself.

And, what's more, Ivy's right. Joyce Turner has been driven over the edge from the sound of it, and I have played a part in it. Oh God, Bill, I'm so sorry, sorry for us all, but most of all for me.

The shop bell jangled, and a voice called 'Shop!' Peggy got up slowly, and found Mr Richard helping himself to a half-pound of butter.

'We've just run out,' he said, 'and Mrs Standing fancies hot buttered toast for tea . . .'

★

The hospital ward had been divided into cosy bays, with a large television set at one end and cheerful prints on the walls, brightening the clinical atmosphere. There were flowers and cards everywhere, and a reassuring atmosphere of illness successfully tamed, under control.

Joyce was sitting up eating grapes, colourful curtains either side of her, half drawn to give her privacy. She looked at Bill without any sign of recognition.

'Good morning!' she said, brightly.

'Joycey?' he said uncertainly, handing her a bunch of freesias bought from a stall outside the hospital.

'What a lovely morning,' said Joyce, in a high, social voice. She laughed, a thin, tinkly sound, and patted her neatly brushed hair.

Bill had seen no staff when he arrived in the ward, and had walked on until he found Joyce's bed. Now a nurse bustled up, and took the flowers from him.

'We must find a vase for those,' she said. 'Aren't they lovely, Mrs Turner?' And then she turned with her back to Joyce and said, in a quiet voice, 'Will you come to my office for a moment, Mr Turner, just a little word?'

Sister's desk was neatly organised, with piles of notes and files, and a small pot of purple African violets placed on a mat in one corner. She indicated a chair for Bill, and then sat down herself, clasping her hands tidily in her lap. Her pleasant, round face looked kind, and Bill waited for her to speak.

'It's absolutely nothing to worry about, Mr Turner,' she said, 'but we think Mrs Turner may have a slight memory lapse, quite common after a convulsion of that magnitude. She seems very happy occupying another world at the moment, and we must just humour her gently.'

'She's escaped,' said Bill quietly.

'I beg your pardon?' said the Sister, leaning forward.

'I reckon she's escaped,' he repeated. 'She was very unhappy at home, has been for years. It's her way out.' He sat hunched and miserable, and Sister walked over and patted him on the shoulder.

'Don't worry,' she said. 'When she's gained some strength, we plan to move her to Merryfields for a week or two. If you are right, Mr Turner, she needs some help, and they have the resources there to give it.'

Bill returned to sit with Joyce, and for a while he listened as she prattled on about shopping and children, and making sure she'd left a note for the milkman. It was as if he were a total stranger, called casually to enquire after her health. He rose to go, leaning over to kiss her on the cheek. She looked up at him with a surprised smile.

'Well, thank you, kind sir!' she said, and waved to him as he walked quickly out of the ward.

Bill collected some chicken feed from the warehouse in Tresham, called in at a pub by the river for a pint and a sandwich, and then drove reluctantly back to Round Ringford. He dreaded the questions and the village concern. Most of all, he realised, he dreaded seeing Peggy. It was all different now, all changed.

He turned into Macmillan Gardens and parked outside his house. There was nobody about, and he walked quickly into the garden and let himself in at the back door. It was quiet, very quiet. He went through to the front room and saw Joyce's toy bear, on his back with his paws in the air, where he had fallen from her arms.

Bill walked over to the window, and drew back the layers of curtains, pulled them all back until the light flooded the room. Then he took the bear and sat him on the windowsill, looking out.

'There you are,' he said. 'You can sit there and wait for her.'

Then he went around the rest of the house, drawing curtains and opening windows, letting in light and fresh air.

Ivy Beasley, walking along on the opposite side of the Gardens to call on Doris Ashbourne, saw Bill at the window, and was shocked.

'He hasn't wasted much time,' she said, as Doris opened her door. 'There's no end to the wickedness of man, is there?'

CHAPTER FORTY-EIGHT

The wood was dank and cold, the wind penetrating through the leafless trees and scattering leaf skeletons, whipping them up in a frenzy and then letting them fall lifeless. It seemed to Peggy, plodding miserably through the mud and brambles, that she was caught up in some rustic *danse macabre*. Only the wind and its victims moved in the wood. Everything else was hiding, hibernating, closed off from the lingering winter.

No colour, no life, no scurrying animals and birds, just a middle-aged woman walking like an idiot through a chilly wood, and nobody to meet at the end of it. Peggy had been unable to stay indoors after the shop shut, and had without thinking walked on and on, and now here she was, in the familiar clearing, wrapping her scarf round her ears and staring over the village below.

She stood still for a few moments, knowing that Bill was nowhere near, but hoping that by some miracle he would come up behind her, put his hands gently over her eyes and kiss the back of her neck.

Nothing caressed her but the cold wind, however, and she made her way back to the road, downcast and convinced that this was the end. She dared not think how she would manage. It had been Bill's strength she had leaned on after Frank's death, but Joyce had staked her claim, once and for all, it seemed. Now we shall see, she thought, slipping around on the muddy road, if I can cope on my own, really on my own.

The weather had not improved next day, and Peggy shivered as she awoke, not having warmed up properly all night. For a few seconds she sleepily planned to stoke up the Rayburn and make a casserole for her supper, mentally adding warm layers to the clothes she would wear in the shop.

Then she was wide awake and remembering that she had still heard nothing more from Bill. The heavy grey sky allowed scarcely any light into her bedroom, and she pulled on a dressing-gown and slippers and went down to the kitchen, turning on the radio for the news.

It was the regular religious homily, and a honey-voiced bishop was exhorting constancy and belief in a world full of paradox and suffering. 'Oh ye of little faith,' he said, as Peggy filled the kettle and put a piece of bread in the toaster.

'Faith?' she said aloud, setting down a plate of fish for Gilbert, who began eating hungrily. 'Faith? Faith in whom? Am I supposed to have faith in Bill, trust all the things he's said to me in the past, wait patiently until Joyce releases him, if ever?' She sat down at the table, poured a dish of cereal and began to eat.

'Or,' she said, putting down her spoon and reaching out to turn off the confident voice, 'or should I recognise Bill's duty to be faithful to his wife, in sickness and in sickness, and tell him to bugger off? Which he appears to have done, anyway . . .'

It was a monotonous morning in the shop, and the rumour of Susan Standing's pregnancy, now rife in the village, had superseded Joyce's drama, so that no one mentioned it, and Peggy heard no further developments. She went through her duties mechanically, making several mistakes in the Post Office and apologising for shortchanging Nigel Brooks on his weekly purchase of butter mints for Sophie.

The shop was empty when the telephone rang, and Peggy grabbed it. But it wasn't Bill, it was Olive Bates, checking on the big order for the wedding. Olive was doing all the cooking herself, had been baking for weeks, and the big freezer in the barn was nearly full.

Peggy put down the telephone with a sigh, and as she did so the shop door opened and Ivy Beasley came in with a chilly rush of air and an expression to match.

'Bottle of lemon barley,' she said, with no preliminary polite greeting.

Peggy put the bottle on the counter, and took Ivy's money. Dare I ask her, she thought, and then, because she was desperate, said, 'Is that for Joyce Turner? How is she?'

Ivy was taken aback. She thought she could be in and out of the shop in minutes, and be on her way to get a lift with Robert into Tresham, where she planned to visit the hospital.

She turned, and seemed about to leave the shop without answering, but then hesitated and said, 'Not good, they say. Lost her memory. Doesn't know where she is. Didn't recognise Bill.' Her staccato delivery was like a hail of bullets and Peggy flinched. At the door, Ivy turned again and looked directly at Peggy, meeting her eyes fiercely.

'Best not to interfere,' she said. 'There's been enough damage done, one way and another.'

That's it, then, thought Peggy, and suddenly desperately wanted to put her arms round Bill and comfort him. Surely he must need her? Well, there was no way of finding out, what with Ringford rules and the impossibility of going to him.

Ivy Beasley stood at the gate of the hospital, looking up at the old, ornate building, and remembered her mother's last days. It had been a grim time, with Mother losing her power of speech, so that Ivy could only guess from her eyes what she wanted to say.

She squared her shoulders and marched up to the reception area, asking for Joyce's ward, and then walking more quietly along the shiny, antiseptic-smelling corridors.

'Good afternoon!' said Joyce. 'How nice of you to come and see me.'

She smiled brightly at Ivy, who knew at once that Joyce had no idea who she was.

'I brought you this,' she said, thrusting the bottle of lemon barley water at Joyce, who took it with elaborate thanks and put it on her bedside locker.

What on earth am I going to say to her? thought Ivy Beasley, whose small talk was limited to Ringford doings and sayings. Since Joyce was clearly temporarily round the twist, these would be of little use. But it was easier than she thought. Joyce chatted on about films she had seen and clothes she had bought, and all Ivy had to do was nod and agree with her.

'You got plenty of magazines to look at, then, Joyce?' she said, gathering up her gloves and scarf.

Joyce stared at Ivy Beasley, her face suddenly rigid with fear, and began to scream.

The word 'magazines' had struck a terrifying, jarring note in Joyce's private world, reminding her of painful reality back at Macmillan Gardens. Nurses came running, and Joyce just went on staring at Ivy, screaming louder and louder.

Ivy hastily put on her coat and ran from the ward, her heart thumping. She didn't stop running until she was out of earshot of the dreadful screams. and then she sat down on a row of chairs outside the baby clinic, surrounded by young mothers and tiny babies. She sat there until her heart slowed down and then she walked unsteadily out of the hospital and down to the busy market place where she had arranged to meet Robert.

Nigel and Sophie Brooks were hunting for old Welsh Gaudy pottery among the junk stalls in Tresham market. Sophie had been given a jug, vivid with rich blue and orange splodgy designs, and had begun to collect other pieces in a casual way. They were hard to find, and in antique shops commanded high prices. But Sophie had found an odd coffee cup on one of Tresham market stalls for a couple of pounds, and had ever since kept her eyes open.

'Look Sophie!' said Nigel. He pointed to a hideous vase, lavishly decorated with gilt and purple pansies. 'My mother had one just like that. Goodness, that takes me back.' He put his arm round Sophie's shoulders, and they strolled on, idly picking up and putting down pieces of pottery, but not finding any Welsh Gaudy.

'Not my lucky day,' said Sophie. 'Let's go and get a cup of tea.'

They walked down the cobbled way between the stalls, and emerged by a café on the corner. Outside, looking frozen and pale, stood Ivy Beasley, clutching her handbag tightly to her, and staring anxiously up and down the street.

Nigel, his arm linked with Sophie's, felt her stiffen.

'Miss Beasley!' he said. 'You look like the maiden all forlorn standing there. Come in and have a cup of tea with us and warm up. The wind is really cold this afternoon.'

He tightened his hold on Sophie's arm and propelled her into the café, looking back to make sure Ivy Beasley followed. But she hadn't, and he saw Sophie safely into a chair and went back to find her.

'No thank you, Vicar,' she said, 'I'm waiting for Robert Bates, and don't want to miss him.'

'We shall see him from our table,' said Nigel. 'Come on, Miss Beasley, come in and have a quick cup. If the worst happens, we can run you home. You won't be abandoned.'

Ivy looked at him out of the corner of her eye, undecided and adrift. She glanced once more along the street, then turned and followed him in.

Sophie smiled at her weakly, and they sat in uneasy silence while Nigel went to fetch tea from the counter.

'Have you been to see Joyce Turner?' said Nigel, setting down the steaming cups. 'Must go myself in a day or two. Best to give her time to settle down. Folks don't always want to see the vicar when they've had a bad time! How did she seem to you, Miss Beasley?'

Ivy Dorothy Beasley took a sip of the hot tea, and began to cry, very quietly and unobtrusively, delicately dabbing at her cheeks with her mother's lace handkerchief. While Nigel stared at her in dismay, Sophie hesitated, then put out a hand and gently patted Ivy's rough, red one.

'It'll be all right, Miss Beasley,' she said. 'Don't worry, these things usually sort themselves out, in the end.'

CHAPTER FORTY-NINE

The weeks leading up to the wedding day had been hectic ones for Olive Bates and Mandy. The air cleared between them, aided by a few well-chosen words from Ivy Beasley to Olive, and they had worked together, arranging the presents, completing the cooking and sorting out last-minute problems. Mandy's mother had drifted in and out, saying how lovely everything was, but not helping much. This suited Olive well, and she happily took over masterminding the whole thing, still with some misgivings about Mandy's suitability to be Robert's wife, but she kept these to herself.

Then, with one week to go, Fred Mills's old, bedridden sister in Macmillan Gardens died, and because of Nigel's many commitments in his other parishes, the funeral was fixed for the afternoon before the wedding.

'How do you expect us to do the flowers?' said Olive desperately to Nigel Brooks. 'Me and Mandy have got it all planned to do them on the Friday afternoon, so as to be nice and fresh for Saturday.'

In the shop, Peggy listened sympathetically as Olive told Ellen Biggs that it was the last straw, and she couldn't see why an old body who was dead anyway couldn't wait for another day or two before being tucked away below ground.

'After all,' she said, 'if we'd got a dead sheep and a decent cold store it could be in there more'n a week with no problems.'

Peggy raised her eyebrows. 'Not quite the same, Mrs Bates, is it?' she said. All we need now, she thought, is for old Fred to emerge from behind the cornflakes.

'So you got to do them Saturday morning?' said Ellen.

Olive nodded. 'As if anybody could make a good job of them a few hours before the wedding! Not to mention the million and one jobs I shall have to do up the farm. I really don't know what to do, and poor Mandy is at her wits' end.'

'Couldn't you arrange the flowers on Friday morning, before the funeral?' said Peggy. 'They'd still be nice and fresh for Saturday.'

'Who ever heard of a church full of flowers for a funeral?' said Olive. 'No, Mrs Palmer, that's no solution, and I shall tell Reverend Brooks he's got to think of some other way.'

'Friday evenin'?' said Ellen.

'Ted's asked all the Bateses from Waltonby over for a bite,' said Olive. 'Mandy's having a night out with the girls from the salon, and Robert's doing God knows what with the Young Farmers.'

Jean Jenkins had come into the shop, and behind her Doris Ashbourne, and now the problem was thrashed out once more from the beginning.

'Well,' said Doris the peacemaker, 'I don't see why you can't have flowers at a funeral. Fred's sister was very fond of flowers. He always grew a bed of tobacco plants under her window so's she could smell them on summer evenings.'

Olive snorted. 'First of all, our Doris,' she said, 'it's not summer, and second, Fred's sister's doing no more smelling.'

'It would please Fred, though,' said Peggy, allying herself with Doris.

'Peggy's right,' said Jean Jenkins, blowing on her cold, red fingers. 'Fred's not making much of losing his sister, but I reckon he must be very miserable inside. Might cheer him up a bit, having lots of flowers instead of a three-parts empty church and a couple of wreaths. There's not many of them Millses left now, you know.'

By now, the shop was full. When the door opened and Nigel Brooks edged in, complete silence greeted him.

'Morning, Nigel,' Peggy said. 'Just the person we need.'

Nigel smiled at her tentatively. He wasn't relishing another village crisis, and the atmosphere in the shop was electric.

'I've always been hoping someone would say that to me,' he said, with a small laugh. 'How can I help?'

He looked around and saw Olive Bates glaring at him, and knew what it was all about. But he waited for Peggy to continue.

'We were all very sorry to hear about Fred's sister,' she began diplomatically. Nigel nodded and muttered some soothing words.

'Pity, though,' she said, 'that the funeral will hinder the wedding arrangements.' She paused and looked encouragingly at Nigel.

He sighed. 'The flowers, you mean.' He looked at Olive Bates, and smiled apologetically. 'Have you any suggestions, Mrs Bates, how we might resolve this one?'

Everybody spoke at once. Then they all stopped and looked at each other, and it was Ellen Biggs who took the initiative.

'Do 'em on Friday morning, and let Fred's sister go in a blaze o' glory,' she said.

They all looked at Nigel, who looked at Peggy. She nodded, and said, 'What a good idea, Ellen. I am sure there would be no objections, and Mrs Bates is a wonderful flower arranger.'

Olive put her head on one side and pursed her lips, but Peggy could see she was pleased with the compliment.

'Fine,' said Nigel, 'the perfect solution. And won't old Fred be pleased? He could do with a bit of comfort, poor old chap. Shall we say any time from half past eight Friday morning, then, Mrs Bates?'

Olive Bates grudgingly agreed, and then began to plan it all with growing enthusiasm.

'Anyway,' she said, 'it'll save me sending a wreath.'

★

The wedding day dawned over Tresham with grey skies and a light drizzle. Mandy got out of bed and stared out of the window, her heart sinking. The weather forecaster had hedged his bets, prophesying that anything might happen.

'Rain before seven, fine before eleven,' said Mandy's mother, coming in with a mug of tea and putting it on the bedside table. She took Mandy's dressing-gown off the hook on the back of the door and wrapped it round her daughter's thin shoulders.

'Why don't you bring your tea in with us?' she said. 'Dad's still in bed, and we can all have a little chat.'

Mandy couldn't think of anything she would like less, but she followed her mother into the front bedroom and sat awkwardly at the bottom of the bed, sipping the hot tea.

'Don't worry, Mandy,' said her father, 'it'll clear up. Trust your old dad.'

For no logical reason, this cheered up Mandy. He'd always been the one to bathe grazed knees and fight her battles with the other kids in the street, and now she half believed that he could work one final miracle for her.

The morning passed quietly, and Mandy's friend from the salon came in and did her hair and nails. They fetched filled rolls from the shop on the corner for a quick lunch.

'Can't have you fainting in the aisle,' said Mandy's mother, encouraging her to eat.

By the time the limousine coasted to a halt outside the house, Mandy was ready and quite calm.

'There you are, my dear,' said her father, as they came out of the front door, waved to the neighbours, and walked down the garden path. 'Told you it would clear up,' he said, and the sun shone warm on his balding head and broad shoulders.

The bells in the ancient tower of Round Ringford church had got into their stride, William and Warren among the ringers, and pulling for all they were worth. The rhythm had settled down, and it was an exciting, heart-warming sound.

At the church gate a small crowd had gathered, and were

gossiping and spreading false sightings of the arrival of the bridal car.

'That ain't it,' said Renata Roberts. 'That's Mandy Butler's mother. She's a smart woman, ain't she,' she added wistfully, as Mrs Butler walked up the church path, her high heels clicking on the stone paving, her lilac suit and small, veiled hat receiving warm approval from the crowd.

Mrs Ross had walked down from the Bagley Road on her own, her little dog safely tucked under her arm, and now stood a little apart, smiling at the other gossiping women. Old Fred, somehow frailer since his sister's passing, leaned on his stick and puffed at his evil pipe. He'd had a word with Olive Bates, said how much his sister would have appreciated the flowers, and promised to come and see Robert and his bride.

Octavia Jones perched on her bike, one foot on the ground, scowling at the guests as they arrived, and criticising their outfits to her friend, Tanya Bright. She had expected her heart to be breaking, but as she stood there chatting to Tanya and her handsome brother, she discovered it wasn't. The wedding ceremony had taken Robert finally out of her reach. It was a bit of a relief, really.

Robert and his best man, John Barnett from Walnut Farm, stood just inside the church porch, waiting to go in. They looked resplendent, if a little ill at ease, in their grey morning suits, worn by special request from Mrs Butler.

'I don't care if nobody else wears them,' she said. 'It just looks so much better in the photographs.'

Inside the church, the winter light filtering through the old grey glass windows fell on white flowers and green foliage arranged by Olive Bates in posies on the pew ends, curving in swathes round the pulpit, filling the font, rising in fountains of ivy and chrysanthemums on the chancel steps, and paying homage in a vase of carnations and fern beneath the plaque commemorating Ted Bates's uncle, lost on a battlefield in Northern France.

Ellen, Doris and Ivy sat in a pew three rows from the back of the church, Doris and Ivy respectably dressed in smart suits and blouses. Ivy's hair was done in the new way, and she had put a pink silk rose in the band of her grey felt hat. Several times at home she'd tried it this way and that, and then taken it out again, listening to the scolding, critical voice of her mother, but finally she'd marched out of the house, banging the front door in defiance, the pink rose still in place.

Ellen Biggs was a triumph. From the wide-brimmed black straw hat, lavishly decorated with scarlet poppies, to her black patent boots, laced very loosely, she was a riot of colour. A royal-blue coat, bought for someone a lot taller, reached to her ankles, and because it was still not spring, Ellen had added the scarlet mohair scarf, which tickled her neck and chin, but made her feel deliciously festive. She was having a wonderful time, spotting Bates family members she hadn't seen for years, and pointing them out loudly to an embarrassed Doris Ashbourne.

Ivy was quiet, and when Robert and John walked self-consciously up the aisle and took their places in the front pew, her heart lurched. But she said nothing, just frowned at Ellen and put her finger to her lips in a fruitless attempt to shut her up.

In the back pew, up against the chill, damp stone wall of the church, Peggy Palmer sat on her own, refusing Doreen's offer to sit in the Price pew. Her hands in her best navy-blue coat pockets were tightly clenched and icy cold. Days had passed and she had not once seen Bill alone, serving him in the shop like a casual acquaintance, asking after Joyce and receiving monosyllabic answers. She had not thought the hurt would be so bad. It was like losing Frank all over again. She had considered not coming to the wedding, inventing a bad migraine, ducking out of it. But then she remembered Robert's kindness after he had found Frank's crushed car, and couldn't lie to him, not on his wedding day.

There was a rustle in the church, as footsteps were heard coming up the path. But it wasn't the bridal party, it was Bill Turner in his best suit, his head up and shoulders back. He walked firmly in, looked around, declined the guiding hand of the usher, and made his way to the back pew, where he sat down next to Peggy. He looked straight at her, for the first time for weeks, and took her small cold hand in his.

'Peggy?' he whispered.

'Bill,' she said, and the relief was overwhelming.

Gabriella Jones received a mysterious signal from somewhere, and brought the meandering, time-filling music to a close. She launched on the bridal voluntary which had accompanied countless brides up the aisle in Ringford church, and all heads turned to look at the door.

Mandy, framed by the arched porch, was a floating cloud of white tulle. She walked in slowly, small and fragile on the arm of her proud father. Her dress was shimmering satin, trimmed with frills of lace and ribbon bows. Bunches of dark red rosebuds had been sewn on her wide, crinoline skirt, and the long veil was anchored with a circlet of the same dark red flowers. It was romance of the highest order, and all that Mrs Butler could desire. Mandy, on her day of days, was an enchanted princess.

Robert's nervous smile, when he saw her standing beside him, broadened with delight, and the service began.

Nigel had done his splendid best for Mandy and Robert, handsome and dignified in his smooth black cassock, crisp white surplice and brocade cope. Once more Ivy's pulse quickened, but she opened her service sheet, and sang solidly out of tune, giving nothing away.

'Well I'm blowed,' said Ellen, in a hoarse whisper, as Greg Jones approached the lectern for the reading. It had been Nigel's idea, and Robert had been willing enough to extend a hand of friendship.

'He might not want to do it, Mandy,' Robert had said, 'him having that defect, and that, but Reverend Brooks says it would be a nice thing to ask.'

Greg had been very touched, but had indeed thought of refusing with an excuse, knowing all eyes would be on him in the church. Then he thought of Robert, and what a nice lad he was, and how they'd upset him over Octavia. So he had accepted the challenge, and rehearsed the passage thoroughly, with Gabriella's help.

The great words of St Paul to the Corinthians rang out, and nobody cared about Greg's odd tone of voice.

' "And now abideth faith, hope, charity, these three; but the greatest of these is charity." '

He looked round from the polished brass lectern, with its eagle in eternal flight, to where Nigel Brooks stood, tall and benevolent. Beneath Greg's neatly trimmed beard it was possible to see a small, forgiving smile.

Cameras flashed as Mandy returned down the aisle, this time with Robert beaming at her side, and then came the inevitable wait while the photographer grouped the Bateses and the Butlers, the bridesmaids and the best man, the grannies and the new-born, in endless permutations.

At last the photographer came to the end of his list. But as he began packing up his camera, Mandy stopped him. Everyone looked at her, surprised that she wasn't delighted to be on the move at last, out of the cold wind.

'One more,' she said, and called over the heads of the wedding guests, 'Auntie Ivy! Auntie, come over here!'

Ivy Dorothy Beasley, in her good grey suit, pink blouse, grey felt hat and its frivolous pink silk rose, stood between Robert and Mandy Bates and stared at the camera, the sun in her eyes and her handbag neatly under her arm.

'Smile, please!' said the photographer. 'Say "Cheese"!'

'Stupid fool,' said Ivy, and smiled broadly, showing her beautiful, even white teeth.